Cast of Characters

Vova Izlomin. The temperamental *premier danseur* of the American Ballet Drama and a brilliant choreographer as well, he treats everyone like dirt.

Natalia Izlomina. Vova's devoted wife, also a dancer, who nursed him back to health after his bout with madness. She's written a book about him.

Charles Graham. The "playboy publisher," who is publishing Natalia's book. He's just divorced wife number three and has his eye on Toni.

Baron de Speranski. The director and former owner of the American Ballet Drama, he has a special arrangement with most of the dancers.

Kate Whitehead. A rawboned, horsey type, she bought the American Ballet Drama and now collects male dancers instead of thoroughbreds.

André Vassine. A soloist, a sweet, talented boy who quit the company because Izlomin was getting all the good parts. Now he's back.

Jeff Ffoulkes. A designer and former dancer. He lives with André and looks out for him. They're the Damian and Pythias of the dance world.

Slava Mladov. Another soloist, very young and wildly gifted. He has a crush on Natalia. He also thinks he can dance as well as Izlomin.

Mikhail Gorin. Also a soloist. Born Mike Gordon, he grew up in Brooklyn and used to be Toni's dance partner.

Elena Perlova. The prima ballerina, a fragile, long-legged blonde who has aged well. She's rewarded herself with a much younger husband.

Kotik Barezian. A dancer and Perlova's fourth husband, who's just been drafted.

Tamara Ribina. The second ranking ballerina, an enchanting young thing who is having a tempestuous relationship with Mike Gordon.

Marina. A pretty little dancer, always ready to console Skeets in Toni's absence.

Paul Samarkand. The *regisseur*. He can't disguise his dislike of Izlomin.

Grigorii. Izlomin's valet, who is ill with ptomaine poisoning and can't dress him.

Bill Stone. An errant photographer, who gets along great with the ballet dancers.

Captain Andrew Torrent. An English-born ballet fancier and a homicide detective, who relies on Toni's knowledge of the ballet company to solve the case.

Toni Ney. A striking, dark-haired, green-eyed former dancer, she's now a newspaper columnist who covers the ballet. She's strangely attracted to Charles Graham.

Eric Skeets. Now a lieutenant in the army, he's home on leave and wants only to be with Toni. But murder, ballet, and Charles Graham are getting in the way of that.

Patrick, the doorman; **Mahoney,** a cop; **M. Daillart**, a ballet teacher; **Tom Jones**, a lordly blue Persian; and **Cleo**, a silky black vixen upon whom Tom has designs.

Mysteries by Lucy Cores

Featuring
Toni Ney-Eric Skeets-Captain Torrent

Painted for the Kill (1943)
Corpse de Ballet (1944)

Non-Series

Let's Kill George (1946)

Corpse de Ballet
by Lucy Cores

Introduction by
Tom & Enid Schantz

Rue Morgue Press
Boulder / Lyons

For Olga
who knows all
about ballet

Corpse de Ballet
Copyright © 1944, 1970
New Material Copyright © 2004
The Rue Morgue Press

ISBN: 0-915230-67-4

Reprinted with the permission
of the author's estate.

Printed by
Johnson Printing
Boulder, Colorado

PRINTED IN THE UNITED STATES OF AMERICA

Meet Lucy Cores

ONE OF THE MYTHS that refuses to die among modern mystery scholars is the notion that strong independent female sleuths didn't begin to appear in American crime fiction until the 1970s and 1980s. Nothing, of course, could be further from the truth. Female authors writing about strong female sleuths were quite prominent in the genre until the post-World War II and Korean War era, when male action thrillers, particular in paperback originals aimed at returning veterans, drove many of them from publishers' lists. Reading tastes, then as now, reflected the general mood of the country. After years of war, America was ready for a time out. Rosie the riveter went back home to become Rosie the housewife. It was the absolute nadir of feminism, a time when you could put a television show on the air called *Father Knows Best* and not risk daily pickets by women's groups. Mickey Spillane could bed his women and blow 'em away in the same paragraph, while John D. MacDonald took misogyny and turned into an art form that most men—and many women—accepted with relish.

But it was an entirely different time for women writers between the two world wars. Having won the right to vote in 1920, women—and women writers—were embracing new lifestyles. Women voters may have been largely responsible for forcing prohibition on the country, but ironically that doomed "noble experiment" also led to increased public drinking by women, albeit in the speakeasies that flourished in most major cities. If women were getting out more, they were also going to college and entering the labor force. The crash of 1929 didn't halt that movement but rather further fueled it. Times were tough and a paycheck was a paycheck, whoever earned it. And when the war came along and took most of the young men with it, women assumed even larger roles in society. Detective fiction reflected those changing conditions.

Lucy Cores' inspired creation, Toni Ney, a dancer turned exercise maven, is a prime example of the kind of strong-willed female sleuth that graced the pages of American detective fiction from suffrage to the bomb. She's smart, self-assured, independent, and not afraid to speak her mind. She likes men but doesn't require one to put food on the table. Work means a career, not something to do while waiting for Mr. Right to come along. Still, she's a bit of a romantic. Like many young girls, Toni dreamed of being a ballet dancer, and, like most young girls, she soon realized that while many are called, only a few are chosen. Instead of being devastated, she became an exercise director (today we would probably say aerobics instructor) at a fancy beauty salon (*Painted for the Kill*), before embarking on a second career as an exercise columnist and dance critic for a major Manhattan newspaper (*Corpse de Ballet*). Her powers of observation are especially keen, which is why ballet aficionado Captain Anthony Torrent of New York's Homicide Bureau seeks her out when he needs a fresh perspective on a case. But Toni doesn't look for crimes to solve. She's on the scene in her work capacity when murder strikes in both of her recorded cases. For the most part, she and boyfriend Eric Skeets earn high marks from Captain Torrent for staying in the background, offering insights instead of digging for clues on their own. Of course, you can't always be good (otherwise we'd have nothing but police procedurals and private eye novels) but Toni is usually joined in her ill-advised clue-gathering by the stalwart Eric Skeets, whose heart is in the right place even if his punches don't always land where they should.

If Lucy Cores' books differ any from other mysteries of the day, it's in their playful attitude toward sex. There's nothing particularly salacious—it's more what used to be called slightly "naughty"—in the narrative but the talk is frank, and the sexual peccadillos of the characters and just the right amount of bitchy asides provide much of the books' humor. There are gay characters, as you might expect in books set in the world of the theater and the beauty industry. Cores doesn't dwell on their sexuality, but this was a period in which gays were seldom identified as such in detective fiction, even in passing, and if they were, it was usually as villains, such as the "gunsels" in Dashiell Hammett's *The Maltese Falcon*. In Cores' books some gay characters are bad, some are good, some are just indifferent, but none are pitied, despised or played for laughs—at least no more than any of the other characters are. Much the same spirit can be found in another contemporaneous two-book ballet mystery series (*A Bullet in the Ballet* and *Murder a la Stroganoff*) written in 1938 by Caryl Brahms and S.J. Simon..

Cores dedicates her second Toni Ney book, *Corpse de Ballet*, to Olga Ley, "who knows all about ballet." But we suspect that Olga Ley was also the inspiration for Toni Ney. Aside from the rhyming similarity in their names, Ley was not only a dancer, like Toni, specializing in ballroom as well as ballet, but she was an expert on exercising, eventually writing two major books on the subject. Her own lean, athletic figure matched Toni's. Like Cores, Ley was born in Russia (St. Petersburg) in 1912 and emigrated to the United States after the Russian Revolution and Civil War. In addition to dancing and exercise, she worked as an illustrator (as did Cores) and a costume designer. She married Willy Ley, a German-born rocket scientist who once tutored Wernher von Braun. Willy Ley fled Germany in 1935 when he learned that Hitler wanted rockets for weapons, not space exploration. Unfortunately, the U.S. government wasn't interested in rocketry and Ley changed careers, becoming one of the foremost science writers of his day. He also dabbled in science fiction, a passion he shared with Olga, a frequent attendee at science fiction conventions, where she dazzled everybody when she appeared in the costume pageants. They passed their interest in science fiction on to their daughter Sandra, who in 1976 edited *Beyond Time*, an anthology of alternate history stories. Olga contributed a story, as did Lucy Cores, whose "Hail to the Chief" speculates that if the Watergate burglars had not been caught, Nixon would not only have served out his second term but would have found a way around the constitutional two-term presidential limit to stay in the White House until 1994.

Lucy Cores was a very versatile writer. In addition to the two Toni Ney mysteries, she published a third comic mystery, *Let's Kill George*, this time a stand-alone, in 1946, before abandoning the form, at least as a writer. She was an avid mystery reader, according to her son Michael, and in her later years particularly admired P.D. James, Ruth Rendell, and Martha Grimes. Among earlier writers, Ngaio Marsh was obviously a favorite. There is a reference to Marsh's Inspector Roderick Alleyn (misspelled, however) in *Painted for the Kill*. Cores was also fond of the classics and once wrote the book and lyrics for an unproduced musical version of Wilkie Collins' *The Moonstone*.

Romance featured in many of her other books, including *Women in Love* (1951), which was based on one of her own early love affairs. The 1952 paperback edition bore the lurid subtitle "She substituted sex for passion." Most of her other romance novels were historicals, including *Destiny's Passion* (1978) and *Fatal Passion* (1989), set in the Regency period. *The Year of December* (1974) chronicles the adventures of Claire

Clairmonte, the onetime mistress of Lord Byron, in Russia. *Katya* (1988) was another novel of romantic suspense set in imperial Russia. There are also elements of mystery in *The Misty Curtain* (1964) in which a young girl attempts to reconnect with her mother, now a princess, who abandoned her as a baby. *The Mermaid Summer* (1971) was set on Martha's Vineyard, where Cores lived for many years, and contained characters easily recognized by her friends there. A short story in *The Saturday Evening Post* was turned into a television series, *The New Loretta Young Show*, which ran during the 1962-63 season. It featured a New York magazine editor who was trying to raise seven children. In addition to her writing, Cores also worked as a book illustrator and graphic designer, notably for Walter J. Black's Classics Club in the early 1940s.

Lucy Cores was born to a middle-class family in Moscow in 1912. For most of her life she thought she had been born in 1914 and only toward the end of her life did she discover the mistake. Since that meant her ninetieth birthday party would be held that much sooner, she was overjoyed. Her family fled Russia after the Communist revolution and she hid out with her mother in Poland and lived for a while in Paris before arriving in the United States in 1921. It's a period of her life that she did not like to remember and refused to discuss. Although her father, Michael Cores, had been a lawyer in Russia, it was not a career he could follow in the United States and he eventually became a professional musician, playing the viola in the NBC Philharmonic under Arturo Toscanini. Her uncle, Alexander Cores, was one of the most celebrated violinists of the twentieth century. Isaac Stern played at his funeral. He was also responsible for teaching comedian Jack Benny how to play the violin badly (Benny could already play it competently). The family musical ability was passed on in full measure to Lucy's younger son, Danny Kortchmar, one of the country's foremost guitarists and a songwriter as well who has played with Jackson Browne, James Taylor, Linda Ronstadt and Carole King (and just about every other legend in the music business) and who today is primarily on the production end of the recording industry.

After learning English, Lucy Cores attended the Ethical Culture School in Manhattan and was graduated from Barnard College. She met and married Emil Kortchmar, the son of Russian Jewish émigrés, in 1942. Although Emil did not go to college first, he attended New York University Law School before he went to work in his father's business, manufacturing screw-machine parts. He eventually took over the business and then sold it in the 1960s, although he continued to run it for the new owners for a time. Until the last year of his life he helped a nephew operate a similar business in New Rochelle. He loved sailing and the family owned several boats over the years. He taught his elder son Michael, who today specializes in restoring old wooden boats, to sail, but Lucy made it clear that sailing was not an activity in which she was interested.

The Kortchmars moved to Larchmont, New York, in 1940s, where Lucy met Frederic Dannay, the half of the Ellery Queen writing team who founded and edited *Ellery Queen's Mystery Magazine*. In 1950, they rented a summer home on Martha's Vineyard, fell in love with the island, and eventually bought a house on North Road where they spent every summer for the rest of their lives. In the 1970s and 1980s they also spent a month or two every winter in Grenada in the West Indies. During those years Lucy made her mark as a formidable poker player and enticed any number of people into joining her in hard-fought Scrabble games. She loved word games and was giving to making puns. She was asked once if she wanted to surf and replied, "They also surf who only stand and wade."

Following Emil's death in 1990, Lucy moved back to Manhattan. She frequently entertained friends and grandchildren in her living room, the focal point of which was a large bowl of M&Ms on the coffee table. She continued to spend her summers on Martha's Vineyard where she swam every day and was a regular at the local library. She died there in her sleep on August 6, 2003, at the age of 91. At the time of her death, she was learning how to use a computer and working on a novel about the Russian poet Alexander Pushkin.

Lucy Cores' sophisticated and charming mysteries are little known today, if only because she survived them by six decades, but they are well worth revisiting. Toni Ney isn't a relic of a forgotten era, trapped forever in the conventions of her time. A few superficial trappings aside, she seems as modern in her outlook as any of today's current female sleuths. The times may change but well-realized characters are never dated.

Tom & Enid Schantz
April 2004
Lyons, Colorado

The editors are grateful to Michael Kortchmar for his very helpful assistance in putting together the biographical portions of this introduction.

CHAPTER ONE

"WHY DON'T you take off your hat and stay awhile?" said Toni hospitably.

Her visitor leaped out of the cat carrier in which she had been brought to Toni's apartment and looked around her wildly. She was a handsome wench, dark of complexion, with bright yellow eyes that shone like headlights in an enigmatic countenance and long ferocious whiskers. Her tail was a silky black plume and she had big feet.

Tom Jones, Toni's own lordly blue Persian, came out of the bedroom and went, "Yeaowr," on a pleased note, as if to say, "What, for me? How nice." He came over to investigate the visitor, who regarded his approach without any particular pleasure. The next minute a black paw flashed, gray fur flew, and Tom Jones was falling back warily, with his ears thoroughly boxed. He sat down at a respectful distance, breathing hard, and regarded the vixen with new attention. Obviously he was fascinated.

Toni watched them with amusement as she hastily poured milk into two saucers. They were now at the beginning of a time-honored routine, to be adhered to faithfully by all self-respecting felines. She patted them impartially, said, "Tom Jones, meet Cleo. Cleo, meet Tom Jones," and fled.

Her entire morning had been like an old-time movie reel with people jittering along at a breakneck speed, and the day bade fair to continue in the same hectic manner. She now had to cover a rather important assignment for her paper—one which was complicated by the fact that the people she had to deal with were as unpredictable as they were exotic. At the same time there was Tom Jones' love life to think of and her own, as well, his in person of the dark Cleo and hers in that of Lieutenant Eric Skeets, fresh out of OCS, who was coming in for a ten-day leave and whom she was supposed to meet at the train.

Lieutenant Skeets at least arrived on schedule. He was out of the gate at exactly 1:03, toting a small traveling bag and showing his beautiful white teeth in a happy grin. He looked different, more solid somehow, in his natty uniform. Not quite the same man, Toni thought while her arms went around the khaki shoulders, and her lips felt the familiar hard pressure of his.

Skeets held her away at arm's length and they scrutinized each other gravely—a slender young man with gray eyes and eyebrows that slanted at a humorous angle, and an extraordinarily slim girl, with dark hair rolled off a spacious and slightly bulging brow and imperturbable green eyes.

Both of them started speaking at the same time, stopped, waited for the other to speak and again began simultaneously. Then they laughed, gave it up and walked away arm in arm.

"Gosh," remarked Lieutenant Skeets, fervently, "but I'm pleased to see you. You, me?"

"Yes."

"Overstating as usual. Here I've been hoping that you'd fall on my neck and gush like any other girl. My golly, girl, just think—it's me here after all those months."

Toni glanced at him mutely. The truth was the sight of Eric in a uniform was moving her to all kinds of unaccustomed emotions, that seemed to gather in a hard ball in her throat.

"Never mind," said Skeets and laughed suddenly. "You look so marvelous. You know, I forgot what you looked like. I kept on thinking of you as looking like that picture you sent me. You were actually pretty in it. But of course you aren't at all. You're—you're just wonderful."

"You mean, like an old shoe."

"That's right. Incidentally, I wish your paper would stop publishing those cheesecake pictures of you. The boys clip them and hang them over their beds with comments and it's very painful to my most sacred feelings."

Toni laughed, remembering a letter from Skeets asking her to send him something more personal in a way of a picture. "Something," he had said restrainedly, "with clothes on." Toni, who had millions of pictures of herself in a scanty bathing suit taken for her daily exercise column in the *Globe,* had to go and have herself photographed fully dressed.

"Now then," said Toni, getting down to business, "what shall I do with you now that I have you here? Let's see if we can fit our schedules together."

"What do you mean, schedules? You intend to devote your whole time to me, I hope.

"Darling, you forget I have a job on a paper. And as luck would have it, I am on an assignment right now. It's all about ballet. I'm supposed to go to a rehearsal in a little while. Want to come along?"

"Ballet," said Skeets dreamily. "Soft music, glossy black coiffures, yards of tulle, lots of pretty legs—sure, I'll tag along."

They repaired for a hasty lunch at one of those French places in the fifties where every aspect pleases and only the coffee is vile.

"Tell me about your assignment," said Skeets. "Is it something for your column?"

Toni explained. Besides her exercise column, she was expected to write up dance recitals and lately had been a steady visitor to the Civic Opera, where the American Ballet Drama had been having an extremely profitable season. She rummaged in her handbag and brought forth a clipping from the *Globe.* "Look, she said. "My own byline, too."

REVIVAL AT AMERICAN BALLET DRAMA
IZLOMIN TO DANCE PHOEBUS
by Toni Ney

April 24: Tonight's performance of the American Ballet Drama at the Civic Opera will feature an event of more than ordinary interest when Izlomin, the celebrated dancer, revives his famous ballet *Phoebus.* Izlomin was at the height of his fabulous Parisian success when he choreographed this ballet featuring himself as the Sun God.

Izlomin made his debut in Paris in 1929. To him, both as dancer and choreographer, can be attributed the neo-Renaissance of ballet which took place in Paris in the 30s. Many of his ballets—*Esclave Grecque, Hyacinth, Cauchemar,* among others—have become standard favorites on all ballet programs.

Phoebus His Best

There is no doubt but that *Phoebus,* the ballet to be revived this evening, was the finest of Izlomin's creations. It has been performed only once before, shortly after its conception in 1935, but was never danced to its end. At its climax, the famous dancer went mad, succumbing to the catatonic schizophrenia which had been developing over a number of years, and to the delusion that he was indeed the Sun God he had danced in *Phoebus.*

Dramatic Comeback

For seven years, "the Prince of Sorrows," as the French newspapers called him, remained in seclusion, nursed by his devoted wife, Natalia Izlomina, also a dancer. According to reports, he would, when able, practice frenziedly the steps for his last tragic ballet. In 1942, the ballet world was startled and rejoiced to hear that Izlomin had been cured, and that he and his wife had applied in Lisbon for visas to the United States. The dramatic story of his comeback, as well as the glamour surrounding his almost legendary figure, have combined to create intense interest in the revival tonight of the once-fatal *Phoebus.* The program will also include *Aurora's Wedding, Rêves de Printemps, Cauchemar* and *Le Roi des Chats.*

"I gather," said Lieutenant Skeets, "that we not only go to rehearsal, we go to the performance as well."

"Well, yes," said Toni. "I'll have to be there. But you like the ballet, Eric—you know you don't mind."

"I don't mind," said Eric. "It sounds as though it might be exciting. Think he'll go nuts again? You know how it is—once a bat, always a bat."

"Oh, dear Vova Izlomin isn't crazy any more, except maybe like a fox. A medical board pronounced him sane before he was allowed to enter the country. He's been getting the most terrific buildup. De Speranski—that's the director of the American Ballet Drama—has been deliberately trying to revive with Izlomin the grand old tradition of the twenties. You know—the good old Diaghilev-Nijinski days when a ballet dancer was a sort of fairy prince. Very glamorous and phony, but the public laps it up."

"Why phony?" asked Eric.

"Because this fairy prince business is nonsense. There are other dancers in the company as good as Izlomin, though he's doing his best to fix that. But he makes the best copy, what with his murky past, and everybody has been writing about him—profiles in *Life,* in the *New Yorker,* and so on. So the *Globe* thought it would be nice to run a story about him in the Sunday section with the emphasis on his private life and lots of pictures. I've taken a lot of them myself on account of the photographer shortage. They've been accepting them too."

"My versatile love," said Skeets. "So you're doubling in flashguns now? I'll hold the lights for you."

"Thank you, dear. I'm taking the rehearsal shots myself with my trusty little Rolleiflex," she patted it fondly, "and Bill Stone's promised to help me with tonight's performance. I'll cover backstage and Bill'll shoot them from the prompter's box—always provided he shows up."

"Yes, there's always that," grinned Skeets. "Old Bill's still around, is he?"

"Usually not when I want him. I've been trying to snare him for the paper but he says a freelance life for him." Toni wrinkled her nose with amused exasperation. "All I want is to have him where I can keep an eye on him. I want very badly to get the pictures of *Phoebus*. Even if they turn them down in my office we can sell them to a magazine."

"Don't you find this Izlomin a bit difficult?"

Toni laughed. "Heavens, no. He is filthy nasty with the members of his company, but I am the press, you know. Besides, he simply lo-offs me because I told him where to get the right kind of sequins for his *Phoebus* costume. Big and shiny like gold dollar pieces." She watched fondly as Eric attacked a large wedge of apple pie. "I hope you don't mind my admiring your appetite, darling. Everybody I know is Four-F with stomach ulcers. Eat good—but try to finish soon, or we'll be late."

But Izlomin was just beginning to rehearse the company when they arrived at the Civic Opera. So they were told by Baron de Speranski himself who came out to meet Toni at the stage entrance, with outstretched arms and an oily twinkle of welcome in his eye. He was a well-fed, genial man with a beautiful and expressive beard and a penchant for proverbs. Disagreeable persons have been heard to attribute his well-fed appearance to years of sucking ballet dancers' blood. Once he had been the sole owner of the ballet but his debts had demoted him to the post of director.

He bent his corpulent body over Tom's hand, bestowed a kiss on it in the heavily continental manner and wrung Skeets' upon being introduced to him. De Speranski always spread himself out like a rug for the press.

"I just wanted to make sure," said de Speranski, "that everything is dze way you want it. Of course we know—certainly you know, Mademoiselle Ney—dzat temperament is something dzat must always be allowed for. Our dear Vova is a bit difficult at times . . ."

"I understand," remarked Toni, "that he and the draft are rapidly getting rid of your best male dancers."

De Speranski turned his eyes heavenward. "Dze war," he moaned. "*Mon Dieu*, draft boards care less than *dzat* about art. Last week Martin—dzis week Barezian—next week maybe Gorin . . ."

"You can't blame Vassine on the draft," said Toni.

De Speranski's face clouded. "Yes," he said, "dze irony of it. Draft couldn't have gotten Vassine so we had to lose him anodzer way."

"Why couldn't what's his name have been drafted?" Skeets' inquired with interest.

De Speranski smiled gently. "He is not dze type. Yes, it is too bad. Poor André Vassine was here just a few minutes ago. He dropped in to pick up some costume he had left behind. When I think of dze poor young man dispossessed of his heritage, stealing upstairs to what had been his dressing room, while his fellow dancers are rehearsing . . ."

"It's probably for the best," said Toni unfeelingly. "He's going to sign up with that new musical comedy and get paid much more than he was getting here."

De Speranski's eyes suddenly glazed over and focused on a point just above Toni's head, a trick he had when the sordid topic of money came up. "It is very unfortunate, all dze same. In my time, of course, art was above all undignified squabbles. I wouldn't have dreamed of releasing a dancer from his contract just because he can't get along with anodzer one. But dear Kate—Mrs. Whitehead, you know . . ."

"I calls her Kate because we wuz brought up together," said Skeets *sotto voce*.

"Pardon? As I was saying, dze minute André Vassine asked for his contract, she threw it in his face. So Jeff Ffoulkes left too. I have no doubt dze whole thing was his idea. You know yourself, André is just like a child. Of course if I had been listened to—but if! Easy to say if. If my grandmother had a beard she would be my grandfather."

Eventually the philosopher took them to the orchestra where he left them with protestations of good will. Toni noticed that they were not the only spectators. There was a couple in the row in front of them. The woman—middle-aged, red-haired, rawboned and ostentatiously tweedy—Toni immediately identified as Kate Whitehead, the backer of the American Ballet Drama. The man was tall and also vaguely tweedy—nobody Toni knew.

Skeets chuckled, gazing at the brilliantly lighted stage.

"Tulle and roses, did I say? But I like it anyhow."

So did Toni. There's nothing quite as revealing in a totally businesslike and unselfconscious manner as the dancers' practice clothes, in which they look entirely different from their sleek performance selves. Faded tights, patched leotards, sweaters and shirts tied at the midriff, wrinkled little flared skirts, hair pulled away austerely from the face and stuffed under kerchiefs and snoods—but, on the other hand, the ribbons of the ballet shoes painstakingly crossed with the knots tucked away in the traditional manner, and faces minutely made up to the last mascaraed eyelash. The boys too looked sleek and stripped for action in their tights, white shirts open to show their manly chests.

The rehearsal seemed to have come to a temporary stop, with the musicians in the pit producing tentative tuning-up sounds and the stagehands busy building a peculiar structure in the background. It consisted of what looked like several large cubes piled on each other to create a series of platforms, with the highest one in the middle. An occasional ramp led from platform to platform. Skeets poked Toni in the ribs and asked for explanation.

"It's for *Phoebus,*" she told him. "The ballet is danced on two levels—the higher one for Izlomin, while the hoi polloi dance on the floor like ordinary human beings. The ballet represents the journey of the sun, and I guess Izlomin will sort of mount from level to level and then down again in time for sunset, as it were. Incidentally, that's another instance of Izlomin's wonderful flair for publicity. Nobody knows what he is going to dance when he gets to the top platform."

"What do you mean?"

"He's keeping it a secret, hinting that it'll be some sizzling combination of steps that'll create a sensation. The only one who knows is Daillart at the Daillart School of Ballet, where he takes his lessons, and of course, like Old Man River, *he* don't say nothin'. There's a precedent for this. A ballerina of the Imperial Ballet by the name of Legnani kept mum at the rehearsals the same way and then on the opening night let loose with thirty-two *fouettes* for the first time in the history of ballet. All the balletomanes are stewing about Izlomin's 'noonday variation.'"

"Somehow," said Skeets, "I can't work myself up into a sweat about it. I'd be much more interested in his going bats again. Which one is this Izlomin, anyhow?"

Toni pointed him out, one among a group of dancers to whom he was apparently explaining some step. His hands were sketching the pattern in the inimitable sign language of the ballet and the dancers were duplicating the motions tentatively with their feet.

The famous dancer was a man in his early thirties, whose whipcord body was sheer muscle and bone, as if stripped of everything except what he needed for dancing. His face, too, with its sharply outlined bone structure, looked as if reduced to its minimum essentials. And there was a queer sense of isolation about him, surrounded though he was, as if an icy wind were blowing from him to the other dancers. It was strange how, in spite of everything, in spite of medical certificates, in spite of his admission to the United States, which would never have taken place if any doubts had remained about his sanity, the members of the company still treated him with a sort of superstitious fear.

"That's the great Izlomin in person," said Toni. "The prince of ballet himself. And there—Mike Gorin, my ex-partner. Do you recognize him—the one talking to Tamara Ribina?

She pointed to a dark young man absorbed in a conversation with an enchantingly pretty and plump brunette of no more than eighteen. "Oh dear," she sighed, "I remember Tamara from when I was still studying dancing. She was in the children's class then, just a skinny little tadpole with long black braids. Just look at her now. Isn't she a Circassian beauty, if there ever was one?"

"She sure is," said Skeets.

"And there's the great Elena Perlova, the prima ballerina. The thin blonde practicing lifts with the red-haired youngster. He's a Yugoslavian import and very good too."

The blonde made a preparation and soared upward in the arms of her partner. She didn't seem to like it, for she stamped her foot and her face grew petulant. "That's another of Izlomin's mean tricks," Toni said, watching them, "pairing Perlova with Slava Mladov. Mike is the ideal partner for her—he's so strong he can make anybody look light. Perlova is wonderful but she's got no elevation and Slava makes her look bad. Now Tamara can do all right without support, even if she is plump. She bounds like a little rubber ball."

"And who is that girl?" Eric indicated a dancer in black tights who had just stepped out of the ranks of the corps de ballet to bring Izlomin a towel.

"That, my pet," said Toni, "is Natalia Izlomina, our hero's wife. She's not a great dancer, although she's often given solos. Technically she's fine and they mostly use her for character parts. Of course the important thing about her is that she's written a book about Izlomin which is coming out in the very near future. It's called *Lazarus Arise* and deals with Izlomin's life and bad times, not minimizing the part she had in helping him to regain his sanity."

"Isn't it a bit embarrassing for him?"

"Oh, you'd be surprised how much publicity of any kind a dancer can swallow. The publishers did a swell job of promotion—just poured on the typical Graham-Dobbs blah. You know, 'We are honored to present this story of a brave and sensitive woman who has passed through a valley of darkness with her husband' . . . The whole thing is not in the best of taste, since the subject of the book is still alive, but I suppose it would take too long to wait for him to die."

The tweedy man sitting with Kate Whitehead turned his head to take a look at Toni. He had fair hair and his eyes shone startlingly blue behind horn-rimmed glasses. Toni thought he looked disapproving. Probably he was the kind who sat in reverent silence through a rehearsal. She directed her attention to the stage where there were signs of renewed activity. The stagehands retired, having done their stint, and the tentative sounds from the orchestra dwindled into a watchful silence, as the conductor took to the podium in his shirtsleeves.

Izlomin pawed in the resin box first with one foot and then with the other and walked toward the platforms with the waddling gait that is the result of a proper turnout, that traditional Chaplinesque leg and foot posi-tion of the ballet dancer. There was a nervous anticipatory movement among all the dancers except Mike Gorin, who went on talking to the pretty little Georgian.

And then there took place a convincing display of the famous Izlomin temperament. Izlomin walked over to the couple and mimed an impera-tive and offensive "Out!" at Mike. The boy's shoulders swung a little and his dark face glowered. He stood his ground. The next moment the im-passive mask of Izlomin's face was convulsed by a grimace of rage, as disconcerting in its unexpectedness as in its exaggerated ferocity. He sud-denly thrust at the other's shoulders and sent him staggering. Mike recovered and came up, crouching like Dempsey, his fists up. Izlomin, on his part, threw himself into a position that was very much like the one favored by John L. Sullivan in his heyday, except that he was "turned out." It would have been funny except for his air of concentrated malignity. He might not have knocked his opponent out, but he certainly was fully prepared to tear him to pieces.

It was over in a minute. There were squeals of excitement from all sides. De Speranski shot out of the wings saying, "*Messieurs, messieurs,*" in agitated tones, and presently Mike was led out into the wings.

"Well," said Eric, "he's pretty free with his hands, isn't he?"

"I told you he was a bad boy."

Izlomin vaulted lightly onto the first platform and stood there, hands on hips. He looked pleased with himself. His voice rang out harshly, and the little Ribina hurried to the middle of the stage to take an attitude. A group of dancers shuffled into formation opposite her.

Skeets gave a chuckle. "You know, now I see that's the way you walk too. Just like all of them. You sort of touch the back of each ankle with the heel of the other foot."

"Doing unconscious *battements,*" Toni agreed. "That's ballet training."

Another command crackled. To Skeets it sounded like sheer gibberish but Toni nodded happily. The rehearsal was on.

CHAPTER TWO

IZLOMIN TURNED HIS SLANTED EYES on Toni and asked quite pleasantly whether there was anything else. He was in an excellent mood—exhilarated by dancing and probably by his clash with Mike. His face was a flat Tatar mask, with a bulging forehead, diagonal slits for eyes and a curly mouth with deep dents at the corners denoting cruelty and willfulness. His broad chest rose and fell deeply but otherwise he seemed unaffected by hours of ceaseless leaping and twirling. The rehearsal had been over for some time now, but Izlomin went on untiringly posing for pictures.

Toni looked up from the floor where she was pawing elbow deep among bulbs. "How about a close-up of some sort? Just as a change from all the action shots?" Izlomin nodded. "Anyssing for you," he said suddenly in horrible English. He went back to French immediately. "I must thank you for the sequins. The man you told me about is working on the costume and it will be magnificent for tonight."

"I'm glad," said Toni. She added, smiling, "Any time you need anything?"

"I need something right now," said Izlomin, "but it is an article you probably have no knowledge of."

"Try me."

Izlomin gave a strange short bark of laughter that left his face unchanged. "*J'ai besoin d'un flic.*"

He needed a cop?

Toni's eyelashes flickered with the unexpectedness of it. But she rose to the occasion nobly. "As a matter of fact, I do know one."

Izlomin looked at her with incredulity which turned to eagerness. Then the impassive mask fell again. "I'll speak to you about it alone."

There were people converging on them from all sides. Mrs. Whitehead, followed by her tweedy companion, and Natalia Izlomina with a tremendous afghan hound on a leash, flanked by de Speranski with a marmoset. Mrs. Whitehead made it first.

"Poor old boy," she said in her rather hoarse voice, "you're sweating all over."

Her large hand clung to his shoulder with a massaging motion. Except for the voluptuous look in her long face, she might have been stroking a cherished hunter after an arduous gallop.

Izlomin's shoulders moved nervously under her hand. The next minute he had shrugged it off and turned to his wife.

"Ah, here are my little darlings." He leaned forward and the marmoset leaped to his shoulder. The dog rose to its hind legs and licked his face, panting sympathetically.

"Hold it," said Toni. "That's a good one. Do you mind holding the lights, Eric?

Eric obligingly imitated the Statue of Liberty while Izlomin held the smile and the attitude until the camera clicked.

Mrs. Whitehead's companion cleared his throat and spoke up. He had a pleasant baritone, with a sort of cultured stutter in it. "Look here," he said. "It'd be rather amusing to get Natalia into this. How about it, Vova?"

Natalia said, "Oh, but Charles," in her soft, queerly accentless voice.

Vova looked perversely blank, but agreed when she translated the remark to him. He eyed the man who had made the suggestion with ill grace. It was clear that his unwillingness to share the limelight included his wife. Toni suggested a pose both balletic and connubial—Izlomin adjusting his wife's arabesque.

Izlomin nodded to that. He detached the clinging marmoset from around his neck and suddenly handed it, with a little bow, to the other man. There was something infinitely insulting about the gesture. Nothing overt—perhaps a certain mocking exaggeration in the bow, in the curve of the arm, the faint insolent smile that brought a flush to the victim's cheek.

"How about posing over by that ramp so I can get the background in?" Toni suggested hastily. The Izlomins repaired there docilely. The gentleman known as Charles remained behind trying to disengage the too-affectionate simian's prehensile grip around his neck. The marmoset gave a sudden cheep of delight, snatched his glasses and decamped.

Toni scooped the animal up just as it was darting past her. It chattered indignantly and there was an absurd little tug of war before it yielded the glasses and was carried away by the clucking de Speranski.

"Thanks," said the owner of the glasses, putting them on again with a sheepish grin. "Crummy little beast, isn't it?" Toni wondered whether he meant the monkey. She was conscious of a small pang of astonishment as their eyes met. His were so brilliantly blue behind the horn-rimmed glasses and so full of bright intense personal interest that she felt an answering emotion of curiosity and awareness. He was tall and well-built, though a bit on the well-padded side. He looked rather like Brian Aherne. Toni had never seen him before. He was obviously a friend of Mrs. Whitehead's but as she walked to the ramp where Izlomin had posed his wife in an impeccable arabesque, Toni found herself thinking of him rather as a friend of Natalia Izlomina, not just because of his intervention in her behalf but because there had been that swift intimate exchange of amused glances between them.

Izlomin was now being the perfect partner. He even wore the beagle look that is the special mark of a *"danseur noble,"* who is supposed to maintain a chivalrous and tender attitude toward the ballerina. The camera clicked, Natalia recovered from the arabesque and curtsied to her husband. She was a slender, soft-spoken woman in her thirties, with smooth brown hair and one dimple, strategically placed in her left cheek. It made her smile very charming. Not even the dimple, however, could dissipate the impression of an implacable will that emanated from her rather placid face.

Izlomin answered her curtsy with a little bow—an exquisite thing it was—and turned away, shaking his head in answer to her "Vova, shall I help you?" An imperious tilt of his head beckoned to Toni, who came along after telling Skeets to wait for her.

She followed him through the rear exit on the left side of the stage and up the adjacent staircase to the first floor. The rooms of the three *premiers danseurs* were around the corner from those of the ballerinas: Perlova, the prima, and little Tamara Ribina, next in rank. This was a rather unusual arrangement since the girls' dressing rooms were on this side of the house and the men's on the other, and the accepted thing is to keep the sexes chastely separated, each on its own side. But Izlomin had insisted on the dressing room he now occupied, and in his capacity of the spoiled darling of the company got it. De Speranski had tried to improve the look of things by putting the two other male soloists, Mike Gorin and André Vassine, in the adjoining room. With Vassine out of the company, the red-haired young Slava Mladov took his place, to the great chagrin of Perlova, who would have liked to see her husband Barezian there.

Toni had to admit that Izlomin had picked himself a nice dressing room. It was large, with a private bathroom and plenty of room in it for an outsize dressing table, with all kinds of gadgets, and a couch with a little table next to it, not to mention a huge trunk filled practically to the brim with costumes. Other costumes hung on the wall, among them the ruffed shirt and black tights of the Dreamer in *Cauchemar* and a luxurious black velvet cape. Against them a tunic of sequins glittered flamboyantly, sending out sheaves of white sparks where the light struck it.

Izlomin explained, "That's the costume I'll have to wear if the tailor won't be able to finish the other one in time. *Hélas!* If I had only thought of asking you about it before, it would surely have been ready for tonight."

Genuine regret quivered in his voice. He took off his drenched shirt and threw a towel around his lean torso, that gleamed with sweat. Then he fixed Toni with a portentous eye. "*Alors.* About the cop. I am in danger and I need one. Tell me, *petite,* how is it you know someone like that?"

Toni explained briefly about Captain Andrew Torrent of the Homicide Squad who was the cop of her acquaintance, not mentioning the circumstances under which they had met but stressing rather the genuine love for ballet they held in common. Izlomin was enthusiastic.

"Just what I need. I must have this Torrent. He is just right for me. It is marvelous. He will help and protect me."

"From what?"

Izlomin's voice subsided into a mysterious whisper. "I told you I am in great danger." Somebody, it seemed, was gunning for him. He mentioned several "*occurrences mysterieuses,*" a rusty nail on the stage, a sandbag that barely missed him, and finally, culminating all these outrages, the fact that his valet Grigorii had been poisoned.

Toni could think of nothing better to say than "How is he feeling?" She thought privately that this was the most unconvincing story she had ever heard. The falling sandbags particularly had a familiar and bogus ring. And a poisoned faithful servitor! "Who? Oh, Grigorii." Izlomin dismissed him with a shrug. "He is as sick as a dog and I must dress myself alone tonight of all nights. But that is not the point." The point was evidently that the valet must have eaten something that was intended for his master. If not for that, it would be he, Izlomin, who would now be sick as a dog, or perhaps, lacking the crude peasant constitution of the valet, even worse. Izlomin blanched at the thought. "You see now why I must have this Torrent?"

Here Toni had an unpleasant thought that caused her to throw a furtive look at the door, which Izlomin had thoughtfully closed before indulging in these revelations. She cursed herself for the thoughtless impulse that threatened to involve her, if not Torrent (whom she certainly did not intend to bother with this nonsense) in the temperamental didoes of a mad Russian dancer.

Disconcertingly the dancer seemed to read her thought. A mocking little smile twisted his lips and he shook his head.

"*Non,*" he said, "I am not crazy. Look."

He fumbled in the pockets of his suit that lay on the couch—a somewhat flamboyant number but custom-made and bearing the label of a reputable and expensive tailor—and took out a few crumpled scraps of paper which he pressed into Toni's hands. Toni looked at them. Couched in bad but sinister French, they warned Izlomin that he had enemies and told him to watch himself or beware of a tragedy in the near future.

"I will have others for you later," said Izlomin and stiffened as someone knocked at the door. He took the notes from Toni and put them into a drawer of his dressing table.

"It is I, Vova," said Natalia's voice.

"One minute," the dancer answered and whispered to Toni urgently, "You will bring him to see me tonight, no?" His eyes commanded her, overriding the protest that rose to her lips. "I will have a ticket for him. He will see Izlomin dance and then serve him, perhaps save his life. *Epatant!*" After a moment's reflection Toni assented. The lure of a ticket to a performance to which all tickets had been sold out in advance might persuade Torrent not to mind too much the obligations connected with it. Torrent did like his ballet. "You will arrange it then. *Bien.* And," he placed his finger on his lips with another of his curiously eloquent gestures, "silence!"

As he opened the door Toni wondered what Natalia Izlomina thought of his being thus secretly closeted with another woman. There was not a flicker of disturbance on her placid face, however. She had changed into street clothes, which were in good taste without the theatrical exaggeration that is characteristic of a dancer's attire for any occasion.

"I hope the interview is over," she said in her pleasant voice, "because Mrs. Whitehead and Charles are waiting. Vova, *tu n'as pas encore pris le* shower?" Her inflection was the indulgent one of a patient mother managing a rather cranky child. She shook her head at Toni. "He doesn't know the meaning of time, *ce pauvre* Vova."

Ce pauvre Vova gave her an evil grin and remarked, "*Madame la gouvernante!*" He added with deliberate unconcern, "By the way, I must have a ticket for a friend of Mademoiselle Ney. Put him in the box or take the ticket away—from you know whom. It is vital. She has been so nice."

"Ah, yes, about the sequins." Natalia went on to say that they made all the difference in the world in the costume. She herself had gone to see the tailor and there was a very good chance that the costume would be altered in time. How could Toni have been so clever?

Vova meanwhile had disappeared into the bathroom, peeling his tights down over his lean hips as he went, and presently there was the sound of a shower being taken. Toni explained about the sequins—she had used them on an evening gown of hers with good effect. They had quite a special golden sheen.

Natalia laughed. "Vova will have to shine for the whole family tonight. I will look a fright, Look!" She swung up her right foot and Toni saw a thick bandage of tape around her ankle. "The doctor says I can't dance without it and it will certainly look lovely in my solo. The Scythian queen with a bandaged ankle—that will be charming!"

Toni commiserated and suggested that a whole slew of heavy barbaric bracelets would mask the bandage adequately. Natalia brightened up and said that that would be fine. Vova had the very thing from his black slave costume in *Scheherazade*. She added, "Do not worry about the ticket for your friend. I will see to it that he will have one."

Toni left, feeling that she was firmly entrenched in the good graces of both Izlomins.

She went back to the stage to pick up Eric and found him in the corridor, talking to Mike Gorin. The latter turned toward Toni with a smile, a capacious Irish grin that seemed to illumine his dark, somewhat sullen face.

"Toni, me darling, I haven't seen you in a donkey's age. I see you haven't put on any weight. Still good for an adagio, eh?" His large hands spanned her waist and he lifted her up in the air without any effort. "Light as a feather," he reported to Skeets and set her down gently.

"Ah, my lost youth," said Toni, recovering from an automatic *plié*. "Mike used to toss me about when I was his adagio partner during my short but delirious career as a dancer. In between I'd nurse my black and blue spots and try to think up ways to avoid more, but it never worked. Any friendship that survives that sort of thing is good for life."

Eric suggested that if that was the sort of thing she enjoyed he would see what he could do about it, and Mike said that you couldn't just do it cold, you needed a lot of practice.

"Nonsense," Eric rejoined amiably. "It's the bruises she misses and I can always supply those." Mike aimed a playful cuff at Eric's chin. Toni thought that for an ordinarily staid citizen, he was remarkably exuberant today.

"While we're on the subject," she said, "that was a fine show you almost put on with Vova. We were worried about you there."

Mike, who had fought in the ring in his day, grinned and then scowled. "I'll have to slap him down yet one day." He added with scorn, "The dumb ballet dancer."

Toni and Eric suppressed a smile at this slighting allusion to a profession of which Mike was one of the brightest lights.

Mikhail Gorin of the American Ballet Drama represented a phenomenon which was of late becoming more and more prevalent in what had been once a purely continental monopoly—a native American ballet dancer. He was originally Mike Gordon, a nice Irish lad from Brooklyn. At the

early age of thirteen he saw a ballet poster and decided that he was going
to be a ballet dancer. What mysterious impulse caused him to choose that
exotic *metiér* he himself could never explain. But there it was. He turned
up his nose at the Irish folk dancing companies or ballroom dancing, which
seemed like more natural outlets for his terpsichorean longings, and grimly
took ballet lessons. His present post as one of the *premiers danseurs* of
the highest paid ballet company in the United States was an impressive
reward of his perseverance.

"I already got hell from de Speranski," Mike went on, scowling blackly.
"As if he didn't know who was to blame. I've always been against this
favoritism. Izlomin is just a worker like the rest of the kids, there's no
reason why he should be treated like a little tin god. De Speranski hates
my guts, though, almost worse than he does Izlomin's, on account of I'm
the shop chairman here and I don't let him get away with any fancy
stuff." Mike took his responsibility to his union very seriously and was
very much the trades-union-conscious Irishman in the midst of giddy Russians. "Only the other day I practically had to pull a strike when he wanted
us to remain on stage for pictures after we'd had our maximum number of
rehearsal hours for the day. Appealing to our honor as artists, the old
goat—" He broke off. "There's the girlfriend."

The coldness with which Tamara Ribina greeted him seemed to gain-
say this statement. At close range she was even prettier than from afar, in
a spicy Mongolian way. Her round dish face and high cheekbones gave
her a definitely eastern look. Her black hair lay smooth as satin around
her small sleek head.

"Toni, how nice to see you. They said you were around." There was
a hardly perceptible Russian accent in her speech, a foreign preciseness,
a faint blurring of the consonants. "I don't see you in class any more."

"I have no time, alas."

"You have quite given up your career as a dancer, yes?" Tamara
patted her on the shoulder sympathetically. "You're so right. It is a terrible
profession. You're lucky to be out of it." Her tone was palpably insincere.
She might have been assuring a jilted friend that the man she had lost was
no good anyhow and she was much better off without him.

"Besides," she went on, with devastating hauteur, "you meet such
boors in ballet." Her ridiculous eyelashes fluttered in disdain.

"Hey," Mike protested, in pained tones. "Don't look at *me*."

Tamara turned on him, black eyes flashing. "Brawling," she said, "brawling before everybody, in the middle of a rehearsal."

"But darling," said Mike, puzzled, "you know it wasn't my fault. Hey!" His black eyebrows moved together. "If you're putting this on just so that you'll have an excuse about tonight—" Tamara's creamy Calmuck skin mantled with an outraged blush.

"Mike Gorin! I'll go exactly where I please!"

Mike shook his head slowly. "Not with that jerk Izlomin. Not if he wants to stay healthy."

"Why, Mike Gorin!" Tamara gasped, her eyes black pools of delighted horror. "How dare you threaten Vova Izlomin! He's a great dancer, and you aren't worthy to tie the laces of his shoes." There was a pause throbbing with emotion. Toni and Skeets departed in a hurry, leaving the embattled couple glaring at each other.

"My, my," said Eric. "All is not well in love's young dream."

"Makes life more interesting," Toni told him. "What's love without Another Man or Another Woman?"

CHAPTER THREE

IT WAS EVENING. The Civic Opera House was now ready for night life. It flashed its array of electric lights proclaiming a gala performance of the American Ballet Drama with Izlomin and Perlova. Toni, who had arrived early, was making her way backstage through the stage entrance from which suppressed excitement seemed to billow forth like smoke. The doorman let Toni pass without his usual comment on the weather. Usually a chatty old soul, he was too busy signing the receipts for flowers which were being brought in by the ton, and going inside to stack the boxes and baskets on a special table in the corridor, from which they would later be delivered to their proper destination.

Toni turned right, passed the first door leading backstage and ran up the adjoining stairs, her jeweled heels tapping smartly. This was a different flight of stairs from the one she had used earlier in the day (that one was farther toward the rear) but it would also take her to Izlomin's dressing room. She was about to report to the latter that he was to get his cop after all.

Dear Vova was getting his way in pretty much everything tonight, Toni thought. Take the program. To a ballet lover it might be merely an artistic delight. To one who was more or less acquainted with the intricate backstage politics it was more than that. It was one man's personal triumph. Of the five ballets scheduled for tonight four were of Izlomin's choreography and the choreographer was dancing in three of them. The curtain raiser, *Aurora's Wedding,* was followed by the much publicized *Phoebus.* Then came *Rêves de Printemps,* a short but lively divertissement, and after that *Cauchemar,* a spectacular affair with mad scenery by a well-known surrealist painter and the kind of modern music with shimmering overtones that sets up unwelcome vibrations in your back teeth. Izlomin's part, that of the Dreamer, consisted of frenetic miming rather than dancing, so that he didn't have to work too hard and would be in shape for the last ballet on the program, that old favorite, *Le Roi des Chats.*

Before Toni had a chance to knock at Izlomin's door, it opened and Natalia Izlomina came out. There was a tiny worried frown on her placid brow. She smiled at Toni, but the frown remained unerased.

"Mademoiselle Ney, you wish to see Vova?"

"Not if it's inconvenient. Merely to thank him and you for the pass."

"Well…" The dimple flashed and Natalia took Toni into her confidence with a look of droll dismay. "There is a great tragedy inside. The costume didn't come." From the way she said it, Izlomin might have been a heartbroken adolescent whose long trousers failed to arrive in time for a party. Toni remembered that Natalia was a little older than her husband. "I hate to seem to want to keep you out, but Vova is a little nervous. Perhaps later…"

Toni said she understood perfectly.

"You know how everything goes wrong sometimes. Vova is so accustomed to having Grigorii dressing him and now that he can't…"

Toni decided that that must be the supposedly poisoned valet. "What's the matter with him?

Izlomina shrugged her shoulders. "Ptomaine poisoning. And just when he is needed most." Her tone seemed to indicate that it was very inconsiderate of him. "Vova won't let anybody but Grigorii dress him, as a rule. I'll help him with the costume and then there'll be just the makeup to put on. The trouble is that I myself have to dress. Well, we'll manage." She gave Toni a friendly nod and hurried away.

Toni was about to follow her example when Izlomin himself came out of his room. In his voluminous kimono of variable Chinese silk, with the marmoset in his arms, he looked mysterious and oriental. His slanted eyes gleamed with anticipation.

"I heard your voice," he said. "*Eh bien?*"

"It's all right," Toni told him. "Captain Torrent will be here tonight and he'll drop in later to thank you for the ticket."

"*Epatant*," said Izlomin. Then his face went watchful as a door opened and closed in one of the rooms around the corner on a feminine voice raised in anger. Mike Gorin tramped furiously to his own room, almost stumbling over Izlomin. The two glared at each other, hackles rising. Then Mike mumbled. "Hello there, Toni," showed his white teeth in a hurried smile and proceeded on his way.

Izlomin watched him out of sight with a funny pleased look on his face. But he too recollected himself, bowed over Toni's hand and told her that she had been wonderful and that he would see her and "the cop" after the performance. Then he too was gone, leaving her alone in the corridor.

"Well," said Toni, "more fun, more doors slammed! What's up? Another lovers' quarrel with Izlomin playing the heavy?"

She decided to drop in around the corner and investigate.

Perlova's room came before Tamara's, and Toni, on her way to the latter, was intercepted by the prima ballerina's calling to her and asking her to come in.

Elena Perlova was seated before the mirror. She had just finished adjusting the silvery wig and tiny diadem of *Princess Aurora* onto her shapely head, had snapped the pink elastic that held it in place under her chin and was now busily pasting on her artificial eyelashes.

She had been one of the *grandes danseuses* of "the golden age of ballet" and was still one of its more luminous lights. She was a memorable Columbine in *Carnaval,* a dazzling glove seller in *Gaieté Parisienne* and, the supreme test of all, a heartbreakingly lovely Giselle.

A fragile, long-legged blonde with a somewhat petulant expression on her oval face, she had worn well. She was still quite a *femme fatale*. She had been married several times. Her fourth husband had been a doddering millionaire and the present incumbent, probably by way of reward, was a handsome young dancer in the company. The tycoon apparently hadn't borne her any grudge for her defection. He had continued her substantial alimony even after she had remarried and had remembered her very handsomely in his will, "in gratitude," as he had put it rather touchingly, "for her having bestowed upon him a few unforgettable years out of her full and valuable life."

"Come in, darling," she greeted Toni. "I saw you at the rehearsal today. Terrible, wasn't it? Have you heard about my poor Kotik? They have taken him into the army. I am so sad."

"They're taking all the best young men," said Toni. "My young man is in the army too."

Perlova extended her slim eloquent arm toward Toni in a gesture of exquisite sympathy and then pointed to a seat alongside the dressing table.

Toni sat down. The two dressing rooms were connected by a tiny bathroom, both doors of which were open, and she could see Tamara sullenly putting on her makeup. She wore tights and a towel and her flat face was sulky, the eyebrows slanting like antennae of an angry bee.

Toni said, "I'd like to take a picture of the two of you. You're both in line."

"Not right now," Tamara called out from her room. "I haven't even got my bra on."

Perlova lifted a malicious eyebrow. "Poor Tamara. She has outgrown all her old bras and has to get a new one, because otherwise she bounce too much."

She dropped a dainty tinkle of laughter, which was echoed by a savage snort from the other room.

"Yes," she continued mercilessly. "Tamara is growing fat again. Pretty soon there'll be complaints from her adagio partners."

Toni suppressed a smile. Tamara's tragedy consisted of her constantly having to make a choice between staying plump and looking divinely pretty close to and a bit heavy on the stage, or dieting and looking wonderful on the stage and haggard at close quarters.

There was a squeal of rage and Tamara appeared in the doorway modestly clutching a towel around the bosom in question.

"I wouldn't worry about my adagio partners," she remarked angrily. "At least I have elevation, no matter what my weight. Certain people may be skinny as skeletons but they can't rise off the floor to save their lives."

Toni registered that as a hit. Perlova had dazzling technique and an impeccable line, but she did lack "*ballon*"—that ability to soar which Nijinski had once described naively as "jumping and just stopping in the air for a moment."

"Don't be a brat," Toni counseled mildly in the wake of the little dancer, who had flounced back to her room.

"I've always preferred Tamara when she's fat," said Perlova with restraint. "When she is dieting she is very disagreeable. Only now she is both fat *and* disagreeable. That's what comes of thinking one is a *femme fatale*. If I were you, Tamara, I'd stick to Mike. He's a dear boy. I know Vova from Paris and he's bad for little girls like you. Is he still saying how he'd like to marry you but there's Natalia to think of?"

"No, he isn't," said Tamara, with violence.

"Oh? Well, then he will. Frankly I don't understand why Natalia stands for this, poor dear."

Tamara banged down a few objects on her table and remarked with some violence that she wished mamma would come in with the Bluebird headdress.

"Everything is going wrong today," she said and added darkly, "If there were justice, I would be dancing Princess Aurora, and not Bluebird."

"Greedy little thing," said Perlova, glancing with some complacence at her own white and gold Aurora costume. "Isn't it enough that Vova sticks you into every one of his ballets?"

"Just little solos. Nobody ever gets a really important part in Vova's ballets except him. You know perfectly well that I agreed to your dancing Aurora last Monday when it was my turn because I thought it'd work out so that I'd have the part for tonight. Just because I can never count right…"

Perlova laughed heartlessly and Toni inquired, "What's wrong with dancing Bluebird? It's just as important."

"No, it isn't. It's just a solo. And besides," there was suddenly a complacent little note in her voice, "I have to dance it with Mike and the way he's acting, it's downright dangerous."

Toni squinted into the viewfinder. "Now that you're decent, sit still and I'll take the picture." She backed into the closet so as to put distance between her and Perlova and get them both into focus. "Why is it dangerous?"

"Because he's so jealous." Tamara froze obediently in her seat. Her incredible eyelashes fluttered coyly against an olive-hued cheek. An irresistible prim little smirk tugged at her lips. "When he gets that way you can't tell what he might do. Why—why, he might even kill one," ' she ended with evident relish.

Toni snorted. The pretty little Georgian was apparently succumbing to an onrush of tribal memories. The worst Mike would do, no matter how

sore he was, would be to take a hairbrush or a ballet slipper to her somewhat oriental derriere.

She snapped the picture and Tamara looked at her reproachfully. "I
thought you'd understand, Toni. But I suppose it's not your fault. After all,
you haven't really danced for a long time."

"True," said Toni, amused. "My sensitivity has been blunted by years
of inaction. See you downstairs, ladies. Thanks for the picture."

She took a last critical look at herself in the mirror before going downstairs. The good old slipper-satin frock (only recently shortened to the
fashionable new length) molded her slim body nicely, with rich oily high-
lights along hip and breast, until she looked as slippery-slick as an eel, and
her hair lay smooth within the sequin-spangled snood. Only the battered
little camera case betrayed her true status as a working girl on a job. She
hoped she would be able to keep this unruffled exterior until she saw her
lieutenant. If she remembered correctly, servicemen on leave liked their
women to be strictly glamorous of evenings, and it was bad enough that
she had to work on his first night home.

Backstage the gala night jitters were in full swing. The members of
the corps de ballet, whose dressing rooms were on a floor above the stars,
were madly shuttling up and down both staircases like angels on Jacob's
ladder. An agitated shepherdess brushed by Toni and ran upstairs weeping loudly. Two others were grimly going through their *pliés*, their noses
up in the air. The *regisseur*, Paul Samarkand, was down on his knees in
the wings, massaging the ankle of the first *soliste*. His harassed air, typical of all *regisseurs* on gala nights, was enhanced by his crossed eyes and
the white lock in his disheveled hair.

Toni patted her camera. Tonight's harvest would be a fine crop of
Degas-like studies. She couldn't use her flashgun during the performance
but her knowledge of ballet was so thorough that she could anticipate and
snap the poses she wanted at exactly the right moment with the lens wide
open. She looked around anxiously but failed to see Bill Stone, the photographer, who had promised to show up early this time.

A bell rang. The stagehands hurried to give the last touches to the
scenery, circling around moving props and shifting spots in a heavy-footed
ballet of their own. A brawny six-footer surveyed his domain, with his
arms folded across his chest, and bawled, "The 'reat'—ain't nobody gonna
fix that 'reat'?" Whereupon a burly subordinate fell on his knees and
delicately adjusted the flowery garland in question.

The girl who had gone upstairs in a tantrum was now flying back, all traces of tears gone, to join the rest of the ensemble that the *regisseur* was aligning for the entrance. On the other side of the curtain the reedy sounds of the orchestra merged with the surflike flurry of applause. Then the national anthem, the opening strains of *Aurora,* and the thrilling susurrus of the curtain going up. The performance had started.

A ballet performance as seen from backstage is a much more casual affair than one imagines it to be. The dancers do not crouch in the wings breathing heavily and waiting tensely for their turn. They paddle around in the semitransparent darkness with their feet turned out a la Chaplin, or lounge in the wings gossiping at the top of their voices. The music sounds far away and casual, like a radio playing next door. Then suddenly in the middle of a sentence, one of the gossipers takes the piece of gum out of her mouth, rises to her *pointes* and floats gracefully onstage. Her stint done she comes back, her breath barely quickened, picks up the wad of chewing gum where she has parked it and in a moment is again immersed in the favorite backstage pastime of blackening the character of a fellow dancer.

Toni, watching Perlova spinning smoothly in the arms of her young husband, thought that there was nobody like her, after all. She heard a tiny sigh, and turning, saw Tamara, who said contritely. "I've been a pig to Elena. And with Kotik going in the army, too. But everything has been so awful."

Toni said there, there, and patted her olive shoulder. They watched Perlova taking bow after bow, giving her funny bittersweet smile to the audience.

"Just for that," said Tamara, "I'm going to the Russian Rendezvous tonight with everybody and not to El Morocco."

Toni wondered why Tamara seemed to regard that as a gesture of atonement. It seemed that a going away party was being given for Kotik Barezian at the Russian Rendezvous after the performance. The snag was that Vova had gotten up a party of his own at El Morocco. ("He would," Toni thought.) This had split the company into two factions, with the larger one led by Mike favoring the Russian Rendezvous.

"I would have come to Kotik's party in the first place," said Tamara, "only Mike got so bossy about it. He's so—well—bullheaded about things. Believe it or not, he bumped into Vova going into the theater tonight and tackled him about it again, in spite of what happened at the rehearsal. Vova just laughed in his face."

She stared gloomily at the stage where Slava Mladov was brilliantly squiring his two partners through the "Florestan and his Sisters" variation. Presently her chiseled little nose went up in the air. This hauteur was for the benefit of Mike Gorin who had just arrived, somewhat out of breath. He didn't look the way he would presently look onstage. He looked like an irascible young Irishman unaccountably rigged out in blue tights and jacket.

"About time," said Tamara to no one in particular. "I was wondering if I would have to go out there alone."

Mike's answering snarl was lost in the applause that greeted the end of the Florestan variation. Slava and his two partners brushed by them. Then the flute trilled the opening phrase of the Bluebird and the two put on the conventional sugary smiles and drifted off.

Toni was watching them going through the flirtatious little variation until subdued yells of rage distracted her attention. Another vivid tableau was taking place backstage. Slava Mladov was sitting on the floor, holding on to his middle. His curled white wig was askew, with the thatch of fiery red hair showing from under it, and tears of rage were pouring down his face. He looked like a fourteen-year-old in a tantrum. One of his partners, the blonde Janet Banks, was also crying bitterly on the *regisseur*'s shoulder.

"He pinched me!"

"She kicked me!"

Toni decided that probably both charges were correct but wondered about the order.

"Monsieur Samarkand, he really did. I won't dance with him. Let Nina be his partner in the finale. I don't know what's gotten into him, he's acting like a perfect devil. I just won't go on if I have to dance with him."

"If you think I want to dance with you, with your damned big feet…" Slava pronounced the last word as "fit." His Balkan accent had thickened under the stress of emotion.

"Slava!" A cool voice interrupted him and Natalia Izlomina stepped into the breach. She was already dressed for *Phoebus* in the barbaric Scythian costume, with the black robe for the "mist variation" hanging over her shoulders. Toni noticed that her suggestion about the bracelets had been taken. "You should be ashamed of yourself. Now you must apologize to Janet instantly."

"What's the matter? Trouble again?" Mrs. Whitehead bore down on the group.

A long mink coat streaming back from her rangy New England figure showed it to be wrapped in a violent magenta gown, a color that throbbed behind your eyelids after you had shut your eyes against it. A thick rope of pearls had been hastily hurled around her stringy neck and occasionally she loosened it with the same gesture that men use when tugging at their collars.

Toni noticed with a queer little twinge of excitement the man who was squiring her. It was the same one whose glasses she had rescued. He had changed his tweeds for evening clothes but his hair was still tousled a la Willkie.

Kate Whitehead inquired ominously, "Who's been helling around here?"

Janet Banks took a look at her, shuddered and dissolved into fresh tears.

"Everything is all right now," said Natalia. "Slava, did you hear what I said?"

Slava threw a sheepish and devoted look at her and muttered a reluctant apology.

"That's better," said Natalia serenely, with an amused glance at the newcomers. "Silly children. Janet, you must stop crying or you will ruin your nice makeup. And you," she turned to the boy again and gave his red hair a playful tug, "come over here and I'll fix your wig for you."

The boy clambered to his feet with alacrity and suffered himself to be led away.

"There, that's settled," said Mrs. Whitehead's friend, evidently much diverted. "Apparently every woman is a mother at heart."

Mrs. Whitehead sniffed. "My dear innocent, let me inform you that not every woman who likes to pat little boys on the head feels motherly toward them."

"What a foulmouthed hag you are, Kate dear," replied the innocent amiably.

Kate dear answered in unprintable terms and announced that she hadn't come here to listen to backstage squabbles. She was going upstairs to give Vova her blessing, and Charles was to wait here for her.

Natalia, who had just finished fixing Slava's wig and rejoined the group, intervened swiftly. But no, Mrs. Whitehead really mustn't—she didn't think that Vova was fit to be seen. Mrs. Whitehead patted her cheek patronizingly and made off. Natalia followed. The set of her shoulders told Toni that she would do her best to protect Vova from intrusion.

Toni went back to her place in the wings and was presently joined there by Mrs. Whitehead's escort. Out of the corner of her eye she saw him take out a pipe, remember just in time, and clamp it unlit between his square white teeth. Toni smiled involuntarily, as one smiles at a mannerism of someone one knows and likes. And then she thought, annoyed, "But I don't know him." A spark of illogical irritation, which seemed to set off another equally astonishing reaction. She found herself saying silently, "I want him to speak to me. I want him to." Shocked, she stared blindly straight ahead at the stage, where Perlova, Barezian and three other men were going through a complicated ritual consisting of passing red roses back and forth. She felt him looking at her.

Then his deep voice said hesitatingly, "I say, that's a fine arabesque."

Toni's hold on her camera tightened. "Yes. Only it's not an arabesque. It's an attitude.

"Really? Looks the same to me. She's standing on one leg, isn't she?"

"Ah!" said Toni. "But while her leg is raised to form an angle of ninety degrees with the body, like in arabesque, the knee is bent and that makes all the difference in the world."

The man took off his glasses and stared at her comically. Without them he looked more like Brian Aherne than ever.

"My word, you do know a lot about ballet."

"That's because I'm a retired ballet dancer and ballet dancers, like elephants, never forget."

"You don't look like retired anything, if I may say so."

"I'm well preserved," said Toni and smiled.

"That's nice," said the man. "I mean your smile. You don't do it very often, do you? You're on the *Globe,* I believe. And this is your beat. I don't know much about ballet myself. Matter of fact, I used to think it rather silly until I met Natalia. She's writing a book for us, you know. I'm in the publishing business. My name is Graham."

Toni added the first name to the last and gasped with dismay. She was remembering only too vividly the disparaging remarks she had made about Natalia's book and by the half-smile on her interlocutor's face, she suspected that he remembered them too.

"Charles Graham," she thought. "Of course, good heavens. The playboy publisher."

She had seen pictures of him in society pages, squiring spectacular blondes at the Stork and successful authors at the Algonquin. She looked at him critically and to her own dismay heard herself say, "Of course you're much better groomed in the pictures."

Graham burst into delighted laughter. "You're wonderful. By George, you are. Look here, what's your name?"

"Ney. I'm not saying an archaic no. My name is Toni Ney."

"Well, Miss Ney, we're throwing a little party in honor of friend Vova after the performance tonight. At El Morocco. Would you consider joining us?"

"Thank you. I'll have to ask my escort."

"Oh?" A fine-drawn eyebrow arched quizzically. "The lieutenant at the rehearsal?"

"The same."

"Engaged to him?"

"Only for the evening, so far."

"Good."

The conversation ended on this rather ambiguous note as Mrs. White-head came sailing back, her face somewhat higher of color than usual.

"Imagine," she said. "He actually slammed the door and locked it in my face, and I think—Charles, I really believe, he threw a ballet shoe at it, the temperamental little bastard."

Toni retired prudently, fighting an unworthy desire to hear more. She was a little afraid of the overwhelming Mrs. Whitehead.

The ballet drew to a close. There was a brief pandemonium as dancers shuttled back and forth for their curtain calls, rushing upstairs to change as these narrowed down to the principals. Even the latter did not take the usual number because of the little time left for changing. *Phoebus* was going on in ten minutes and everybody was in it. Those who had not danced in *Aurora* came down dressed in their *Phoebus* costumes, as Ethiops, Greeks, Scyths. Some of them already wore the garments they needed for their first emergence on the stage as Morning Mists, long trailing burnoose-like affairs that were fixed to their heads by means of thin silver fillets and cascaded down to the ankle, hooding their faces and covering their costumes. As the stage slowly darkened in preparation for the ballet, they seemed to disappear in the shadows, as if they had been shadows themselves.

Toni watched them absently. It looked as though she would not be able to see the ballet from up front with Skeets.

"Waiting for someone?" a voice caroled helpfully behind her. A weedy young man with a sparse blond mustache and longish blond hair put down the photographic equipment with which he was loaded and beamed at Toni tentatively.

Toni beamed back. She didn't bother to scold Bill Stone for being late. Their extremely pleasant relationship was based on an attitude of patient resignation on her part, coupled with a weary realization that Bill was really trying. She had even given up questioning his excuses, which were a bit on the weird side—something like "sorry to be late, but there was a man-eating tiger loose in the subway." Trouble was, you couldn't tell with Bill. Once he explained his failure to show up at a very important assignment by a casual mention of a holdup in which he was involved. The next day his pictures of it were spread all over the front page. That was Bill Stone.

Toni fastened on the photographer with the savage joy of a mother lioness recovering her lost cubs and promptly popped him into the prompter's box. When she came back again to pick up her coat, which she had left lying on a packing case, the ballet was almost ready to start. She was just about to start for up front when Izlomin appeared in the entrance. Like Richard Corey, he glittered as he walked. He passed quite close to Toni but the impassive gilded face he turned to her showed no awareness of her presence.

He took his place at the extreme end of the ramp. Toni's last glimpse of him as she left by the little door that led up front showed him going through his *pliés* in a deliberate, almost ritualistic manner. There was a loneliness and strangeness about him that suddenly brought his dark history to Toni's mind and made her see him for a moment as a protagonist in some as yet unperformed drama.

CHAPTER FOUR

"THERE HE IS," said Skeets to Toni, who had just squeezed into her seat. He pointed out Captain Andrew Torrent, who sat in a row ahead, his sandy pompadour bent over the program.

"He looks a little puzzled," Toni remarked.

"It's the program notes," said Skeets. "Why do they always sound as if they had been written by a pompous foreigner and translated by his dear friend with the help of Chevalier's French dictionary? 'It is just before dawn,' " he read rapidly as the lights dimmed, " ' and we find ourselves before the refulgent palace of Phoebus, Lord of the Sun. The gray mists, symbols of the passing night, perform a stately dance in their crepuscular robes'—ouch!—'and are scattered by the first rays of the sun. The gates fly open and the radiance-suffused Sun God commences his diurnal journey. He passes over many lands and climes. The wild Scyths, the ancient Greeks, the dusky Ethiops pay him homage in dances expressive of their race and civilization. His omniscient and amorous eye'—tsk, tsk—'falls on an Ethiopian maiden doing her work in the fields and a desire for her inflames him. Yet ere the willing maid can bestow the utmost of her virgin favors on him, she falls dead before the divine fire he emits. He mourns her but life must go on. He follows his predetermined course until the night mists gather again, dimming his refulgent rays.' "

Skeets chuckled. "Apparently your friend Izlomin burns them upon stage as well as in private life."

The curtain rose on a darkened stage, a few columnar strokes on the backdrop indicating the gates of Phoebus' palace. The woodwinds breathed an uncomplicated tune and the voices of the choir, brought in especially for the occasion, rose pure and sweet. A long line of gray figures snaked slowly across the stage. It was a simple but effective sight, this unstopping procession of shadowy shapes, with only the fillets on their hooded heads glimmering dimly as they went.

Toni confided to Skeets that the effect of the unbroken line was obtained by pressing all the members of the company, even the soloists, into the procession. "They're going round and round and the ones who go off into the wings are running like hell this very minute to get to the other side of the stage and come on again."

"So it's really not as restful as it seems. By the way, when is this conga line going to stop?"

As if in answer, the voices died away and the brief silence was broken by the faint shimmering crash of the cymbals. The line of the "mists" wavered, broke its moving continuity, drawing itself into a semicircle of frozen figures that strained away from the palace gates from behind which a faint golden glow was beginning to illumine the stage. Then they resumed their measure, now grown erratic and ragged, until three male dancers in golden armor, brandishing golden spears, came leaping out of the wings to drive them off the stage.

"Now, they're all madly tearing off their mist costumes," said Toni, "and putting on their headdresses, or whatever they had to leave off, and getting ready to come out for the next stint."

A clarion trumpet call and the right hand gate slid open, disclosing a shining figure standing motionless on a platform. A subdued gasp went up from the audience as they took in the sight of the golden warrior. He might have been a gilded statue except for the tremulous glitter of the sequins that covered his attire. He shone from the tip of the helmet that surmounted his impassive countenance to his spangled sandals. There wasn't an inch of him that wasn't somehow gilded. He even wore gold-colored tights and sleeves merging into his gilded hands. It was hard to look at him when he finally moved into his dance and his sequins caught white fire from the spotlight.

The ballet wore on, a typical Izlomin production, strictly classical so far as choreography was concerned, without any Balanchine pretzel effects or Massine mugging, but lush of costumes and decor. Izlomin's solo, a stately adagio, was followed by a wild oriental dance of the Scyths, with much leaping and twirling.

When Phoebus reappeared on a higher level, Skeets whispered to Toni, "Do you realize that the guy is always on the stage? He simply can't bear to leave his public."

That was quite true. His solos were always done in a bright spotlight with the rest of the stage dark. On the other hand, he himself never wholly disappeared, remaining as a dim glow behind the transparent scrims that were lowered upon him after every solo to call the audience's attention to the gambols of the corps de ballet.

The high point of the ballet followed a brief classical interlude. Skeets didn't need Toni's whispered explanation to know that what was coming was the mysterious "noonday variation." There was an almost visible thickening of attention in the audience as the golden figure, now on the apex of the ramp, exploded into a veritable fireworks. A series of pirouettes on the ground, then in the air, like a golden spring uncoiling, then sensational *entrechats* culminating in a straight drop downward to the next lower level, with his feet still fluttering like the wings of a humming bird as he flashed out of the spotlight into darkness. The audience burst into wild applause that went on and on, with the result that the Ethiopian tribes who had meanwhile pranced in were forced to caper to inaudible music. Even the applause drawn by Phoebus' *pas de deux* (still on two levels), with the Ethiopian maiden danced by Tamara, palled in comparison.

The ballet came to a flamboyant end as Phoebus reached the lowest platform on the opposite side of the stage from where he had started. Another scorching solo and then the gauze scrims slowly veiled the spinning figure of the golden dancer until it was merely a faraway fiery glow, really reminiscent of the sun before it sinks beyond the horizon. The final curtain came down as the mists began snaking in. This time they were really crepuscular, Eric remarked.

Izlomin was called back for innumerable curtain calls which he took from the various levels of the ramp, apart from the rest of the company, on whom he called twice before settling down to the serious business of taking his bows alone. He scooped up some flowers laid at his feet and bowed extravagantly.

"He prides himself on remaining in character, when he takes his curtain calls," said Toni, amused. "That's why all the climbing around like a mountain goat. The rest of the boys and girls don't like it very much. Look, Slava Mladov and Perlova took only one bow and Mike just skipped his. Of course it's definitely Izlomin's ballet."

"I suppose this is what you'd call a dazzling performance," said Skeets, adding his bit to the frantic applause.

Toni nodded. "Not quite as dazzling as he would have wanted it to be." She went on before he had a chance to ask what she meant. "I'd better go backstage now and see how Bill's been getting along."

"Hey," Skeets protested, "light, will you? Stop running around."

"I've got work to do, darling. Remember? Wait for me in the lobby. I'll come back before the show is over. Take care of Captain Torrent, will you?"

She clambered out over the knees of the unconscious balletomanes who were still applauding, their eyes glazed with rapture.

Skeets sighed and joined Torrent, who had decided that he had done his share of clapping and was making his way along the aisle. "Alone again," he mourned. "Captain Torrent, didn't you see a slender dark-haired girl with me here a minute ago?"

"She'll be back," said Torrent soothingly. He was a sandy-haired, ruddy-complexioned gent, with a small reddish mustache and a deliberate way of speaking that occasionally betrayed his English extraction, a man pleasantly phlegmatic when off duty and disconcertingly sharp when on.

"Yes, and then what? She'll take you to talk to that whirling dervish and I'll be deserted again. Do you suppose, incidentally, that there is anything to that hoopla he's handing out, or is it the good old persecution complex?"

"I haven't the slightest idea. I'm just here to see a ballet, don't you know. Fancy, they're still clapping. How about getting us a drink at the bar?"

"You're on, Captain."

Izlomin was still taking curtain calls as they plowed through the crowd and pushed on to the bar, preceded by two rabid ballet fans, who were deep in discussion. One claimed that Izlomin had been doing *entrechat sixes* with one *entrechat huit*. The other one insisted with equal conviction that it had been *entrechat huits* with at least one *entrechat dix*, maybe two.

Skeets shook his head. "There must be something about ballet," he remarked. "Imagine worrying about how many times a guy crosses his feet while he's in the air. You didn't happen to count, did you?"

Torrent conceded that he hadn't. "I expect Toni will tell us." They sat through a pleasant performance of *Rêves de Printemps.* This was an early Izlomin piece, in which he seemed to take himself less seriously than in others, and its theme was the effect of spring on a demimondaine, a high-school girl and a spinster aunt, danced respectively by Perlova, Rosalind Reed, and Natalia Izlomina, with the handsome young Barezian strutting through the role of the unconscious object of their affections. The curtain came down to hearty applause, although nothing to compare with the Izlomin ovation, as if the audience were saving up its energy for the next number where Izlomin was appearing again. Torrent and Skeets again repaired to the bar, where presently Skeets spotted Toni, who was looking for them. She returned his wave and came toward them swiftly. Her face was composed, as always, but Skeets, adept at reading that particular landscape, immediately knew that something was up.

"Anything wrong?"

"I don't know," said Toni slowly, "but they don't seem to be able to find Izlomin."

CHAPTER FIVE

THE TWO MEN looked at her with an identical expression of incredulity. Torrent spoke first. "What do you mean, they can't find him?"

"Just that, Captain Torrent. He wasn't in his room and he's due to go on any minute and so far he just isn't there."

"Well, where is he?" Skeets asked somewhat illogically. "I mean, who saw him last? Did he go home or something?"

"The doorman swears that he didn't see him leave. Besides, the idea of Izlomin's leaving his own gala performance is a little peculiar. You don't know ballet dancers, my friend. They hobble onstage with broken ankles, wrenched knees and a fever of a hundred and six."

"Then what happened?"

Toni shrugged her shoulders. "I don't know. It's rather odd, considering."

"Couldn't he have gone to the john? Ballet dancers are only human, you know."

"All too human," Toni agreed. "But they've looked. They're looking for him right now, in all the dressing rooms, in the storage room below— everywhere they can think of. You have no idea of the uproar that's going on there. De Speranski is going to have a stroke, or so everybody hopes. Of course," Toni added, "they might have found him by now."

It looked as though they hadn't. The audience returned to their seats after what seemed like an unusually long intermission, to be greeted by a surprise. The curtain parted to let out de Speranski. His face purple in the glare of the houselights, he held up a pudgy hand and his voice shrilled jerkily across the subsiding noise. "…great regrets…owing to art indisposition…dze part of dze Dreamer will be danced by Mikhail Gorin." An excited buzz arose, that continued even after the curtain had risen on a Dr. Caligari-like room with buzz-saw walls and a figure in black tights and a white shirt motionless on a cot.

Toni and Eric paid but scant attention to the sick dreams of an impressionable poet. Their eyes kept wandering away from the costumes, designed by the well-known surrealist and rife with lobsters, melting clocks, and strangely shaped fungi, to seek out Torrent's still figure in the front row. Presently he seemed to have made up his mind. He got up, motioned to them and left his seat. Skeets and Toni followed, shrinking under the barrage of dirty looks and muttered imprecations.

"I think," was Torrent's low-voiced comment as they met in the aisle, "we'd better look into this business. Take me backstage, Toni."

Toni nodded and led the way to a little side door to the left of the musicians' pit, guarded by a man in evening clothes. Torrent showed the man his badge, and as he started to stutter calmed him with a cold look of his authoritative blue eye, and got in a few questions. As a result he knew as they went on that Izlomin had not come out that way and something about the people who had come in.

"This would seem to indicate that he's still inside," Torrent told Skeets and Toni, who followed him in, all bright-eyed like a brace of intelligent young hunting dogs.

On stage Mike Gorin was crawling on the floor, miming perfectly justifiable horror at another unpleasant surrealist apparition that had just arrived on the scene to add to his troubles. Backstage a distracted group milled about ineffectively in semidarkness, getting in the way of stage-hands and electricians. Its center was a gesticulating, forehead-mopping de Speranski, surrounded by Kate Whitehead, Paul Samarkand, Natalia Izlomina, a harried-looking middle-aged woman, whom Toni identified as the wardrobe mistress, and a few curious dancers hanging around on the periphery. Charles Graham was also there, though not part of the group.

Torrent approached them with Toni at his side, while Skeets tactfully hung back. De Speranski turned a bloodshot eye on him and barked hysterically, "I am very busy now, please. No time." He took in Toni's presence and added, mindful of respect to the press, "Excuse, please."

Toni explained briefly about Torrent, who supplemented her remarks by another display of his badge. The effect was pronounced and varied. De Speranski, turkey red and bulging of face, became incapable of speech with only the distracted wagging of his beard to express his emotion.

"A copper," said Kate Whitehead. "Well, I'll be damned."

"A detective," Natalia Izlomina echoed her softly. "And Vova wanted to see you. But why?" Several emotions flickered across her face but one that remained was that of unmistakable relief. "Please," she said eagerly, "you must help us now."

De Speranski's voice finally emerged out of his congested throat. It squeaked ludicrously. "But dzis is…" he cleared his throat and tried again. "But why should Vova…"

"We can ask him that when we find him," said Natalia impatiently. "The important thing is to find him. Captain Torrent…" A gesture laid the task in his hands.

"Well," said Torrent, "when was he seen last?"

De Speranski made a helpless gesture. "Well, all of us saw him, naturally, while he was taking his curtain calls."

"Anybody speak to him? You, madam?" he looked at Natalia. She shook her head.

"I had to go away to change for *Printemps* immediately after *Phoebus*. I didn't have the time to speak to Vova." She was still dressed in her Spinster costume, its sedate 1890 lines looking somehow right on her. Her face was drawn and anxious under the unexpectedly perky hat with its bunches of cherries.

"Well, did anyone else speak to him?"

Kate Whitehead spoke abruptly. "Nobody had a chance to talk to him because right after he took his last curtain call he scooted upstairs talking to what's his name?" she jerked her head toward the stage. "Gorin."

Toni blinked at this picture of brotherly affection.

"Then Gorin might know something." Torrent's sharp eye fastened on the plump harried woman who, while she fastened a bilious green costume on one of the dancers, looked as though she wanted to say something. "You're the wardrobe mistress, aren't you? Anything on your mind?"

The woman straightened up, and the apparition she had been working on fixed a loathsome mask on its bland and childlike face and stalked off toward the wings. Well, she said, she had gone up to offer her services to M'sieur Izlomin. She had had no occasion to do that before since he had his own dresser, but seeing that the latter was unavailable and seeing that Madame Izlomina had personally asked her…

Toni wondered whether Torrent noticed that, like everybody else, the wardrobe mistress was reluctant to deal with Izlomin.

Anyhow, she came up and knocked at his door. There was a low-voiced but animated conversation going on in the dressing room, which stopped as she asked whether Izlomin needed her help. He peeked through a crack in the door and shook his head at her. She saw that he still wore his makeup and his costume, which was rather odd, considering that he was supposed to be getting ready for *Cauchemar*. She got the impression that he didn't want to be interrupted in his talk with whomever was inside with him. He just nodded assent to her proposal that she come back later and closed the door.

"Any idea who was with him?"

No, she never saw that person. But she thought later that it was someone from the dressing room next door, because when she knocked there, nobody answered her.

"Gorin, perhaps?" mused Torrent. "Incidentally, is he coming out soon?"

The *regisseur* assured him that the ballet would last another twenty-five minutes and that Mike remained onstage all that time. Torrent returned to the wardrobe mistress' story. She had gone back to Izlomin's room about five minutes before the end of the *Printemps* ballet, to find him gone, and had reported it to Mr. Samarkand. Here Mr. Samarkand himself, assisted by de Speranski, launched into a somewhat incoherent report of their search for the missing dancer, one that covered the downstairs business offices, other dancers' dressing rooms and even the basement storage room.

"And nobody has seen him since he went up to his room, outside of this lady here? None of the dancers?"

Samarkand fixed him earnestly with his crossed eyes and said hollowly, "The dancers were all in their rooms getting ready for *Cauchemar*— very complicated costumes, as you can see for yourself. They wouldn't see him wandering around unless he actually came into their rooms. They all say he didn't and I believe them. I'd like to see Vova condescending to visit a corps de ballet dressing room—I beg your pardon, Natalia."

"You say the doorman didn't see him go out?"

A chorus of assent.

"Well then," said Torrent sturdily, "he must be hiding somewhere around this building and we'll find him."

Hiding was an unfortunate word to use, particularly against the background of the caterwauling music and the nervous agitation of the people around him. It made one think of an insane game of hide and seek through shadows and dusty corners, the fugitive finally tracked down and dragged out of his hiding place shaking with sly and silent laughter.

A vision in a white tutu, with a cluster of white roses in her dark hair, darted toward them from the stage and said breathlessly, "Well, have you found him yet?"

That was Tamara. Toni remembered that she was dancing the Beloved in *Cauchemar.* She went on, "Did you look upstairs? That's where he went. Maybe he's still there…Oh, dear." She stamped her foot in exasperation and dashed back to the stage.

"Wait," said Torrent, following her. "What do you mean?"

"I saw from around the corner, up the other stairs."

"Wait," said Torrent impotently and got a look that branded him an idiot.

"Wait? I'm on right now:' She rose to her *pointes* and *bourréed* off gracefully. Torrent, who had followed her in his eagerness, barely stopped short of the glare and motion that was the live stage and turned back.

"I think I know what she means," said Toni.

"I'll give you a chance to explain," said Torrent. Then turning to the others, "Madam, do you mind taking me to your husband's dressing room? And you too, perhaps, to explain the layout of the building?" This to de Speranski.

Toni attached herself unobtrusively to the small procession that moved toward the exit in the back. As she went, she caught an indignant look from Skeets, deserted once more, and answered it with a tiny apologetic shrug of her shoulders. There was nothing she could do for Lieutenant Skeets, except enlighten him as soon as she herself knew.

They made their first stop on the second floor, where the stars' dressing rooms were located, and Torrent's glance veered questioningly to Toni.

She told him, "Tamara must have meant that she had gone out of her room, which is around the corner from the men's and saw him go upstairs using this staircase"—pointing to the one near Izlomin's room—"rather than the continuation of the one we used just now."

"Well, where does it take you?"

Izlomina said, "Also to the third floor, but at a little distance from the dressing rooms of the girls there. But why should Vova? There's no reason for him to go there. Besides, the girls would have told us about it."

"There are other floors beside the third?"

De Speranski, who had been mauling his beard in his agitation, answered affirmatively. "Dzere are more dressing rooms on dze fourth and fifth. Dzose on the fifth aren't used, however. Much too high for our *artistes*," he said with a faint paternal leer.

"All the dressing rooms on this side of the house are occupied by—

er—the female of the species, right? The men's are on the other side, I assume. How would one reach them from here? I suppose by going downstairs and crossing the stage?"

"Yes, but wouldn't he have been seen by stagehands and others? And nobody saw him downstairs once he went up," said Natalia.

"It is true," said de Speranski, "dzat he could have used dze back gallery on dze fifth floor to cross over to dze other side. But again, why? Dzere's even less reason for him to visit dze boys dzan dze girls—beg your pardon, Natalia. And dzere's nothing else except dze rehearsal halls on dze other side on dze fifth floor."

"We shall look into them," said Torrent, "but first let's take a look at Mr. Izlomin's own room."

Torrent gave it a quick going over, peering into the bathroom and even behind the huge baskets of flowers that crowded the room. He ruffled through the costumes, noting that the spangled tunic wasn't there and that the black tights and white shirt for the Dreamer part hung on the wall, as did Izlomin's street clothes.

"Apparently," said Torrent, "he didn't change, at least not in here."

He looked speculatively at the huge trunk and his eyes narrowed.

"Costumes not in use are kept in this trunk," said Natalia. Torrent hesitated imperceptibly, then he pulled away the black velvet cape that had fallen on the trunk and lifted the lid. Natalia's ballet slippers flashed beneath her dove gray skirts and she was at his side, her hand pressed to her mouth, sick terror in her eyes.

"Take it easy," said Torrent, propping the lid up against the wall. "There's nothing there, except a lot of old costumes, as you yourself said. Come and look for yourself."

Natalia gave him a pallid smile. She was visibly shaken. "But—but you thought he might be there," she said in a low voice. "I could see by your face you expected him to be there. Captain Torrent, you think he may be—" she stopped.

"Nothing of the sort," said Torrent cheerfully. "I'm sorry I frightened you. It's just that we are kind of used to being thorough. Part of the training, don't you know."

Natalia took a deep breath. "I've been silly," she said resolutely. "We will find Vova, and all will be explained."

But when Toni recollected the whole incredible evening later, that was the point at which she placed the sudden change in atmosphere, a change from vague discomfort to a downright conviction that this was going to end badly.

They mounted the next flight of stairs in a tense silence, only de Speranski wheezing unhappily as he toiled after them and muttering something about a well-known Russian proverb that "you must go slowly and you will cover a greater distance." They stopped only for a brief time in the third-floor dressing rooms, emptied by the ballet now in progress. Torrent, who noted duly that these dressing rooms were around the corner from the stairs they and Izlomin had used, asked whether these stairs were much in use during the performance. It was Natalia, a denizen of this floor, who told him, no, as a matter of fact, they weren't. Not until the end of the performance when the girls were leaving the building. The other stairway was much more convenient when you wanted to reach the stage in a hurry. Torrent nodded. Like Toni's, his impression was strengthened that Izlomin had not wanted to be seen during his inexplicable promenade.

Then they suddenly began picking up his track. It was when they were starting for the fourth floor that Torrent saw something glittering on the steps and bent down to pick up the minute glittering fragments of what both Toni and Natalia identified as a golden sequin from the *Phoebus* costume. The search of the fourth-floor dressing rooms proved fruitless, but the elderly electrician on the first fly gallery (to which you go by turning to the right from the landing and falling down three steps) had some information for them.

He had seen a figure dressed in something shiny pass the landing and go on up. This was after *Rêves de Printemps* had started. Yes, he could be even more exact than that, he said, making off to peer at a schedule thumbtacked on the wall. It was just after he had put a red slide into the spot to produce a "rosy effect," exactly six minutes after the ballet started. That would make it at 10:01. Yes, he had been here all the time, taking care of the lights. That was all he had to do. Most of the scene-shifting took place from the fly gallery on the other side of the house. Glancing over the rail, Toni saw the stage as a bright rectangle, segmented by parts of the flats that hung there swinging slightly in the semitransparent darkness, like huge sheets hung up to dry. Curiously foreshortened figures scuttled about the stage. It was an intriguing crow's-nest view. She turned from it reluctantly as Torrent said, "I guess we go on up."

"Excelsior," said Toni obediently, and followed him.

The next floor, the fifth, was deserted, its dressing rooms mute and dusty, the doors standing open. Torrent looked into each of them, switching the lights on dust and disorder. But the third one evoked a slow whistle from him. Toni rose on tiptoe to look over his shoulder.

"Somebody," she said, paraphrasing the Three Bears, "has been here and was sitting in front of that dressing table."

The dust on that dressing table, one of a row, had been wiped away. The mirror on it was polished. A towel lay carelessly on the floor under a chair which was standing at an angle to the table, as if somebody had recently got up from it. Natalia pounced on the towel with a little cry and stood holding it palely until Torrent took it out of her hands.

"Gilt," said Toni, excited. "It's the gold stuff Izlomin used on his face, isn't it?"

Izlomin's wife nodded, her eyes blank with surprise. "Yes, it is. I don't understand. Where is he then?"

It was a cry of pure bewilderment. Torrent answered, "Well, obviously he was here a little while ago. The gold paint on the towel indicates that it must have been after he danced *Phoebus*. The wardrobe mistress saw him with his makeup still on, remember?" He thought for a while, twirling the towel by the edges. "Grimy, isn't it?" he said absently. His sharp blue eyes rested thoughtfully on a rectangular imprint in the dust on a nearby table. It might have been that of a box or a small suitcase.

De Speranski dropped heavily into the chair vacated, presumably, by his *premier danseur* and proceeded to do some good Moscow Art Theatre emoting.

"*Mon Dieu*, how could he have done dzat to me? Vova, Vova, *comment pouvais tu?*" He stopped his lamentations to listen. "*Voilà! Cauchemar* is over now and Slava will have to dance *Le Roi des Chats*. What a scandal! Dzere is a Russian proverb—"

Torrent did not wait to hear it. "You mean the ballet is over? Good, we can ask Gorin about Izlomin. Maybe that'll give us something else to go by." He broke off to go down on one knee and pick up another pinch of tiny golden fragments. "Obviously he took his makeup off here. He may have changed here too."

"But his clothes are below."

"Perhaps," said Torrent, "he had another suit of clothes waiting here. Madam, have you tried calling your hotel?"

"No, but—You mean he left the theater after all? But that's bizarre. Why? Why?"

"That I can't tell. I think it's a remote possibility that he did, since there's some evidence that he did change his clothes. As you know, he felt himself to be in danger, enough so to want my advice and protection, as he told Miss Ney here. Perhaps he felt suddenly that the danger had become too acute."

"What danger? I demand to know what danger," exclaimed de Speranski, swelling like a turkey cock and slamming a clenched hand on the table. A cold look from Torrent deflated him.

"But the doorman said…" Natalia objected.

"The doorman may not have noticed. They usually pay more attention to people going in than those going out."

"Dzat is true," said de Speranski. "Dzat fool of a Patrick. You know perfectly well, *chérie*, dzat all doormen are of an inexpressible stupidity. What do you advise dzen, Mr.—ah…?"

Torrent suggested that a call be made to the hotel or any other place where Izlomin might logically be supposed to make tracks. "Also somebody might collar Mike Gorin and ask him what he knows. Suppose you two go down right after we've taken a look at the fly gallery on this floor. I'll join you downstairs as soon as I've taken a look at the other side of the house." He herded them out of the room, talking soothingly as he went.

Their look at the second fly gallery brought no information. It was just another long narrow balcony full of ropes and wires wound around rows of thick wooden pins, while other coils of ropes seemed to crawl snakelike along the cement floor. Torrent snapped on the light, a bulb hanging at the end of a wire, and the thick snakes stopped crawling. But Izlomin wasn't there.

He waited until the dancer's wife and the bearded director left before he turned a frankly puzzled face to Toni.

"This is the craziest business I've come across yet. A guy, seemingly in possession of his senses, gives a brilliant performance, then sneaks out of his dressing room, picks out a dirty room to change in and disappears. Do you suppose he went nuts after all?"

Toni said that that seemed to be the only explanation to the senseless behavior of Izlomin. "The only thing is, I can't imagine Izlomin walking out on a performance even in the throes of starkest madness."

"Screwy," said Torrent decisively. "Could you perhaps tell me why, after he wiped the paint off his face, he felt it necessary to wipe up the dressing table? Look." He shoved the grimy towel in front of her interested eyes. "The dirt is over the gold smears. And there was some of the gold rubbed into the table. What do you suppose caused this great yen for cleanliness?"

They walked back along the fly gallery and turned at right angles to enter the back fly gallery by which they could cross over to the other side.

"A gilt complex," said Toni promptly. "Any psychiatrist will tell you. What's the matter?

Torrent was staring back at the fly gallery which they had just left with a strange still look on his ruddy face. Toni followed the direction of his gaze and swallowed a scream. The next moment Torrent had given her a little push in the direction in which they had been going, and himself turned back.

"Get some stagehands," he told her. "I won't be able to haul him in alone."

He left her precipitately. It was a long moment before she could tear her eyes away from the inert bundle that hung outside the rail, that swayed and glittered faintly as its sequins caught the dispersed light that reached it from below.

CHAPTER SIX

"YOU CERTAINLY PICKED YOURSELF a fancy corpse this time," said Detective Mahoney, shaking his head in wonderment.

The body had been hauled back into the fly gallery and was now lying on its back, its arms flung abroad in the stiff yet abandoned way that the dead have. Death seemed to have spread an ashen veil over him, dimming even the bright sequins that studded his costume. His gold-colored silk tights were smeared and stained. His face, naked of grease paint, showed little of the customary congestion, Torrent thought, looking at it with a practiced eye. It had grown small and wizened, with the white slits of eyeballs glimmering mockingly between the puffy eyelids. He still wore his hempen collar around his neck.

"So that's Izlomin," Torrent thought. He remembered him spinning radiantly and then soaring in that sensational leap, and was conscious of an odd pang of regret, as if he were looking at a dead bird. He wondered what Izlomin had wanted to tell him. Now, he thought grimly, he would have to find out the hard way.

Mahoney was saying behind him, "That's a hell of a rig to hang yourself in. That's what this guy did, isn't it, chief?"

Torrent nodded absentmindedly. "Looks like it." He moved to the rail. "See? Looks like he had picked up one of those thinner ropes—God knows there are plenty of them here—tied it around his neck and tightened the other end around the rail. Then he moved this cluster of ropes aside, leaving a sort of loophole for himself to squeeze through," Torrent indicated a fissure in the jungle-like tangle of ropes running from the grid to the rails, "right here. Then he straddled the rail and slid down—and well, there he was. Funny part is we didn't see him here when we first looked. He was hanging outside, don't you know."

He looked at the body again with a sort of baffled resentment, and then snapped out of it and became his own crisp self. "What's happening below?" he asked.

"I sent the widow home with one of the men, like you said. She's a cool one, ain't she? Identified him without batting an eyelash. And this Russian with the beard—what's his name? Buttinski?"

"De Speranski."

"He made an announcement from the stage, and everybody went home. And we're taking everybody's name backstage."

"Okay," said Torrent. "I'll be down soon." He turned to the waiting crew. "All right, boys. You can print the place. See what you can get. After you're through here, I want you to go over one of the rooms in the back."

"Please, everybody!" The big policeman's voice had a frayed sound. "Would you kindly mind sitting down and waiting until Captain Torrent gets around to talking to you, please?" His face grew purple and he raised his voice to cover the distracted babel of French, Russian and English. "I said *please.*"

His bellowing voice must have struck a reminiscent chord—a memory of a distracted *regisseur* finally losing his head at a rehearsal, perhaps—because it had some effect. The frantic dancers who had been trying to bypass him in order to get out turned back and went to sit dejectedly on chairs, packing cases and sturdier props.

"I feel sorry for the cop," said Toni to Skeets. "He must think he's in the middle of a nightmare."

"I see your point," Skeets agreed gravely. "I myself have seen something like this after having eaten not wisely but too well."

He pointed to one of the dancers who still had on a costume she had worn in *Cauchemar.* It consisted of a bilious green leotard with a bright red lobster tastefully appliqued along the abdomen. Her head was wrapped in tulle, which obliterated all features, with a single strand of seaweed wandering dankly in the middle of what would ordinarily have been her face. When she sat down with a resigned sigh and began unwrapping the tulle, the effect was unsettling to say the least. Toni watched the policeman's fascinated gaze constantly jerking back to her. A shudder passed like a ripple along his broad back.

The other figures were scarcely more reassuring. There was the inevitable figure in pink tights with a bunch of roses springing out of its neck to take the place of the head. There was an exquisite Louis Quinze gent, whose air of polished elegance was considerably spoiled by a hole in his middle from which some artistically executed viscera were hanging out. Another nightmare-like shape had just removed a death mask, uncovering a rosy and pouting countenance. Everything considered, Toni didn't blame the policeman for blanching.

The first excitement past, they huddled together, casting fearful looks upward to the fly gallery, where lights were burning brightly and huge shadows moved. Mike, still wearing the black tights and white shirt of the Dreamer, wasn't looking up, though. He stared at the ground, his large hands opening and closing nervously. He seemed to have forgotten all about Tamara, who, having recovered from a healthy bout of hysterics, was now tearfully perched on a packing case behind him, her huge black eyes fixed unwinkingly on his rigid back. She looked as though she would have liked to creep closer to him, an impulse which was kept in abeyance, Toni guessed, by the presence of her mother, a large and grenadier-like matron with a mustache.

Perlova drooped wearily nearby, her slim arm wound possessively around the neck of a sinister character in black domino, who, upon taking off his mask, revealed the good-natured and somewhat stupid visage of her young husband Barezian. Her own face looked suddenly washed out and old.

Kate Whitehead also waited for Torrent, looking incongruously at home with the weirdies in her outrageous magenta gown. She had refused to wait in de Speranski's office and was grimly sitting bolt upright in a chair, flanked by a wilted de Speranski and Charles Graham.

The latter was perhaps the only one who remained detached from the excitement. His interested blue eyes roved around with a spectator's mild curiosity. There was something almost impertinent in his detachment. All this might have been a private show put on for his amusement, a trifle loud but entertaining. Occasionally his eyes stopped on Toni, speculatively. Toni presented an unresponsive profile to this impertinent scrutiny, but she felt her cheek growing warm under it, as if under a sun ray trained through a magnifying glass. Why the hell does he do it? I hate people who do that to one. I won't look up. She looked up nevertheless just as the bright blue gaze slid away and a suspicion of a smile quirked the mobile lips.

There was a nudge in her ribs.

"I was making censorious remarks about you," said Skeets. "Didn't you hear me?"

Toni lifted her eyes from the careful examination of her own toes and smiled at him warmly.

"I always turn the traditional deaf ear to censorious remarks. What did you say, Lieutenant?"

"I was saying that I am disappointed in you."

Toni batted her eyelashes inquiringly.

"Yes, I am. A fine newspaperman you turned out to be. A scoop like this in your lap and you just sit here. Another guy would be sending carrier pigeons to the desk."

Toni looked at him inscrutably. It was quite true. She had missed her chance. Just after the body was discovered she could have rushed out and called the desk. But the shameful truth was that she just hadn't thought of it in the excitement. Remorse gnawed at her like a cankerworm. But she continued to say nothing, merely looking a shade more inscrutable than ever.

"Aw, lay off Toni," said Bill Stone. "She's just a columnist. Nobody expects her to cover a big story like that. Besides, we'll square them." Mr. Stone felt very pleased with himself and with good reason. He had a scoop in his camera. While wandering around in search of Toni, he had come up to the fifth floor just as Torrent was cutting the body down, whereupon he had taken a few pictures of this operation in a quiet and unobtrusive way and modestly retired the way he came.

Detective Mahoney arrived on the scene. He too winced at the garish crew disposed in dejected attitudes around the stage and it was with evident relief that his pained eye located Toni's more conventionally garbed form.

"Captain Torrent would like to see you, Miss Ney. In what's his name's dressing room."

Toni got up with alacrity. "Thanks. I'll find my way. I know where it is."

She was almost on the second floor when a thought struck her, and she retraced her steps down to the corridor outside the stage. She walked lightly and quietly, a small excited smile on her lips, past the stage entrance door. The doorman was engaged in earnest conversation with a policeman who was taking notes and neither noticed her swift passage. The doorman was saying, "I tell you there was only Mr. Ffoulkes who left after *Phoebus*—sure, I woulda noticed. I got as good eyes as you." Ffoulkes, eh? But Toni didn't stay to listen further. She was bent on reaching her goal, de Speranski's own office at the far end of the corridor. It was open, thank God, and nobody was inside.

Toni shut the door noiselessly and flung herself at the telephone. It seemed like eternity before the night editor answered her.

"Look," said Toni, "I've only got a moment, so spread your ears." She talked fast, her voice low and emphatic.

"So far, they say suicide, but that's not final," she answered the spluttering query on the other end of the wire. "Yes that's right, he's the man who was mad in Europe. Well, now he's dead in the United States. Incidentally you might put in some stuff about the ballet being unlucky. Last time he tried it he went insane and now... What? Oh the ballet is just a ballet and he danced it very well. Read my review tomorrow. Yes, that's what I'm doing—covering the performance. That's life, isn't it? I'll try my best. I'll be over as soon as they let me out of here. With the picture of the corpse." She hung up on that. It seemed like a good exit line and besides Torrent was waiting.

They carried Izlomin's body past her as she was going up. She flattened herself against the wall and watched the stretcher ride by, with its burden looking pathetically flat and small under the sheet. Light and stiff like a skeleton of a bird. She was glad that she hadn't had to see it. That glimpse of the glittering bundle hanging outside of the fly gallery was enough.

She arrived on the second floor a few seconds before Torrent and was explaining her presence to the policeman stationed on that floor when Torrent himself appeared.

"O.K., Moran." He nodded to Toni. "I want you to take a look with me in Izlomin's dressing room. The one he normally uses when he isn't thinking of hanging himself," he added with a touch of grimness. "I still haven't quite doped it out, don't you know, why your friend Izlomin should feel it necessary to use another dressing room in that contingency or why he should take such good care to clean his face before leaving this world for the next."

"Maybe he didn't like what he saw in the mirror after he got the greasepaint off." Torrent's grave face didn't relax and she went on, "So you think it's just plain suicide?"

"Plain? No. Very fancy. Also I'd feel happier if I knew why Izlomin had to clean up the table so that there wasn't a single fingerprint left. Yes, ma'am, a very fine cleaning and polishing job was done on that table. The only fingerprints left are those of de Speranski. I know they were his because I saw him leave them there myself. Well, here we are. I want you to look around and see if you can spot anything that's out of line. You'd know better than I what belongs in a dancer's dressing room and besides you've already been here tonight."

"Not tonight," Toni corrected him, obediently looking the room over. "I was here during the rehearsal when Izlomin showed me the notes."

"To be sure, those notes." Torrent was at the dressing table now, his hands moving swiftly among the assorted objects scattered on it. "In which drawer did he put them? Here? And here they are. Is that what he showed you?"

Toni shook her head. "No, there's another one here now. Remember, I told you he said he'd have more to show me later?" She glanced through it. " *'Prenez garde, vous avez des ennemis qui n'hésiteront pas...'* " She translated for Torrent, " 'Take care, you have enemies who will not hesitate...' That's all. Whoever wrote this didn't finish the sentence."

Torrent put the notes away carefully. "Now do you suppose you could locate a nice lucid suicide note for me?" He moved through the room slowly, examining every nook and corner with intense scrutiny.

He stepped over to a small side table and picked up a tray holding a pitcher half full of orange juice and an empty glass. He looked at Toni inquiringly.

"Izlomin always swilled orange juice like mad," she told him. "Very careful of his health, dear Vova was, and somebody had told him about vitamins."

"Not today, though. The glass shows no trace of having been used. Unless he washed it after drinking."

Toni laughed scornfully. "Who, Vova? Wash a glass? Why, that's sacrilege." Her brows drew together thoughtfully. "Now that you mention it, who could have washed it for him? He didn't have his valet to do for him."

"Ah, yes," said Torrent. "To be sure. The poisoned valet. I remember about him. Perhaps Mrs. Izlomin washed out the glass. I'll have to find out."

He drifted toward the bathroom, singing softly to himself the valley-de-sham aria from *Ruddigore*. Torrent had kept a national fondness for Gilbert and Sullivan.

"Wet," he said breaking off and drawing his finger along the shower curtain. "Somebody's been showering. Izlomin?"

"Indubitably. Vova always bathed the body sacred before dressing for the performance. Sort of a ritual. Come to think of it, he made a ritual out of everything he did. That's part of the grand style he affected. Other members of the company hopped in and out of clothes and rushed onstage without very much fuss. But Izlomin had his prestige to think of!"

"He shared this bathroom with the boys in the next room, I suppose." Torrent stepped over to the door that led to the adjacent dressing room and tried to turn the knob. It didn't turn.

"Then you don't know about the great Bathroom Affair?" Toni said, her eyes gleaming with amusement. "Why, it was a *cause célèbre*. When Izlomin snagged this room for himself, it was naturally taken for granted, as you just did, that the other boys—Mike and Vassine, who was then in the company—would share the bathroom with him. But they didn't know Vova. He had a clause in his contract stipulating that he should always have a private bathroom. The boys were requested to use the washroom across the way, and Vova locked this door with great pomp and circumstance and much gloating and tossed the key away. There was an awful to-do about it. Nobody talked about anything but Izlomin's bathroom for days. It even got into Lyon's column."

Torrent was shaking his head incredulously as he went back to the dressing room to resume his prowling. Toni followed him. She was fascinated by the number and variety of the floral offerings. There was one strange concoction of yellow orchids forming a sun-shape with rays. It bore Mrs. Whitehead's card. And of course, roses, roses and more roses.

There was one charming basket full to the brim with anemones, whose clear vivid hues made Toni's mouth water. Toni picked it up and glanced at the card that came with it. Torrent found her studying it with a puzzled expression.

"Nothing significant," she said slowly, in answer to his query. "Just a little unexpected." She read it aloud. " '*Je sais qu'aujourd'hui au moins tu seras un Phoebus éblouissant.*' Meaning, 'I know that today at least you'll be a dazzling Phoebus. Signed André Vassine.' "

"Well?"

"It's just—Well, André Vassine was Izlomin's only serious rival in the Ballet Drama. He's a wonderful dancer, in an entirely different way. He and Izlomin were at each other's throats all the time, but dear Vova had a bigger pull. So Vassine had to quit. Under the circumstances this missive is awfully sporting, shall we say? I mean one would expect something like, 'I hope you trip and break your neck.' " She added reflectively, "Unless it's his idea of subtle sarcasm."

"Probably," said Torrent. "So this Vassine was by way of being Izlomin's enemy?"

Toni gave him a droll look. "You're already thinking in those terms. Well, you'll find plenty of people who would have liked to see Vova cut off at the neck, other than Vassine, who wasn't even here tonight, though he seems to have sent a…"

She stopped. "Go ahead," said Torrent. "Finish what you started to say."

"Though he seems to have sent a friend. I just happened to remember. The doorman said something about Ffoulkes being here tonight. Jeff Ffoulkes is Vassine's best friend. They live together—I mean, they share an apartment. Jeff is an artistic and highly talented Englishman who has done a lot of designing for the Ballet Drama. He broke off with it though when Vassine quit. I don't know why I should tell you all this irrelevant stuff. It's just that I inevitably remembered Ffoulkes when I mentioned Vassine. Most people do."

Torrent gave her a tight smile. "I'd be much obliged if you'd just keep feeding me stuff, whether it seems relevant or not. I'm afraid we're again involved in a field of which you know more than I do. Anything else you can think of?"

"Everything else looks all right to me," said Toni, after giving the room what she hoped looked like a professional onceover. They left the room.

Torrent was in a hurry now. There were at least two people downstairs who might tell him something about Izlomin and he wanted to get at them as soon as possible.

Toni quickened her step to keep pace with him. She said, "Then what is it, after all, Captain Torrent? Suicide or—what? Is there or is there not a smell of the fish about it? Incidentally, I hope you realize that you are talking to a newspaperwoman."

"By George," said Torrent, "so you are. Damned if I didn't forget. Well, well. I'd better watch what I'm saying around you."

He beamed at Toni paternally. It was pretty obvious that he didn't take her very seriously in that new role.

CHAPTER SEVEN

"I WONDER," SAID TONI, thoughtfully, "what Torrent will say when he finds out about Izlomin's down on Mike. I think he won't like it at all...Eric?"

Lieutenant Skeets, who was sprawling gracefully against a large packing case with his officer's cap over his eye, elaborately imitating relaxation and sleep, merely snorted. He was disgusted. Torrent had given Toni her choice between going and staying around until he had given a statement to the reporters, who were by now besieging the doors of the Civic Opera. "Probably your paper has sent a representative, but after all, you were here first," he had added kindly. Toni had thanked him and elected to stay.

"For heaven's sake," Eric said wearily, "can't you understand that you've got a scoop? All those reporters are beating their brains out trying to get in and you've got what they want and you won't do anything about it. It's immoral, that's what it is."

Toni had merely given him a limpid look. "Oh, I don't think it's fair to take advantage of my fellow workers, do you?" Skeets' jaw dropped to his first button. "Besides, the longer we wait the more news we'll have. Maybe Torrent'll have something definite for us. That'll be better than going off half-cocked with a vague story, no?"

"No," said Skeets firmly and shut his mouth. Something had happened to the girl he loved, no question about it. A slight curdling of the brain.

"Never mind, darling," said Toni, soothingly. "It'll all be over soon."

The activity now in progress on the stage resembled the preliminary stages of a new production. On one side Mahoney and a helper were going through the routine of separating the wheat from the chaff, the helpful from the ignorant. Some of those questioned were turned loose and allowed to go home. Others shuttled on to Torrent, who was seated in the center of the stage, like a bigshot producer interviewing the principals. Just now he was questioning Mike, and Toni couldn't make out whether any earthshaking revelations were being made. She rather thought not by the discouraged set of Torrent's shoulders.

Torrent tapped a pencil on his notes and tried to curb his growing irritation. His hope that Mike would contribute something to explain the weird aspects of Izlomin's demise was having a short shrift. Moreover, questioning Mike was like pulling teeth.

"All right," said Torrent, "Then you came over to him and what did you say?"

"I said, 'I want to talk to you.' "

"And what did he say?" Torrent prompted patiently.

"He said all right."

Pause.

"And then?"

"Then we went up together."

"Talking?"

"Yes."

"What about?"

"First of all," said Mike woodenly, "I congratulated him on the performance. Then—then we talked about the party."

"The party?"

Mike nodded, like a mandarin. Torrent gave him a puzzled look. He knew Mike fairly well from his Brooklyn days and had followed his career with interest. It was because of Mike that he had first become interested in ballet himself. He remembered the boy, a dark and deadly serious Irish lad practicing his steps in a Brooklyn gym, undeterred by the hoots of the un-balletically minded and ready to back up his *cabrioles* with his fists. There was no driving Mike back to honest work. On the side he gave classes in gym, built up candidates for the police force, did some fighting in the ring, but the important thing had been his ballet classes.

Torrent smiled a little. He thought he knew what Mike's trouble was.

This was the first time he had met Mike in his official capacity and not as a fan and that was making the young dancer uncomfortable.

"Relax, Mike," he said in an undertone. Mike's eyes darted to his from under the heavy black eyebrows and Torrent thought he saw something childlike and helpless suddenly showing in them—an appeal, perhaps. The expression flickered away, leaving his dark face set and sullen as before. "What party? I'm a stranger here."

Mike explained about the Russian Rendezvous versus El Morocco situation and added, "We had a meeting of our unit and decided that everything should be done to have good attendance at Kotik's party. As shop chairman, I was delegated to tell Izlomin of our decision and the reason for it, and explain that it would be helpful if he showed up, also, even for a minute, before going on to his own party."

"And did he say he would?"

Mike grinned wryly. "Not that baby. Union solidarity didn't mean a thing to him." For a moment he looked like himself again. The interview went faster. He had been with Izlomin when the dresser knocked on the door. Then he had gone to his own room and started dressing for *Cauchemar.*

"I was supposed to dance the Man in Black. But as it turned out, I had to take Vova's part, and Barezian had to dance the Man in Black."

"I see. Izlomin's room is next to yours. Did you hear him leave?" Mike shook his head. "Did you hear anything at all of an unusual nature?" The answer was no. "Was there anything odd about Izlomin when he was talking to you?"

Mike considered this for a moment and then said cautiously that Izlomin had seemed excited.

"Excited?"

"Well, jumpy like. Excited."

Torrent felt strongly disposed to kick his inarticulate witness in the pants. The last man to talk to Izlomin and he couldn't describe what the man was like. "How excited? Did he climb the walls or did he just bite his fingernails?"

Mike gave this his consideration and said, "Well, no, I wouldn't say that. He just seemed kinda restless. Couldn't sit still. Jumpy. As if he had something on his mind."

"All right," said Torrent, beaten. "You may go."

He watched the boy go away with a step that grew lighter with the distance he put between himself and the table, and his mind was far from easy about Mike.

Tamara Ribina was next to be interviewed. She passed Gorin on her way to the table and stopped to give him a look—a strange look, thought Torrent who had glanced up from his notes just in time to catch it. Almost as if she wanted to tell him something. But Mike didn't see her. He was hurrying away blindly, blundering over boxes and chairs, like an animal released from a trap and scurrying for the woods.

Tamara's testimony was equally disappointing. She had been getting dressed for the role of the Beloved in *Cauchemar.* She happened to leave her room and caught a glimpse of Izlomin, still dressed in his *Phoebus* costume, going up the back stairs. Apparently Toni had interpreted her earlier remarks correctly. Izlomin did use the stairs near his room, the ones which would take him to the protected side of the higher floors, where nobody in the corps de ballet dressing rooms would notice him.

Was he carrying anything with him? Tamara shook her head. Her face looked white and pinched and her eyes were enormous. She looked frightened and young, much younger than her years, so that Torrent found himself thinking uneasily that these were probably late hours for her. He let her go, reflecting gloomily that she and Mike were the only people from whom he had hoped to get some enlightenment, and he had failed. Certainly he expected nothing from Mrs. Whitehead, who was advancing upon him with much sound and fury.

Mrs. Whitehead had nothing to contribute save her grim decision to stay around until the whole goddamn mess was cleared up, if it took till next summer. Torrent soon found out that she hadn't been close enough to Izlomin to speak to him the whole evening. She implied darkly that things might have been different if she had. The imperturbable Mr. Graham, backed by de Speranski, eventually prevailed upon her to leave.

Toni marked their going with considerable relief. She had felt self-conscious to the point of awkwardness under the bright interested gaze of Mr. Graham, which had rested on her all too often. It was an unusual sensation for her and it made her angry. Some of the tension in her went with them and yet she was aware of an illogical pang of disappointment. She had braced herself for a farewell disconcerting look and smile from Graham and was pretty sure that she could meet and sustain them without betraying any of the ridiculous flutter that bothered her. And naturally he went without a backward look.

Probably, she said to herself, this is the last of Mr. Graham. Just as well. Toni resented people who made her uncomfortable. One of the reasons Eric was so indispensable was that he was one of the few people with whom she was completely at ease. She turned to look at him with renewed and affectionate attention. Sweet old Eric! Slumping there, so disconsolate because she had failed her paper. She tweaked the black lock that had fallen across his brow.

A short while later the two of them, followed by a heavily laden Bill Stone, made their way to the street. All around them reporters were hurrying to phones to communicate to their offices the brief statement Torrent had given them. Toni gave them a careless glance and inhaled the sweet night air.

"We might as well walk to the office," she remarked. "It's a minute's walk from here."

Bill merely grinned. "Me for the nearest darkroom. Those films are burning my pockets."

He shifted his paraphernalia from one drooping shoulder to the other and Eric remarked sympathetically, "Boy, you'll have nothing to fear in the army. A full pack is nothing to this and at least it stays in one piece."

"Don't pity him," said Toni, "he feels it no more than the camel feels his hump. Incidentally, Bill, did you have any information to give them? Like seeing Izlomin suddenly seized by madness on the stage in front of your amazed eyes or something?"

"No, I never saw that," Bill returned seriously. "But Torrent said he'd like to see the pictures after I develop them. Well, I'll get back to the studio and get to work."

"Not on your life," said Toni, taking a firm hold on him. "You'll develop those pictures in the *Globe* darkroom. You think I'm insane enough to let you go? Eric, you've had a busy evening. Do you want to leave me to my career or are you coming along?"

"I'm coming," said Eric grimly. "You're going to hear some bad language from your boss, my girl. You'll need somebody around to punch him in the nose when he really forgets himself. Not that I blame him."

"You're making me feel so feminine, darling. Come on, then."

A truck with the black and green insignia of the *Globe* drew up at the curb and the driver tossed out a bundle of papers hot off the press. Eric glanced at them idly, stopped short and looked hard at the headline which proclaimed, supplanting the war news for the moment, FAMOUS DANCER MYSTERIOUSLY DEAD AT GALA PERFORMANCE.

Eric read it, his lips moving silently. Then he looked at Toni with eyes whence all faith in humanity was gone.

"You rat," he said softly, "you secretive conniving little rat."

Toni gave him a sweet brave smile of one long misjudged and at long last vindicated.

Torrent left the Civic Opera building and climbed into his car. He had by now passed through the various stages of sleepiness, fatigue and boredom that are a part of routine work and now his mind was clear and razor-sharp. People he had interviewed and facts he had amassed were falling into clean-cut categories. He could see what he had and what was missing. What he had was obviously a poser. Izlomin, an artist, and a man with madness in his past history, had finished his dance, had received an extraordinary ovation, had gone to a place where there were ropes available and had hanged himself. So far there was no answer to the question, Why? unless it was in the unanswerable logic of madness.

But behind this big question there lurked others—discrepancies, contradictions, evasions and coincidences. They surged up mockingly from between the orderly rows of his notes. Was it really possible, for example, that nobody should have known anything about Izlomin's peculiar actions? Granted that he had suddenly gone mad, it somehow seemed incredible that this should have escaped notice. The aberration was not pronounced enough to attract Mike's attention, unless his description of a "jumpy" Izlomin was just a piece of gigantic understatement. And what was wrong with Mike? Was there any connection between Vassine's charming note to his rival, that had so surprised Toni, and the presence of his friend—what's his name? Ffoulkes—backstage

Then he became aware of another discrepancy.

The wardrobe mistress had said that after talking to Izlomin, she had knocked at the door of the adjacent dressing room, occupied by Mike and Slava Mladov, and got no answer. Now Mike was in Izlomin's room at the time, by his own admission. But Slava—Torrent visualized the pale freckled face of a scared adolescent over a thin tense body in chartreuse tights—Slava Mladov had said that he had gone to his dressing room directly after *Phoebus* and was there while Mike was talking to Izlomin. Did the wardrobe mistress make a mistake or had Mladov been out of the room and was now lying about it for some unknown reason? If so, again why?

Torrent had a hunch he would come across a lot of that sort of thing before he was done. He needed background badly. He needed to understand the psychology of these people before he could hope to understand why they did things. Luckily, he thought smiling, he knew someone who could tell him. Toni seemed to be extraordinarily well informed about the slightly mad doings behind the scenes.

All this, however, would have to wait on the report from the Medical Examiner's office, where the thing that used to be Izlomin, dancer extraordinary, was now submitting to all kinds of odious familiarities.

In the meantime Toni had arrived in her office, where she was immediately pounced on, pounded on the back, kissed on both cheeks in Gallic manner and sternly cross-examined until the last drop of information had been wrung out of her. Then she was told to write an earwitness account for the morning edition around the pictures now being feverishly developed by Mr. Stone. But Toni was allowed to leave for half an hour to get some coffee after she had dutifully pounded out her review of the performance.

"Where to?" asked Eric respectfully. Ever since Toni's coup, he had been almost obsequious in his manner. Toni suggested the Russian Rendezvous, which was within walking distance from them. There was a reason for her suggestion. She expected to find there most of the principals in the melodrama that had taken place at the Civic Opera.

The Russian Rendezvous was famous for being exactly that. Not only did Russians, in the professional sense of the word, meet there, crowds came to see them meet. It was the natural stamping ground of the various Cossack Choirs, the Philharmonic, the ballet companies, and other birds of a genre who flock together. The pretty ballerinas made a practice of dropping in after the performance to show off their new beaus and furs and chatter in Russian, French, or, if they knew neither, in carefully distorted English, conscious of the attention they were getting.

A look showed Toni that her hunch had been right. The tense hysteria of the Opera had been transferred here bodily, its center the long table around which the members of the American Ballet Drama were seated.

"Well, well," said Toni. "Kotik's party is being well attended, after all." She explained briefly and Skeets looked intelligent.

"I see it all," he pronounced gravely. "Izlomin had got wind of the fact that his party was going to be boycotted in favor of the less illustrious Kotik. His oriental instincts told him that the only way to save face was to hang himself."

"I thought that you were supposed to hang yourself on the gate of the person who offended you."

"Maybe his mother had trained him not to swing on other people's gates." He dodged a light cuff from Toni as they came abreast of the ballet table, where Toni was cordially greeted and place made for her and her military escort.

Skeets looked around the table. The boys had taken off their makeup and the girls had put on a different kind, in which a faint exaggeration still persisted. Their eyelashes were still too black and their eyelids too slumberous; their mouths were so many red poppies and their tongues were clacking madly.

"Mike isn't here," said Toni reflectively. "Neither is Slava nor, of course, Tamara. But on the other hand..." Eric followed her gaze toward two men who were facing them across the table. Unlike the chattering horde around them, they were silent. One was a rather beautiful young man, beautiful rather than handsome because of a certain betraying softness in his features. Sooty eyelashes, silky black hair with unruly curls spilling over a low white forehead, a small chiseled nose and a fresh lovely mouth. Skeets wondered who their possessor might be, since he had not seen him backstage. His companion was a man of about thirty-seven, sandy, lean-jawed, with bright friendly eyes. The pipe at which he was reflectively sucking, a worn tweedy jacket and a certain toothiness about the smile he directed at the newcomers gave him an indefinable British aura. His voice when he finally spoke added to that impression.

"Well, Toni," he said, "nice to see you." He pronounced it "naice."

Toni made the introductions. Lieutenant Skeets—Jeffrey Ffoulkes, André Vassine. The handsome youth started at the sound of his name, like a skittish horse, and directed a startled look and a mechanically charming smile at Toni and Skeets.

"I understand," said Mr. Ffoulkes, "that you've come from the scene of the tragedy. Horrible." His Adam's apple slid up and down the length of his throat. "But then it was quite to be expected. The management was insane to allow him to revive that ballet with its unfortunate associations for him. It proved to be too much."

"Is that what you think?" asked Skeets. "That he went mad after dancing the ballet and did himself in while *non compos mentis*?"

"That seems to be the only explanation, doesn't it? Why, the man was unbalanced. You know the story of the first production of the ballet, I suppose. It was a dangerous experiment to repeat it. But of course the management cares for nothing but publicity."

"I didn't think he was crazy," said Toni.

Skeets added, "Certainly his dancing showed nothing like that. It was quite something."

"Was it?" said Vassine, speaking for the first time. His voice was boyishly husky, with a pronounced foreign inflection. "You liked his dancing? That variation, for example?"

"Well, it was spectacular. Didn't I hear something about an *entrechat dix*?"

"Two *entrechats dix*," Vassine corrected sternly.

"To come back to Izlomin's madness," pursued Ffoulkes, who seemed to be as interested in that aspect of Izlomin's personality as Vassine was in his dancing. "I admit that he may have appeared perfectly sane to outsiders but to us who knew him closely, who had the opportunity to observe him every day—no!"

"You are right, Jeff." It was Perlova who spoke. "Vova was always a louse, even when I knew him in Paris. But he was never quite as unpleasant as he was here. He was very mean to my poor Kotik. It got so Kotik was glad to go in the army, to get away from it all, weren't you, darling?"

The sensitive Kotik grinned fatuously and rubbed his head against her arm.

"What about André here?" said Ffoulkes. "You all know how sweet-tempered André is. But after all there are limits. When they were reached we simply had to leave." He shrugged his shoulders. "I knew the American Ballet Drama would miss André more than he missed them."

"Particularly now," Toni remarked. "With Izlomin gone, there'll be a dearth of *premiers danseurs*."

Ffoulkes shook his head with a little smile. "Oh, they wanted André back before that. I spent an hour or so with de Speranski tonight. He wanted André back and hoped I would use my influence with him. We will drive a harder bargain now, naturally."

"By all means," said Toni heartily. "Make that old buzzard cough up some of his ill-gotten lucre. Did you speak to Izlomin at all, Jeff?"

Ffoulkes shook his head. "I wanted to, though. I'd wanted to say, good work, Vova. It was, you know. No matter what we thought of Izlomin the man, Izlomin the dancer was something else again."

After making this remark in a rather self-conscious way, Ffoulkes turned away to talk to someone else. Toni remarked in a general way that Mike didn't seem to be here and was told that he had dropped in before, but had left in a hurry.

"Slava isn't here either," piped up Eric's other neighbor. She craned her swanlike neck across Skeets' manly chest and the huge *chou* of purple veiling that surmounted her small sleek head tickled his nose. "Could he be—do you suppose, Toni, that he is comforting Natalia?"

She giggled musically. Eric removed the *chou* from under his chin and beamed at the small pansy-like face under it. "What's so funny about that remark?" he inquired gently.

"Well, Slava is so silly about it," the girl explained. "The way he carries on, it's as if he really had a serious affair with her instead of just having a crush on her." She let loose another tinkling cascade of laughter. "He's been acting all grown up ever since Izlomin told him to stop hanging around Natalia."

"So Izlomin warned him to stay away from his wife," said Eric ominously. "Aha."

"He was just picking on him. Vova used to pick on everybody. He was an old meanie."

"He couldn't possibly," said Eric with horror, "have been mean to a beautiful child like you?"

"Oh, he didn't notice me. I'm nobody. I'm just corps de ballet."

"You look all right to me, honey. What's your name?"

"Marina." The girl's slim white fingers toyed beguilingly with the brass buttons nearest his heart. "And yours, Lieutenant?"

"I've got to run," said Toni unfeelingly, "or McNulty will have my scalp. But you don't have to, Eric."

Eric surged gallantly to his feet, casting a regretful look at his new acquaintance and muttering unconvincing not-at-alls. The next minute they were again speeding along Fifty-fifth street back to the night desk and McNulty.

"That Marina," said Eric, cutting a hopeful eye at Toni. "She's a sweet child, isn't she?" Toni, who knew the sweet child's exact age, the number of her marriages and other connections, kept a charitable silence. "Did you notice how I pumped her? There's a lot of information to be gotten out of these simple innocent little ballerinas."

"You're the one to do it," said Toni. "You seem to have a way with them."

"Aha, you noticed?" Eric inflated his chest and thumped it in an exhilarated manner. "What a night. Bracing, eh what?"

"*Trés* fresh air," Toni agreed. "A fine night for wolves."

CHAPTER EIGHT

THE ROSY-FINGERED DAWN was having a fine time painting the sky red when our heroine staggered out into the streets after having assisted at the birth of an early edition. The Izlomin affair headline had shrunk to a reasonable size in proportion to the war news, but it had a huge inside spread with a slew of pictures. Toni had to stand by to write captions for them. Eric had stuck to his guns gallantly, but inactivity finally got him down and he had begun to yawn prodigiously, great tearing yawns with puppylike wheezes at the end. When it became apparent that Toni would be called on to write Izlomin's biography, since she had most of the facts at her fingertips, she sent him home.

At about seven she called the Homicide Bureau and spoke to Torrent about the pictures that Bill Stone had developed. She could bring the contact prints over if he still wanted them. Torrent did. There were, besides, things he wanted to ask her.

"Good," said Toni. "We'll swap information."

"Oh," said Torrent. Toni had a feeling that he was smiling. "The newspaperwoman angle again, right? Well, come on over. What did you do with your boyfriend?"

"Oh, he couldn't stand the pace," Toni said. "Apparently life in the army unfits one completely for city existence. I'm coming over."

She bought a few morning papers on her way over and had the satisfaction of seeing that the *Globe* had really scooped them. The reviews of the performance were obviously written in ignorance of the tragedy. "Unfortunately," wrote one critic, "an indisposition prevented Izlomin from appearing in anything save the much touted *Phoebus*. Perhaps it was just as well, for after his brilliant performance in that ballet anything else that evening would have seemed anticlimactic. He seemed to have sprung to a much higher stature with a youthful electric quality taking the place of the rather academic coldness that, this reviewer at least feels, often spoils his style. Nor was any of his impeccable technique lost. His pirouettes, both fast and slow, his tigerlike leaps, and the sizzling perfection of his *entrechats*—two *entrechats dix* are almost a history-making event in the annals of ballet—are a fitting answer to those who have felt that Mr. Izlomin has been overpublicized at the expense of his younger colleagues."

"I brought you all the pictures we took," said Toni, scattering them on Torrent's desk. "Mine as well as Bill's. Pretty good harvest, don't you think?"

Torrent lifted a sandy eyebrow at one of them and Toni grinned shamelessly.

"Yes. That one brought us a lot of kudos."

A floodlight had been hauled up to illuminate things when they were lifting Izlomin's body into the fly gallery, so that Bill had been able to take his picture like a gentleman, without any fuss or use of flashgun and with a nice long exposure.

"I bet Bill'll get some sort of photographers' award for this. It's been given half a page on the inside spread. And they've used others. Mine among the rest," said Toni, pleased. "I only wish I had followed my impulse and snapped Izlomin's picture when he came down for *Phoebus*. There was something so—well, strange and lonely about him. You'll probably think I'm rationalizing, but I had the oddest feeling, to which I will henceforth refer as premonition, when telling the story." She gave a sudden gamin grin.

"Did you speak to Izlomin, by any chance?"

"Heavens no. You don't talk to Izlomin before he goes on. He bites off your head if you do. Mrs. Whitehead tried to and got the door slammed in her face for her pains. That's a funny thing about Whitehead. Everybody fears her. Little ballerinas tremble when she shows up at rehearsals and de Speranski doesn't approach her otherwise than on his belly. But she got along with Vova beautifully—took his tantrums and all. She used to treat him like a racehorse before a race, very respectful-like. Those are the pictures you want, I suppose."

They showed Izlomin leaping, twirling and posturing in a blaze of white sparks. Some were blurred because of the fast action, and the angle from which they had been taken gave him a large Mussolini-like chin. Torrent laid them aside without comment and went through others, mostly Degaslike backstage studies.

He paused with a half-smile over two of them that obviously went together. Both had Mike and Tamara in them. In the first one they were snapped from the wings as they were taking their curtain calls hand in hand, Mike all gallantry and Tamara all pretty submission. The second one showed them a moment later in the wings glaring at each other.

"I did that, with my little Rolleiflex," said Toni. "Like it?"

"What was the row about?"

"Oh, it's an old story. Mike was jealous of—" Toni stopped. Light-hearted backstage gossip that is such an integral and delightful part of ballet suddenly lost its inconsequential charm.

"Go on," said Torrent bleakly. "I've got to know those things."

Toni said unwillingly, "I suppose you'd have found out anyhow. Mike and Tamara had been going together and Izlomin's been giving her the eye and she's been flattered and Mike's been sore. But hell, everybody's been sore at Izlomin at one time or another."

"So I gathered, said Torrent. "Look here, Toni. I'd be obliged if you could get me enlargements of these. Moreover I want you and Bill to go over them carefully and mark on each the time when it was taken, as nearly as you can remember. It'll help us to establish who was where and to refresh their memories. Some people have been awfully vague, like your bearded friend de Speranski. A picture like this," he pointed to one, "showing him in the wings just before *Phoebus* might help start him on a train of recollections."

Toni said slowly, "You seem to be interested in people's movements even before Izlomin disappeared. Why?"

Torrent stacked the pictures neatly into a square pile. "Well, it looks as though Izlomin's death wasn't his own idea after all."

"You mean he didn't hang himself?" Toni breathed, green eyes dilating.

"Your friend Izlomin was dead by the time he was hanged."

"Oh my goodness," said Toni inadequately. She sat very still for a moment. "I thought this business about sudden madness had the smell of the fish about it. But how did he really die then?"

"Suffocated. We have reason to believe that he must have been unconscious before he was killed. There are no marks of struggle or violence on the body and the marks on his throat were made after death, so it looks as though he had been stifled first by something soft put over his mouth."

"Like Desdemona," said Toni thoughtfully. "He must have been unconscious all right. Vova was not the sort of character to allow liberties like that without a struggle. And he was a pretty muscular specimen. Was he hit on the head or something?"

"Nope. No bruises or contusions. Probably drugged."

"When did all this happen?"

"Well, it's hard to put it at the exact time. The M.E. says from nine to ten with leeway on both sides. As a matter of fact, we know it must have been after ten because he was seen at that time."

"By Tamara and by the electrician on the first fly gallery. How true. Then there was something behind those threatening notes, after all. And I was so sure that somebody was being silly and that Izlomin was being dramatic."

Torrent nodded. "Yes. Those accidents did sound very phony. Now I'll have to look into this business of the poisoned valet. I'll be seeing Izlomin's widow later in the day." He began again to hum the valley-desham tune. "I'd like to get some dope on those people, Toni," he said, stopping the humming. "Are you willing to serve as shortcut?"

A small impish smile flickered on Toni's lips. "For a consideration. May I call up my paper and tell them that it's murder, he says? I'll call from here so you can stop me if I say anything that would be of comfort to the enemy. All this is new to me, you know."

"You're doing all right," Torrent remarked dryly as Toni settled herself cozily on his desk in the best journalistic tradition and called her office.

"Thank you for those kind words. And how about ordering me coffee so I won't fall asleep in the midst of important revelations?"

This request being granted, and the news being communicated to the incredulous and admiring editor, Toni settled down comfortably in the large leather chair in which Torrent was wont to lull his victims into a precarious feeling of security with his soft-spoken gentlemanly ways, and allowed her brains to be picked.

"Slava Mladov? He's been a sort of beau page to Natalia Izlomina, so far as I can make out. Everybody's been teasing him about it, and I understand Izlomin himself had found it necessary to be nasty to him. But madame has been pretty nice about it and has treated the kid decently. That's all he is really, just a kid, in spite of being a dancing marvel. A good deal of Peck's bad boy about him. I expect it's the red hair. He wasn't fifteen when he came here three years ago and he had already had a few seasons at the Zagreb Opera House under his belt. I sound like those odious little thumbnail sketches they put in programs. Let's see, what else? He was a Sokol in his own country. That's an athletic organization like our Boy Scouts only more so.

"The cross-eyed *regisseur*—that's Paul Samarkand. He's a character. Used to be a swell dancer and knows his ballets by heart, which is why he is a *regisseur*. He's eccentric as hell—chases imaginary cats all over the room during rehearsals and looks for them behind draperies. But he's very kindhearted. Had no use for Izlomin, who, he claims, was a stinker in Paris and hadn't changed. Izlomin didn't care for him either because he preferred Vassine's style."

"Yes, the mysterious Vassine," said Torrent. "Tell me about him."

"He's not mysterious at all. He's sweet," said Toni. "He used to come in and take the same classes as I did at the Daillart School and he'd borrow my toe shoes and stuff them surreptitiously inside his own soft ballet shoes. He had a mad desire to dance on points, like the rest of the girls. But he was really a sweet boy I am not being nasty when I say that. He wouldn't hurt a fly, and he's as affectionate as a lapdog and as soft and pliable as wax. Somebody is always running his life. A couple of years ago it was his mother. It was a standing joke that Vassine was the only male dancer extant to own a '*mamasha*'—that's the balleto-Russian term for a stage mother. She was a bit under four feet and she kept him under her thumb. Then she died of cancer, suffered quite a lot toward the end, I hear. Luckily by that time Jeff Ffoulkes had taken him under his wing. He's been looking after his interests ever since. He's designed his costumes, fought for good parts for him, and even got him a better contract out of de Speranski, who, needless to say, was swindling him mercilessly."

Torrent dealt in a few more personalities and at the end wanted a collection of reactions to Izlomin's disappearance. Toni supplied him with them, after a little reflection.

"Well, I think the madness angle was uppermost in their minds. De Speranski tore at his beard and moaned like a banshee about how he might have known and he always was afraid of something like that. The Whitehead screamed at him to keep his mouth shut, but you had a feeling she agreed with him. Natalia was icy cold and icy pale. I think that's the way she gets in emergencies. You know, they pounced on her with the glad news right after the curtain came down in *Printemps*. She didn't have a chance to take more than one curtain call."

"I wondered about that from my end," said Torrent. "She was good as the Spinster."

"Well, she's a good character dancer. And naturally what she would give her eye teeth for is a juicy classical part like something in *Swan Lake*. And she isn't so hot at that, although I understand she is a superlative teacher. She taught, you know, while Izlomin was sick… Yes, reactions. Samarkand was sort of pleased in a glum sort of way because while it was a mess all right, he knew Mike could do the part, having done it before, and he didn't much care what happened to Izlomin. I don't know how Mike felt, because I didn't see him."

"I can imagine," said Torrent heavily. Toni tried to fix matters.

"I wouldn't think of Mike's quarreling with Izlomin just in terms of jealousy. It might have been trade union grounds, which doesn't sound very ominous, does it? You've heard about the after-performance party, haven't you? Well, Mike had tackled Izlomin about it before the performance and got no satisfaction out of him. That may have riled him, rather than the Tamara business, which he probably didn't take seriously. Mike is awfully strong on union solidarity."

"Wait a minute," said Torrent, waving union solidarity aside, "before the performance?

"So I was told. Why?"

"Nothing." Torrent's face darkened and Toni had an uneasy feeling that her remark had added to his worries about Mike.

"Well, I think you've picked my brains clean, at least that's how they feel." Toni's slim body stiffened in a convulsive yawn. "I'm going to stagger home and go to bed. My cat must be entertaining the gravest suspicions of my behavior."

As it turned out, Tom Jones had other worries. His romance was having tough sledding. When Toni came in he and his dark lady were nose to nose in the middle of the living room, watching each other steadily. Tom Jones was making soft conciliatory noises to which the black vixen responded by low snarls. Tom Jones gave Toni a perfunctory glance. He had circles under his eyes and a martyred expression. Toni gave him his breakfast and he merely shrugged his shoulders as if to say, "Who wants to eat now?"

Toni left him to his troubles. She crawled into bed and fell asleep as if poleaxed.

The hotel apartment in which Izlomin had lived still bore the imprint of his peculiar personality. There were hangings on the walls and rugs on the floor and a cornerful of icons, all the trimmings with which a true Russian inevitably tries to make himself comfortable and soften the impersonal correctness of a hotel room. Pictures of Izlomin plastered every inch of the wall: coy and petal-covered in *Spectre de la Rose,* black-satin-slinky in *Roi des Chats,* a curious faun with a bestial and oblique glance, a lithe Spaniard, a mocking Harlequin. In the corner opposite the one with icons there hung a sheaf of ballet shoes, covered with inscriptions.

The door opened and Natalia Izlomina came in. Her round face was pale and bore a rather touching look of exhaustion. She answered Torrent's greeting with a faint smile and sat down. In her black dress she looked prim and demure. Torrent remembered what Toni had told him—that other members of the company called her the governess.

He told her about the new development in the case, watching for reactions as he spoke. She seemed to take it quite calmly. Only her pupils grew enormous and her lips went thin and pale. It occurred to Torrent that her reaction was that of complete and devastating fury.

"Before I ask you any other questions," said Torrent, "do you have any idea who might have murdered your husband?"

Natalia Izlomina shook her head slowly. Her breast rose and fell under the thin black fabric of her dress. "No. I wish I knew." Her voice was low and a little hoarse. "When I think of the black years we've lived through, and now this. Dead years, when nothing kept me going except that I just knew that we would have to be happy and famous again. And now everything is gone again and no hope this time. Yes, I wish I knew who did it."

She pressed an immaculate handkerchief to her lips and was herself again. Torrent produced a sympathetic noise and watched her curiously. He thought, unfairly, that while she looked and sounded a bereaved wife, she spoke like someone who had built up a fine thriving enterprise, nursing it lovingly through bad times, only to have it wantonly and spitefully smashed.

"Your husband—I am sorry to have to say this, Mrs. Izlomin, but my impression is that he wasn't too well liked."

"No," Natalia agreed quietly. She smiled a little. "You see, Vova was greedy. He hadn't danced for so long that he wanted to make up for it. And then he was spoiled by—" she hesitated. "By the management."

Torrent thought he understood the meaning of the hesitation and did not pursue it further. Instead he asked, "You were not aware, were you, that your husband wanted to consult me about some danger that threatened him?"

"No, I wasn't." Natalia spoke eagerly. "Do you know what it was about, Captain Torrent? The first I heard of it was when you told me. I knew that Vova was planning something with the help of that girl, Miss Ney, but I thought it was something about costumes. Did he tell her?

For answer, Torrent dug into his wallet and brought out the threatening notes. Each one of them was carefully spread out within a cellophane wrapper, very handy for picking up fingerprints in a quiet and unobtrusive way, which was the way Torrent preferred to do things. "These notes were sent to your husband a few days before his death. Do you recognize the handwriting?"

Natalia took one of the cellophane-protected notes. A little cry escaped her, and the note fluttered to the floor. She stooped to pick it up and when she straightened again, the shock, or terror, that had momentarily flickered in her face was gone. Torrent might have imagined it. Only he didn't think so.

"No," she said. "No, I'm afraid I don't."

"No idea who might have written them?"

She shook her head silently. "Quite," said Torrent and pocketed them, his face expressionless. "Now, ma'am, did you notice anything unusual about your husband's behavior during the past few days?"

She hadn't. Torrent turned to the day before. Natalia obediently recounted Izlomin's actions during the entire day, arriving finally at his appearance at the Opera House at seven-thirty. He had come in before her and when she visited his dressing room she found him terribly upset because his costume, the one with Toni's sequins, hadn't arrived.

"It was a tragedy," said Natalia. "He even forgot all about little Tamara. He said—"

Torrent stopped her. "Little Tamara?"

"Why, yes, the little Ribina. She was in his dressing room when I came in." Natalia smiled an indulgent smile, behind which there was a tiny prick of malice. "Oh, Vova can't be without his little *affaires de coeur*. They are never quite as important as *les paillettes*. Besides, Tamara has her own young man."

Yes, thought Torrent grimly, a young man whose dressing room was next door to Izlomin's and who would hardly relish his girl's visit to the latter. Having dismissed Tamara lightly, Natalia went on with her recital. The boy from the costumer's did arrive to deliver the new costume, just as she went to telephone about it, and to take the spare one to be likewise glorified.

"Vova was jubilant. Of course he was still put out by the illness of Grigorii." (Torrent had to think a moment before he placed the name as that of the poisoned valley-de-sham.) "He doesn't like to have anybody else touch him. If Grigorii isn't there he prefers to dress alone, with me helping a little. You see, Vova gets very high-strung before he dances, particularly if it's a new ballet. And he is so used to Grigorii that he doesn't mind him at all. He's just part of the routine which Vova follows." She stopped as if just becoming aware of having used the present tense. "Used to follow," she said in a curious flat tone as if trying it out for sound.

"Tell me more about the routine."

"Well, for one thing, he wouldn't tolerate visitors in his dressing room half an hour before the performance. When he'd come in, he would first of all go through his exercises. Then he would take his shower. Then he would begin dressing. Presently he would drink his fruit juice, which would always be waiting for him on the little table near the couch, not later than twenty minutes before he went onstage."

Torrent interrupted here to ask about the clean glass he had discussed with Toni and received the answers he expected, that Vova had drunk his orange juice and that she had not at any time washed the glass.

"He would take a drink upon coming back from dancing every number," said Natalia. "To come back to his routine before the first ballet. He would put on his makeup last of all. Vova was always very serious about that part of it, makeup and coiffure. He claimed it was just as much a work of art as actual dancing. Everything in art," said Natalia somewhat pompously, "must be an integral part of a harmonious whole. And as he made himself up, Vova would become the character he portrayed. It was like magic."

"It must have been. When did you leave him?

"A little while before *Aurora's Wedding* began. I came back later. With Mrs. Whitehead. She wanted to speak to Vova and of course I knew it was a bad idea. I asked him if it was all right for us to come in and he shouted no. He came to the door and glared at us and slammed it. Mrs. Whitehead tried anyhow. She's so stubborn. And Vova was abominably rude. He threw something at the door when she tried it and he yelled. So we left. I could have come in, probably, but I thought it might make Mrs. Whitehead feel better if I didn't. She was a little hurt, I'm afraid. So I never did see Vova again."

Torrent glanced at her questioningly and she corrected herself. "Not to speak to, I mean. I suppose it was a good way to see him for the last time, dancing and whirling above me in a golden glow. And yet," she added, in a changed voice, "I think I had a premonition. While Vova danced, I saw him, yes, but I—I didn't feel him there. It was as if he was already gone, just a shell of him left. It must have been a premonition. Then I had to change for *Printemps* and so I had to hurry away before he was through with his curtain calls."

Torrent listened patiently to the rest of the story he already knew told in Natalia's soft painstaking voice. Occasionally she looked up from her intertwined hands as she stopped to remember some detail of the frantic search before Torrent's arrival on the scene, and Torrent, looking into her dilated eyes, had a hunch that she was probably getting one hell of a headache. "Just one more thing," he said when she finished. "I'd like to see this valet chap, this Grigorii. Could you supply me with a little of his background before I do?"

A little was right. Natalia only knew or was interested in that part of it which impinged on their life. He used to be a dresser in some rundown theater in Lisbon. He waited on Vova during a benefit performance there, Vova liked the way he worked and hired him. Torrent thought it was a good idea to speak to him and Natalia offered to take him to his room and to serve as translator, if things bogged down.

"I don't speak Russian any too well," she explained on the way to his room. "Just from being with Vova and all the Russians. I am French, you know. Vova and I talked French."

Torrent commented on the excellence of her English. She smiled dimly and said, "London," by way of explanation. "Vova," she added, "refused to learn any English, either in London or here."

Grigorii lived in a little room, like a doghouse. He was a shaggy taciturn man with a shock of black hair from under which his eyes looked out at the miserable world with the disillusioned stare of a constipated sheepdog. He had a little dab of a mustache, like Voroshilov's, or to less charitable eyes, like somebody else's. Torrent found him sitting on his bed, strumming a melancholy guitar and very drunk. His English was less than monosyllabic and Torrent had to have recourse to Natalia's help. He questioned him about his health. Grigorii, apparently touched by this solicitude, brightened up and burst into impassioned speech, patting his stomach affectionately. Torrent could distinguish the word "cafeteria" balefully repeated from time to time.

Natalia translated. Grigorii seemed to blame his troubles on several tuna fish sandwiches he had eaten at a cafeteria lunch. An hour or so later he was seized with acute stomach cramps and vomiting and had to be taken home. A doctor had been to see him, but Grigorii seemed to distrust that profession as a whole and had taken his cure into his own hands with the help of a bottle of vodka.

Torrent left, after requesting Natalia to write out for him the full name of the faithful valley-de-sham and the name of the doctor who attended him. In an hour he was to be at the Opera where all the members of the company he wanted to interview would be gathered for questioning, a convenience provided by the management. He remembered the cautious treatment of the word by Natalia and decided that it was a good idea to see the backer of the American Ballet Drama, the redoubtable Mrs. Whitehead. He remembered the raucous voice, the pale long face over a dress of regrettable magenta—the recollection of the color sliced through his brain like a headache. He hoped that Mrs. Whitehead favored other colors in the morning.

Mrs. Cornelius Whitehead II lived in a lavish establishment on Park Avenue, complete with butler, noise-stifling rugs, tapestries on the walls of the foyer, monumental staircases and elevators to the second floor. The chatelaine herself was out riding but was expected back soon, and the butler, upon being firmly handled and shown Torrent's badge, finally showed him to the library, muttering as he went.

Torrent didn't have long to wait. A quarter of an hour later Kate Whitehead's rangy figure appeared in the doorway and he noticed with relief that the color scheme was much easier to take. She looked almost human in her riding habit. She stared at Torrent, swishing her crop against her dusty jodhpurs, while he recalled himself to her memory.

"Ah, yes. The copper. Sorry I kept you waiting. I went riding, you see, and lost track of the time. Made things more bearable," she said gruffly and strode to the buffet like a man. She flipped the doors open on a trove of dark appetizing-looking bottles. "Scotch?"

Torrent declined and watched with some admiration the stiff dose she poured down her own gullet. It was his private opinion that this was not the first drink Mrs. Whitehead had had this morning. There was that certain glassiness in her eye, that certain stiffness in her carriage. She reminded him of nothing so much as a country squire, a tough article who could hold his liquor like a trooper and ride when others might have found difficulty in walking. And then he saw that her eyes were red with weeping.

"Well," said Mrs. Whitehead, pouring herself another drink, "what can you tell me about poor Vova? Who killed him?"

Torrent looked at her. "The official report last night was suicide. What makes you think he was killed?"

"Don't be silly," said Kate Whitehead acidly, "and don't goggle at me with that stonewall expression. I didn't believe that suicide stuff for long. Why should Vova kill himself? He had everything to live for. He had just danced a brilliant ballet, he was about to dance another. He had everything he wanted, and," she added with a magnificent arrogance, "I was going to marry him."

Torrent digested this in silence. His first reaction was that perhaps Izlomin's situation mightn't have been as wonderful as it looked at a first glance, if it was necessary for him to marry Kate Whitehead.

"I know what you're thinking," said that lady, and amazingly her next remark proved that sure enough she did. "You're wondering why Vova should want to marry an old battle-ax like me." Torrent, taken by surprise, recovered enough to murmur politely, "Not at all."

"Of course you were. Don't lie to me. As a matter of fact, it would have been a damn good thing for Vova. I'm no yearling but I have compensating qualities. I wouldn't have interfered with his life and I would have insured his future. Listen, all dancers, no matter how good they are, are only good for a time. After that what have they got? They're like horses, only with less sense. Somebody's got to take care of them. I would have taken care of Vova after his legs gave out, just as I would have of any thoroughbred."

Torrent had a disconcertingly vivid picture of an aged and decrepit Izlomin let out to pasture.

Mrs. Whitehead rambled on. "Never cared for anything but horses before. Nothing like 'em. Same feeling about ballet dancers though. Ever watch them during a ballet class? Just like a good stable. Legs like steel springs and rippling muscles under velvet skin and even the same dumb look. Wonderful." She hiccuped with great dignity. "Well, get on with your business, man. What do you want to know from me?"

"You say, ma'am, that you were planning to marry Izlomin. Was his wife aware of that?"

"Natalia?" Mrs. Whitehead' made a contemptuous gesture. "Vova told her, naturally. That cold-blooded fish! Vova was sick and tired of her. He had wanted to get rid of her for a long time."

"And was she willing?"

"Of course not. She knew she had hold of a good thing. She wouldn't let go."

"But then?"

The woman disposed of the whole matter with another contemptuous gesture. "I was going to buy her off, that's all. Natalia likes money. She would have given him up, all right. I suppose she was entitled to being paid off for the years she spent taking care of him."

"Did you discuss the matter with her?"

"No, I left it all to Vova. I've let her know how I felt, though. Like mentioning a few things I could do for Vova and have done."

"For example?"

"For example, the little surprise I was preparing for him. Vova's relatives were mostly nasty tempered bastards like himself. The only exception seemed to be an aunt of his who was decent to him when he was a little boy. He was quite fond of her. She was the only relative he didn't drop after he became famous. You'll probably read about her in that book of Natalia's. Well, the last they knew of her she was still in France. I got her out. She's in Lisbon now waiting to be shipped here. It took a little doing," said Mrs. Whitehead complacently, "but I usually get what I want."

Torrent, with a look at her traplike jaw, agreed that it was probably so.

"Yes," said Mrs. Whitehead somberly. "I'd always get a horse I wanted no matter how much it cost me. But then," she ended on a deep sigh, "sometimes after you get them, the best of them break their legs and have to be shot."

She downed another slug. Torrent deftly interposed questions into the alcoholic fog that was gathering about her and was able to expand a little the previous picture of her movements during that evening. She even recounted with some wryness Izlomin's keeping her out of the dressing room, the part she had omitted before. That was all. Mrs. Whitehead expected Captain Torrent to report his progress to her personally.

Captain Torrent thanked Mrs. Whitehead for her cooperation and produced one of the threatening notes to Izlomin. She didn't recognize the handwriting.

"Looks as if somebody in the ballet had a cute idea. Everybody hated him, you know. He was a high-spirited bastard. Mean," she said proudly. Torrent had a feeling as if she were speaking of an animal she owned rather than a man. "Even I've been tempted at times to smack him down, and I loved him."

"Have you any idea who could have…?"

"Killed him? Yes, I have," came the unexpected answer. The woman's eyes suddenly glowed with an ugly green fire. "It's his wife who did it. That's who. That damnable little prig."

"Motive?" Torrent inquired gently.

"Because he was going to leave her for me, of course, you nitwit. She couldn't stand anybody else having him so she killed him first. Not that I expect you to see past her virtuous little act."

"Just so," said Torrent, adding a curlicue to a doodle he had drawn in his notebook. "That's very interesting. A while back you gave me the impression that you considered Mrs. Izlomin a cold fish, a woman mainly interested in money. That doesn't quite chime with your present picture of a madly jealous woman, ready to kill when her love is scorned, don't you know."

Mrs. Whitehead made an angry sound and strode to the window.

"However," Torrent addressed her back, "we shall investigate every possibility, of course. Good day, Mrs. Whitehead."

He left, unanswered. He reflected as he went that he had at least a partial understanding of Mrs. Whitehead's role in the ballet. She kept a stable of ballet dancers, obviously. It was equally obvious that her preference ran to the stallions.

CHAPTER NINE

TONI OPENED HER EYES and looked dourly from the ringing telephone to the clock, which showed that she had been asleep all of two hours and fifty-five minutes.

It was the day desk calling. The news reporter had learned that Torrent was questioning a lot of people at the Civic Opera, but he couldn't get through for love or money. It was up to Toni, who knew everybody there, and who had been so wonderful at handling Torrent anyhow.

"What is all this beautiful friendship between you and this dick? Is he paying your rent by any chance? Those depraved policemen…"

"Nothing of the sort," Toni assured him primly, "just a little black-mail."

"You don't say? What'd he do?"

"Shot a man who wouldn't let him have his sleep," said Toni and hung up.

The two cats leaped up on the bed and watched her dressing.

"Any progress?" Toni inquired with interest.

Tom Jones nipped his playmate's black ear in a proprietary manner. Cleo biffed him and fled under the bed. "Excuse me," said Tom Jones and followed her, his fluffy tail flicking out of sight as Toni headed for the shower.

Half an hour later and only a little more than half awake, Toni breezed through the Civic Opera stage entrance. Apparently she was still a per-sona grata.

Torrent had taken over de Speranski's office (at the latter's express request) while Mahoney stood guard in the outer office, where the mem-bers of the company had been got together for the purpose of inquisition. He greeted Toni cheerfully; he remembered her from Lais and shared his chief's regard for her.

"He's talking to the guy with the beard now," said Mahoney, shoving a flat palm a way under his chin to indicate the length of said beard. "Hey, this is some case, Miss Ney. Reminds me of the days we used to raid burlesque houses. But these chicks beat the burlesque dames. Younger, for one thing. I'll tell the chief you're here the minute I get a chance."

Toni was immediately surrounded by the chattering ballerinas who, having told each other everything they had to say, welcomed the sight of a new listener.

"Did you hear that Vova…? They say Mrs. Whitehead is going to dissolve the company now that Vova…We're going on just as if nothing…All this is making me lose weight, I tried on my *Swan Lake* costume this morning and it's loose…I'm so scared—just feel my heart…That detective…I don't think he's so terrible with that cute little mustache…"

The possessor of the cute little mustache squirmed a little, not because he had overheard the remark but because de Speranski's carved chair felt uncomfortable against his back. Two photographs of Izlomin, conspicuously placed on the desk, stared him in the face. One was taken in 1935 and one in 1943. Both showed him in his *Roi des Chats* costume and both bore the inscription: *"A mon très cher ami, à qui je dois tout! Vova."*

"You say Mr. Ffoulkes joined you in this office in the beginning of the ballet performance. What was the subject of your discussion?"

"Dze possibility of André's return to our company," de Speranski told him. "A ballet dancer's place is in a ballet company. Dzose who dance in musical comedies soon lose dze technique."

"Was Ffoulkes the one to discuss this with?"

A smile appeared in the beard. "He is dze one to decide. I will be frank, both Jeff and André were a great loss to dze company. Ffoulkes is a very clever designer. His costumes for *Labyrinth,* for *Chessgame...*" De Speranski kissed his exquisitely kept fingertips. "I was very much against letting dzem go. I believe, sir, in sanctity of contracts!"

"Quite," said Torrent. "The reason for their leaving was their inability to get along with Izlomin, I believe."

De Speranski made his eyes as big as possible to lend more emphasis to the affirmative closing of them and the slow portentous nod. *"De mortuis*, of course, my dear Captain, but he didn't like people near him to be too good. And he had pull. But I made it my business to stay on good terms with dze boys. As a Russian proverb says, 'do not spit into a well, you may want to drink from it.' "

"Anyway, you were with Mr. Ffoulkes in this office most of the time?"

On the whole, yes. He had been called out of the office once or twice. As for Ffoulkes, he had taken that opportunity to visit Mike and Slava in their dressing room. Then they went backstage to watch *Phoebus* from the wings.

Torrent wanted to know whether de Speranski had noticed anything out of the way that happened during the performance, anybody acting in a strange or unwonted manner.

"Acting strange!" said de Speranski. "My dear sir, you are talking to one who has worked with ballet dancers for thirty years and you expect me to notice when anyone acts strange? When do dzey act any other way? I don't know what makes dzem do some of dze things dzey do— take unreasonable dislikes to one anodzer, refuse to wear a costume because it's unlucky, try to run out two minutes before going on because dzey have forgotten a lucky charm, or go on dancing with a broken ankle before dzey think of giving up a part. I have given up trying to understand dzem. I only revel in dze beauty dzey bring and dzat I, in my small way—"

Torrent interrupted by asking whether any of the dancers did act as he had described. He was particularly interested in the one who had tried to leave in the middle of the performance. It turned out to be nothing sinister. It was Slava Mladov, who wanted to run upstairs after a forgotten good luck piece. His partner, Perlova, objected strenuously and de Speranski had to interpose his authority to keep him where he belonged. Yes, he stayed and danced, without the charm.

Torrent came back to Ffoulkes. "Did he stay around after the ballet?"

No, he left right after the ovations started, stopping only to say goodbye to de Speranski. "He had promised to let me know his decision before he left, and he did. He was going to advise Vassine to come back."

"Nevertheless," said Torrent to himself, "I'll have to check up on Mr. Ffoulkes, even if he seems to have left too early to be of use to us."

He went on to check up on the director's whereabouts, particularly during the time when the wardrobe mistress came down with the news of Izlomin's disappearance. De Speranski at first claimed that he couldn't remember all the places that he, as director, had to visit, then it turned out that he had been in the men's room. He, too, described the vain search of the theater with Mrs. Whitehead, Samarkand and Natalia.

Torrent jotted down the last line and thanked him for his cooperation. But the director lingered. "You must understand, Captain Torrent, that you are dealing with very delicate human material here. Artistic temperament. When balance is upset, performance suffers. You are lover of ballet yourself, Captain, so you will understand when I say dzat any consideration on your part will make me very grateful." He added delicately, "Not to mention Mrs. Whitehead, who is a rich and influential woman."

Torrent's cold blue eyes rested on him with dislike. "The artistic temperament seems to have developed some homicidal aspects. I can't go easy on anybody until we have placed the blame where it belongs, no matter how rich Mrs. Whitehead is and how grateful you are. Now if you don't mind sending Mike Gorin in…"

De Speranski left, perspiring fatly and insisting that Torrent had misunderstood him.

"What about it, Mike?" said Torrent. There was almost a plea in his voice. "You don't understand how bad it looks. Look at the record. You and Izlomin were on bad terms. You had quarreled and nearly come to blows over a girl. Yet after his performance you come over to him to tell him something and he ignores everybody else and goes up with you as if you were his best pal. Obviously you had something to tell him that was important enough to make him forget how he felt about you. Now that's the last anybody sees of him. The next thing we know he's hanging from a fly gallery rail. You are the last person to have spoken to him. We've got to know what you had to tell him."

"I told you what. About the Barezian party," said Mike doggedly. He was lying, Torrent knew, not convincingly but stubbornly, and he would stick to the unconvincing lie till the cows came home.

Torrent sighed. He much preferred the subtler liars, the kind that tried to make their fabrications works of art, so perfect and esthetically satisfying that eventually they grew to love them for their own sakes and went to pieces with sheer artistic dismay when something slipped.

He said wearily. "Don't give me that. You talked to him about that before the performance."

Mike's eyes flickered. He muttered, "Well, we talked about it again." He added with a weak grin, "Maybe he owed me money."

Torrent disregarded the sally. "When you were with Izlomin, did you see him take a drink?"

"No, I don't think so. I don't remember. He may have."

"Did he do anything else—take his makeup off, start to undress?" Mike shook his head. "And yet he was supposed to be preparing for the next number. And he was supposed to be very fussy about being ready on time. How do you explain that, Mike? Still claim that you were talking about the pretty unimportant matter of Barezian's party?"

"Union matters aren't unimportant."

"To Izlomin they were." There was silence. Torrent took out the threatening notes and gave one of them to Mike. "This mean anything to you?"

Mike deciphered the French laboriously and handed them back to Torrent with a puzzled frown.. Either he was really seeing them for the first time or he was a consummate actor. "Looks like a kid's trick to me. I don't know who wrote it, though."

Torrent dismissed him with a curt nod. "I'm not in a mood to play ring-around-a-rosy with you, Mike. If you won't talk, I'll hold you as a material witness. Before you go I want you to write out a few words and give them to Mahoney."

Mike left. His shoulders drooped, but his swarthy face was set with stubbornness and something like despair.

Tamara Ribina followed him, as she had the night before. But this morning she looked frankly scared, ludicrously like a little girl sent in to see the principal. She let herself down on the edge of a chair, where she sat tensely, her huge black eyes fixed unwinkingly on Torrent.

The latter offered her a cigarette, which she refused. But he could see that the homely little action seemed to reassure her. A man who offers you a cigarette can't be so terrifying.

"Now, Miss—Ribina, is it? We've been going over everybody's stories hoping to get anything we may have missed last night, don't you know. Supposing we go over your movements again. Let's start with when you came to the theater."

It was at about seven-thirty, earlier than usual, she admitted, because she had a date with someone. Yes, it was Izlomin. "He wanted to have a serious talk with me," she explained.

"Do you always have your serious talks before the performance?"

A faint smile dimpled around the girl's lips. She blurted out, blushing, "Mamma won't let me go out with Izlomin. She—she thought he was too old for me."

"How old are you?"

Tamara raised a weary eyebrow and began to say twenty when it apparently occurred to her that after all this was the police. "Eighteen."

"And you only go out with the boys that mamma approves of?"

"Oh, no," said Tamara loftily. "Mamma is awfully old-fashioned. But she was really serious about Vova."

"I see. Well, what was the important thing he wanted to tell you last night?"

"That's just what it was about, my going out with him, I mean. He said to tell mamma that he was going to marry me and that it's all right for him to see me whenever he wanted to."

Torrent sighed and asked a question that he had asked of another, older woman a while ago. "What about Izlomin's wife?"

"He said it would be all right about the divorce. It would take a little time but he wanted to be sure that I would go out with him in the meantime. He said I was to regard myself as his affianced wife."

"Were you pleased?" Torrent inquired, somewhat at a loss as to the dancer's reactions.

"I should say so," said Tamara. "That'd show him a thing or two."

"Whom?"

"Oh," said Tatiana, growing vague, "a certain person."

She went on with her story. After Vova's announcement Natalia had come in and Tamara had gone back to her own room to get into her Bluebird costume. She saw Izlomin next when he appeared on the stage as Phoebus.

"You were the Ethiopian girl, weren't you?" said Torrent, consulting the program. "And very good too."

"Thank you," Tamara breathed. "It's a good part if only I didn't have to roll all the way across the stage when I die. It's so hard on the hips."

"Must be brutal," Torrent agreed. "Then you went to your room to change, right? Now then, you told me yesterday that you saw Izlomin again."

"Yes," said Tamara in a whisper. Her face was getting that haunted look again and this time Torrent's reassuring smile had no effect.

"Look here," said Torrent uncomfortably. "Don't be so scared. I'm just checking for details, like did you see him or hear him first?"

"Well, I heard voices and there was Vova on the stairs." She stopped too late and Torrent pounced.

"Voices? Then he wasn't alone?"

"Yes, he was," said Tamara loudly and looked at Torrent in abject terror. "I meant a voice. His voice."

"To whom was he talking?" Silence. "As far as I know there was nobody on the floor except you and the two boys. Was it one of the boys?"

"No!"

"You perhaps?" said Torrent with mild irony. A look of relief flashed on the girl's round Mongolian face. "Yes, that was it. He was talking to me."

"What was he saying?"

Tamara foundered. "I—I don't know. That is, I couldn't hear him."

"Now don't you see how strange that sounds, Miss Ribina? First you hear voices before you see Izlomin, or he sees you. Then you claim that he was talking to you and you can't even tell me what he said because you couldn't hear him. Why don't you just tell me whom he was really talking to?"

Tamara suddenly opened her shapely mouth and began to bawl like a little girl, her face all screwed up. Apparently she had come to the end of her rope.

"Come on, there's a good girl," said Torrent, not unkindly. "Don't you see that all this stalling· around isn't making it any better for whomever you're protecting? Why don't you tell me who it is? I mightn't share your belief in his guilt."

Tamara glared at Torrent through drenched eyelashes, from which mascara was beginning to run in black streaks. "I don't either believe he's guilty," she shouted defiantly. Realizing her error, she abruptly stopped crying, gave Torrent a trapped look and fainted. It was the phoniest faint Torrent had ever seen. She sank down as lightly as thistledown, her dark head pillowed on a gracefully extended arm. Even her toes pointed. It might have been the finale of the *Dying Swan*.

"Oh lord," said Torrent between laughter and annoyance. He bent over her prostrate form. "Look here, Miss—"

The door flew open and a large and opulent woman flew in, her black eyes snapping with rage. She swept Torrent out of her way and threw herself down beside Tamara, pillowing her head on her capacious bosom. Torrent fancied that he saw an expression of relief flit across the little dancer's supposedly inanimate countenance.

"What have you been doing to my daughter, you—you policeman? It is the third degree, yes?" she demanded fiercely.

"Just asking some questions," Torrent answered meekly. He was wondering whether Tamara was eventually going to look like her mother.

"Asking questions," the matron retorted with withering scorn. "You have fainted her, look, with your questions. My poor little one."

"Shall I pour some water on her?" Torrent asked.

Here Tamara decided to revive. Torrent allowed her mother to fuss over her, helped her to a chair, sent for some water and went on with the questioning.

"I'd like you to stay here, Mrs. Ribina," he told Tamara's mother. "Just to keep your mind at ease about the third degree, don't you know."

They went over the same ground, with the difference that Tamara, unable to muster another swoon, confined herself to a mild fit of hysterics. Torrent thought that mamma was beginning to look thoughtful. Thereupon he dismissed them.

"According to what you told me, Miss Ribina, you were the last person to see Izlomin alive. Any time you want to add to this statement…"

He ushered them out courteously, smiling a little at the immediate outburst of impassioned Russian on the other side of the door. A funny little scene! But last night Tamara had told her story without any signs of fear, while today…Of course, last night Izlomin was supposed to have committed suicide, while today everybody knew that it was murder.

Torrent decided to make a break in the routine and see Toni.

"What were you doing to Tamara?" Toni inquired with some amusement. "I saw mamma rushing to the rescue."

She looked grave when Torrent gave her an abbreviated version of the interview. "I suppose she thinks she has kept her dark secret, the poor little ostrich."

"I daresay," said Torrent. "I wish you'd do something for me, Toni. Tackle that young idiot, Mike, will you? He has a lot of respect for you. Tell him it's very, very wrong to keep things from the police."

Toni agreed albeit dubiously. "I doubt that any good will come of that. Mike can be as stubborn as a mule. Do you think he's badly involved in this mess?"

"To the ears. Probably also protecting someone." Torrent broke off and gave Toni an avuncular smile. "Now that you're a newspaperwoman, I suppose I should add that this is off the record."

"Naturally. I shall tell them at the office that Captain Torrent has nothing to say at present but is expecting important developments in the near future. Isn't that the phrase? Good-bye, Captain Torrent."

She headed for the nearest drugstore and began to make telephone calls. She called the hotel where Eric was staying and was told that he had gone out. Then she called her office and was promptly saddled with another task. Didn't she know the dancer's widow personally? Good. Interview her.

Toni groaned. "So I'm a sob sister now."

She was told to snap out of it. "You want to write an exercise column all your life? You should be grateful for the opportunity."

Toni reported that the only opportunity she would be grateful for just now was that to catch up with her sleep. Before hanging up she was told that her boyfriend had tried to get her at the office and would pick her up at the Civic Opera at one-thirty.

Toni put through a call to the Hotel Southern and upon giving her name was eventually connected with Natalia Izlomina, to whom she stated her errand.

"My paper is writing a brief biography of your husband for its Sunday section. We'd like you to look it over and see if it meets with your approval. We hate to intrude on you at this time, but your husband was an important public figure, a legendary one, really, and we feel it's important to present a true picture to the public."

"Wait a minute," said Izlomina. Her voice receded and Toni guessed that she was consulting someone. Then she said, "Yes, you may cone over, immediately, if you wish."

Toni thanked her and hung up. She struggled for a moment with the problem of what to do about Lieutenant Skeets, who would miss her at the Opera. Finally she left a note with the doorman and hopped a cab. She still had to stop at the office to pick up the copy she wanted Izlomin's widow to approve.

She encountered a surprise in Natalia's living room.

"You have met Mr. Graham, I think," said Natalia. "My publisher."

Graham said, "Yes, we've met. I'd asked Miss Ney to join us at El Morocco last night,"

"Really?" said Natalia, without interest. Her face retained its cool pallor, yet somehow there was a feverish look about it. The crisp tendrils of hair at her temples looked as if they had been curled by inner heat. Toni, like Torrent, decided that Natalia was suffering from a bad headache.

Graham went on, "We are thinking of putting out a little pamphlet about Vova's tragic death as an addendum to the book. It would be incomplete without that. Do you suppose Captain Torrent will be able to come to some conclusion in time to be useful to us?"

"Charles, you are incredible," said Natalia, coloring faintly with annoyance. "Asking such questions. I told you I don't care."

"Ah, but it's very important, darling," said Graham easily. "And Miss Ney is such a perfect person to ask, with her intelligence and her knowledge of the ballet, and her acquaintance with the police." Toni gave him a quick impassive glance. He simply couldn't be as simple and ingenuous as he made out.

Natalia leaned forward, her clear hazel eyes fixed earnestly on Toni's. "There is something I want to ask you, Miss Ney. About Vova. You see, I was so surprised about those notes. He never told me about them. Is there anything else?"

Toni assured her that there was nothing. Except—after a brief hesitation she told Natalia about the supposed poisoning of Grigorii. Natalia's eyes widened.

"But—but that's absurd. It was just ptomaine poisoning. The doctor said so." She pressed her hand to her forehead. "And yet those notes were written and Vova is dead—murdered!"

"Don't, my dear," said Graham gently. Natalia paid no attention to him. Her eyes held a dry glitter as if of unshed tears.

"That's what torments me so. I am to blame for Vova's death. You see, it isn't true that I haven't known about his suspicions. I have. But I made him keep quiet about them. I frightened him into being silent because—" Her hands twisted. "It's so easy for people to look at a man who had been ill, and say 'Aha, it's coming back.'" (Toni remembered Izlomin's sidelong look and his "*Non*, I am not crazy.") "And people in the company didn't like him. It would have been so easy to start a little whispering. The persecution mania. He thinks somebody is after him, you know what that means. But he was right. I knew that I helped his murderer kill him the minute Captain Torrent showed me those notes."

She fell silent and in a moment was calm and self-possessed again.

"I'm all right now. And I'll look at what you've written about Vova, Miss Ney, if you wish." She took the sheaf from Toni's hands and rose to her feet. "I'll read it in my own room," she said with a little smile. "Somehow it is so hard to concentrate when you know that people are waiting for you."

"So," said Graham, when the door closed behind her. His eyes were laughing. "You won't give me advice."

Toni said dryly, "I was a little handicapped by the presence of the subject's widow."

"And now," said Graham, "you're ticking me off for talking so heartlessly, as if the book were all that mattered, and poor old Vova not yet cold in his grave. Strictly speaking, he's not in his grave at all, is he? Your friend Captain Torrent is still working on him."

"Captain Torrent is not a ghoul by profession," said Toni. "I believe the body is now in the hands of the Medical Examiner's office."

"True. What a beautiful loyalty you have to your friends, Miss Ney. Now you're thinking that I haven't. But Vova wasn't a friend of mine. Only his wife, who is a remarkable woman. And I keep forgetting that she probably doesn't see him as the bastard he really was. I'm terribly absentminded, you know. Can't remember anything unless I write it down. And I keep calling you Miss Ney, because I can't remember your first name."

"Toni."

"I'm Charles. And now," he bounded up from his chair and ran a hand through his rumpled hair, "I fear I must leave you. I have a very important engagement at one."

"The watch on your left wrist seems to show that it's now a quarter to two," Toni remarked with interest.

"Too true, alas. I knew it half an hour ago but I had to wait and see you. Goodbye, Toni."

"Goodbye," said Toni, putting her narrow hand into his large one. "By the way, there is one piece of advice I can give you about your book. Change the title. It's *Lazarus Arise,* I believe. And," she said, withdrawing her hand, "he won't, you know."

CHAPTER TEN

AS HE LOOKED at the pale, freckle-dotted, carrot-topped face of the boy he was questioning, Torrent thought that this seemed to be his day for dealing with frightened adolescents. He wondered whether Slava Mladov was frightened because of something he did or something he knew, or whether this was the standard Continental reaction to police questioning. Just now he was engaged in trying to clear up the discrepancy between the wardrobe mistress' statement and his.

"But I was there," said Slava earnestly. "But yes. She's a stupid old woman. I said, '*non*,' when she asked if we needed her and I thought she heard me because she went away. She must be deaf, I think, the stupid old bitch," he added in a sudden fury. "I heard her knock on Vova's door. I can even tell you what she said. 'Monsieur Izlomin, you need me? All right, I'll come back later.' That shows I was there, isn't it?"

He sounded like a bad boy presenting a laborious alibi for a broken window.

"While Mike was talking to Izlomin in the next room," said Torrent, "did you happen to overhear any of the conversation?"

"No. I hear nothing."

"No arguments? No loud voices?"

"Oh, no." Slava thought a little and said cautiously, "I guess I did hear a little something about the party for Kotik Barezian.

"And then Mike came back and began dressing for *Cauchemar.*" He went on hurriedly, giving Torrent a definite impression that he was slurring over something. "And then we heard Mrs. Whitehead. She came knocking at Vova's door. 'Oh Vova, are you there? Oh Vova.'" He mimicked her in a wicked boyish falsetto.

"And was Vova there?"

Again the wary look. "I don't know. I guess not. The door opened and closed and he didn't say anything and she went away. Tramp, tramp with the big feet like she was disappointed." He grinned like a young fox.

Torrent's shoulders moved in a resigned shrug. Everybody had kept something back. Why not the Whitehead? Slava was still laughing noiselessly, but his eyes were uneasy. Torrent was reminded of an anxious urchin going through his tricks to keep the grown-ups' attention from some mischief he had done. He returned to the subject from which the digression had taken them.

"How long was Mike in there talking to Izlomin?"

"He came back right after the wardrobe mistress left. He wasn't in there long."

It would have to be a short time. *Phoebus* was over—he glanced at the schedule Samarkand had given him—at 9:40. The ovations kept Izlomin on the stage until 9:50. He was seen going off on his mysterious wanderings at about 10:00. So Mike must have been with him from 9:50 to 10:00 unless—Torrent thought of Tamara's testimony and felt gloomy. He grilled the boy until he fidgeted like a worm, noticing unhappily the telltale signs of evasiveness: the way his coffee-colored eyes shifted, the dull splotches of color staining his cheeks. But he stuck to the story of Mike's early return.

Torrent abandoned the subject. "You yourself were on pretty bad terms with Izlomin, weren't you?"

Slava didn't look concerned. "So what? I'm not the only one. He picked on everybody. He always gave Kotik Barezian bad parts in his ballets. And he tried to get Perlova out of the company, because she gets as much applause as he does. Mike Gorin once did four *tours en l'air* in *Roi des Chats.* Vova told him not to do it, all he wants is three *tours.* He hates to see anybody get ahead. He kept his wife so busy taking care of him that now she can only dance character parts. And Jeff Ffoulkes can tell you a boy in his Paris company killed himself because Vova never gave him a chance to dance. He was Jeff's friend, so it's a true story. He's a lousy selfish bastard."

"Was," Torrent corrected dryly. "Incidentally, did you write these?"

The young dancer's eyes slid over the slips of paper in their cellophane wrappers. He dropped them and leaped to his feet. "It's a lie, it's a goddamn lie. I never—"

"Pipe down, son," Torrent advised amiably. "If you didn't, do you know who did?"

The boy shook his head a little, as if there were a roaring in his ears that prevented him from hearing well. Then he shook it again, more emphatically, for "no."

"You can go now. Give Mahoney a sample of your handwriting."

Slava went, a thin young Apache, moving with a feline grace that seemed to soften the angular sharpness of his boy's body.

"That's right," said Elena Perlova. "Mike came into Tamara's dressing room just before *Aurora's Wedding. Mon Dieu*, how he was furious. All about being in Izlomin's room and listening to his silly proposals. He should have known, of course, that Tamara was just doing that to teach him a lesson." Torrent wondered sourly why all women thought it necessary to do that to men in whom they were seriously interested. "In the old days—*peut être*! All Vova had to do was crook his little finger. *C'était du prestige, dormir avec* Vova. But now it's different. Besides there was no necessity, Tamara is getting along very well. It is true her arms are a little Moscow…"

Torrent watched her as she prattled on. She was wearing a suit of a dark ripe crimson, a color you associate with overblown roses just about to shed their petals. It was her favorite color, Torrent surmised, remembering that she had worn it in *Rêves de Printemps*. It gave her an air of chic melancholy, a cachet of old world elegance that went with her exaggeratedly slender waist, her pale, almost faded cheeks and the faint shadows around her beautiful blue eyes that seemed larger than they were because of an artful thin line at the corners. She had long aristocratic feet, unlike the small stubby feet of the average ballet dancer. Torrent had no way of knowing it, of course, but their aristocratic length gave her a lot of trouble. She had to tape them before putting on her ballet shoes but even that didn't prevent the bunions that are the fate of all ballet dancers with long feet.

Torrent remembered that she had known Izlomin in Paris. He asked her, "Was Izlomin always a woman chaser?"

Perlova rolled her eyes expressively and launched on a long and probably libelous account of his varied love life.

"What about his wife?"

"Natalia?" Perlova was startled. "She is very realistic. She knows Vova can't do without her. He always comes back. Besides, she is very cold, that one. I suspect she doesn't mind if Vova takes his satisfaction elsewhere but naturally only if there is no danger of losing him."

"But supposing he wanted to marry someone else?"

"Ah, that would be different. *Ça serait une catastrophe.* But he never." She smiled her funny tricornered cat-smile. "He always says he will. 'How I would like to marry you, petite. But my wife, you know. Let us do the best we can under the circumstances.' He tries that on everyone." She rattled off a list of names from the company. "He even tried it on me last year and I told him, 'Vova, you forget. I knew you in Paris.' Besides I was already interested in Kotik. That is my husband, whom the army has taken from me. Do you think that it will be a long war, Captain Torrent? Because it will be terrible if it is a long war and Kotik will come back and find that I am old."

"No war can possibly last that long," said Torrent, slightly surprised at his own attack of old world gallantry. She must really be a charmer to have evoked it. It was too bad that she had been too busy dancing to notice anything.

And like the others, she knew nothing about the notes.

It was evening now, and Toni relaxed limply on her couch in front of the fire. She had had a busy day. She had worked feverishly over her interview with Izlomina, with the editor brandishing a whip over her head and telling her that women reporters don't know the meaning of deadlines.

"I am not a woman reporter," Toni had snarled back, nettled. "I just do the exercise column and cover dance recitals, remember?"

The editor had patted her on the head and had said that she was too a woman reporter.

"The widow was very sweet about everything and gave me a hell of a good interview," Toni told Eric, who was magnanimously doing the dishes, after having talked Toni into cooking a simple but effective dinner at home. "The story is that she expects to find solace in dancing and in writing about the dear departed. Let me help you with the dishes, Eric. I've just read an article about how very un-morale-building it is to let your soldier boy do KP duty when on leave."

"Under the circumstances," said Eric, "it's a pleasure. You stay where you are."

Toni lay back. "Nice to have a man puttering in one's kitchen. Did you see our friend Torrent?"

"Just for a minute. He's beginning to look all grim and British. He thinks, sadly, that people are lying to him."

"Who?"

"Oh, just everybody." Eric sighted down the already shining surface of a carving knife and gave it another wipe. "Yes, I almost forgot. There's another development. It came up at about the same time as I did and poor old Torrent had to question people all over again from another angle. It seems old Izlomin was doped up. The Medical Examiner found a good stiff dose of—what was it again?—morphine-scopolamine in him. It's a drug that puts you to sleep awful fast. In ten minutes you start getting wobbly. In twenty you're fast in the arms of Murphy. Hey!"

Two miniature cyclones, black and gray, swept by, circled the kitchen and returned to the bedroom whence they had issued. "How long does this sort of thing go on?

"Depends on temperament. Cleo seems to be a reluctant virgin. Anyhow she plays hard to get. To date, she's scratched his ear and probably given him a couple of black eyes if one could see under the fur. But when he gives up, she comes around and switches across the room in a provocative manner. But to come back to that drug business. It's very interesting."

"Torrent seemed to think so."

"I mean the twenty minutes part of it. Izlomin had to be killed not sooner than twenty minutes after he was doped, because he was unconscious when he died. Shouldn't this help us somehow? Like mathematics. X plus twenty, you know."

Eric thought it over. "It does at that. But it makes it bad for your friend Mike because figuring it that way, Izlomin must have been doped while he was still in his room. Look, Izlomin was seen going to the fifth floor at about ten. Now let's assume that he was drugged at ten-five. In twenty minutes he's asleep.

"Give him five more to make sure that he's really out. Then suffocate him. Then string him up, five or ten more minutes at the very least. That brings us," Eric counted on his fingers, "to about ten-forty. Now according to the schedule I got from Torrent, *Cauchemar* started at ten-thirty. At ten-forty you and Torrent were snooping around upstairs, leaving me behind in a very callous and inconsiderate manner, I may add. You should have run into the strangler."

"True. Anyhow, ten-forty doesn't agree with the time of his death as established by the medical examiner."

"And besides, the ballet had started. Everybody was on stage or accounted for."

"No. That's a bad time," Toni agreed. "The time the murderer would do his dirty work is when Izlomin's absence hadn't yet been noticed. Or while everybody was frantically looking for him in the wrong place."

"That would be during *Printemps* or the intermission following. Now let's apply the X plus twenty test to it."

Toni sighed. "Do we have to tell Torrent about this? Because it shows that Mike must have been with Izlomin while he drank the stuff in his room."

At that very moment Torrent was saying to Detective Mahoney, "It's a cinch that Izlomin must have got that drug inside him while he was still in his own room. Otherwise, if we allow twenty minutes for the drug to work, it'd place the murderer on the spot at about the same time as we went up." Here he went through the same logical process as his young friends. The incomprehension on his satellite's face didn't bother him. Mahoney would figure it out eventually. "Now if we assume that he got drugged right after he came to his dressing room at nine-fifty, by ten he's on the fifth floor fast asleep. The murderer suffocates him—don't ask me why, maybe he snored too loud. About this time they are looking for him downstairs and in the corps de ballet dressing rooms. Yes, that's the right time. Now what about Mike?"

Mahoney vouchsafed no answer. He knew that his superior was merely thinking aloud.

"Nothing good there. Mike's gone upstairs with Izlomin. Must have— his girlfriend practically admitted that she saw him. He might have been up there doing away with Izlomin while all the hue and cry was going on."

"Didn't the wardrobe mistress see him when she came back the second time?"

Torrent shrugged, an impatient shoulder. "That's just the trouble. She inquired next door all right, after she found Izlomin gone. But it was Slava who answered. The kid stuck his head out the door and she didn't see whether Mike was inside or not. She merely got the impression from what he said that Mike was there. But actually...It looks bad, all right."

Mahoney remarked, after a respectful pause in deference to Torrent's evident distress, "Besides, Mike musta been the one who spiked the drink. He was right there, wasn't he?"

"It ain't necessarily so," said Toni to Eric, who had just finished preparing his own special and inimitable brand of martinis. Watching him she thought approvingly that the army had taught him control and deftness. "When would Mike have a chance to drug anything with Izlomin watching him? He wasn't doing anything but talking to Mike—thank you, darling, this looks fine and tastes even better—and he would have noticed him monkeying around."

"There are ways," said Eric ominously. He had settled himself on the couch next to Toni. "You can always say 'Look! Behind you!' or some such good old standby and work fast while he's looking like a dope. For example you never knew that while engaging your attention with fascinating chitchat, I poured a gallon of potent aphrodisiac in your drink."

"As a matter of fact," said Toni, "I did notice it. But I switched the drinks.

"In that case," said Eric. He put his drink down and kissed her. Toni closed her eyes. His lips felt cool and hard and a little sticky from the martini. But somehow it was as if he were kissing her through a cotton wadding. She didn't feel stirred, merely contented. Eric sighed and laid his head against her shoulder, his close-cropped hair prickled her cheek softly. The fire that he had blotted out for a moment glowed rosy against her closed eyelids.

Torrent shook his head and leaned back in the swivel chair. "No, I don't believe Mike spiked the drink while he was talking to Izlomin. This morphine scopolamine comes in tiny little pills that you have to poke at for some time before they melt. Mike couldn't have done it without Izlomin noticing."

"Then maybe it wasn't given him in the orange juice like you seem to think," Mahoney suggested.

"It's the best bet. Besides, the glass was very carefully washed out. Izlomin wouldn't have done that and nobody else admits to doing it."

"Couldn't he have been drugged before he went to dance *Phoebus?*"

"Not and be able to dance. He never drank anything right before dancing, and if he drank it long enough in advance to give the drug a chance to work, he couldn't have dragged himself out of the room, let alone onstage. No, he drank it right after he came back from dancing *Phoebus*, and I think the drink was tampered with during *Phoebus*."

"I get it," said Mahoney, enlightened. "That's why you've been trying to find out if anybody was missing while the ballet was going on. That's what you thought they might be up to. Well, any luck?"

"Oh, yes," Torrent laughed shortly. "Mike Gorin left the stage right after he danced his last solo. He didn't come back in time to take a curtain call."

"You don't say." Mahoney wagged his head. "See what happens when a decent Irish boy from Brooklyn gets mixed up with a bunch of crazy Rooshians."

That was one way of looking at it, Torrent admitted. He was hoping that the next day might shed a little more light on the undoubtedly screwy aspects of the dancer's death. By now he had a fairly complete set of fingerprints and handwriting samples, which should prove helpful as far as the threatening notes to Izlomin were concerned. The interesting part about these enigmatic missives had been that one of them, the unfinished one, sported a set of fingerprints that were neither Izlomin's nor Toni's, who was the only other person to handle it, except, presumably, the person who wrote it. The fingerprint experts ought to be able to match it with one of the batch he had collected and if not, there were a couple of other possibilities that Torrent had not had time to look into during his long and tiring day.

Eric broke the comfortable silence. "I have a hell of a wonderful idea. Let's get married. We're engaged, aren't we?"

Toni considered it. "I guess so. Not that I've ever formally announced it to a girlfriend or confided it to my diary."

"I've kept it informal to save the expense of buying an engagement ring. Seriously, how about it?"

"I suppose so," said Toni and yawned irresistibly. "If you want to."

Eric sat up and shook her. "If I want to! Don't be so damn obliging. Don't you want to? I don't believe you do, at that!"

"Well," said Toni apologetically. "It's not that I *don't* want to. It's just that it's so nice the way it is and you know how I am about changes."

Eric's voice was gentle. "Yes, particularly emotional ones. You don't even dare to sign your letter 'with love' and spell it right. Or pronounce it right. It's always 'loff.' Makes it less serious that way. Noncommittal little beast."

"Eric, you aren't upset, are you?" Toni peered anxiously at his face. "Of course I'll marry you. Tomorrow, if you want to."

"You'll marry me," said Eric grimly, "when instead of saying 'it's nice the way it is' you'll say, 'we can't go on this way.'"

Toni, who privately couldn't see herself saying anything like this, under any circumstances, laughed. "Darling, I couldn't work up anything but mild contentment right now if I heard that Hitler'd been shot. Give me a night's sleep and you won't know me. I'm simply numb just now."

"This reaction is new to me," said Eric thoughtfully. "Usually women gibber with delight when I propose. Or else suddenly become affected with some nervous disorder, like a tic. I remember one girl who kept twitching…"

Toni snuggled closer to Eric and closed her eyes. *He isn't hurt*, she thought happily. *Sweet old Eric*. She fell asleep.

At midnight Eric gingerly removed a numb arm from around her and gently shook her awake. She stumbled groggily to the door after him to wish him good night. Eric looked at her standing there, her slim body swaying with sleepiness, and caught her in his arms.

"But you do love me, Toni?"

"Silly," said Toni, "of course I loff you."

She only understood a moment later the rueful expression with which he removed his hands from her shoulders to place them around her neck and go through a very realistic pantomime of throttling her.

The telephone rang about ten minutes later, after Toni had already climbed into bed. Long enough, she thought smiling, for Eric to have ducked into the nearest drugstore. It turned out to be someone else though. "Is this Toni Ney?"

"Yes," said Toni. "Who is this?"

She knew though, as her heart gave an absurd hurting leap. "This is Charles Graham. Did I get you out of bed?"

"Well, no," said Toni, scrupulously fair. "I'm still in bed." She heard his deep chuckle.

"Well, I hope to get you out eventually. Look here, I know this is outrageous, but would you consider joining me at the Stork?" He went on diffidently over her silence. "You probably think I'm being very brash but it took me a small struggle to call you. I so badly want to see you."

"All right," said Toni abruptly. She hung up over his thanks and directions and sat a while staring at the reflection of her pale strained face in the mirror.

"Hell!" she said. "Damnation." Because suddenly she realized the reason for her inexplicable lack of enthusiasm about Eric's proposal.

Mr. Graham rose from his table to meet her. "You did come. How splendid." He hovered over her solicitously as she sat down, hurriedly ordered a champagne cocktail for her as if she were a traveler from a far land in need of sustenance, and sat back and beamed at her.

"What I like about you is your lack of archness. You wanted to come and you did, without fuss and flutter. That is rare."

"Frankly," said Toni, "you intrigued me."

"Frankly," said Graham with an ingenuous smile, "I counted on that."

He was being boyish and charming and Toni recognized the deliberateness of it. The main thing that concerned her, nevertheless, was that he had found it worthwhile to expend his charm on her. Unless...

"Was there anything special you wanted to see me about?"

"No." He laughed. "I'm a man of iron whim, you know. I just wanted to look at your lovely little poker face again. But now that I've got you here I feel strangely abashed. Perhaps we'll end by seeking refuge in ships and shoes and sealing wax."

"Graves and worms and epitaphs is more like it."

"How true." Mr. Graham tried hard to look grave. "But I'm not really concerned with Vova's death, as I told you. All I care about it is the book about him and thanks to the fundamental lowness of human nature, I think we're sure of having a best-seller now." He looked at her drolly. "At least now your demands for common decency will be satisfied. You didn't like the idea of a book like that being written while the subject was still alive."

"You needn't have taken me quite so literally," said Toni, deadpan.

Graham stared, then laughed. "Ah, but you're the type of public we're trying to reach. At least I am."

"Tell me," said Toni, coming to the subject that had interested her ever since her interview with the widow. "What kind of person is Natalia? Is this going to affect her very badly?"

Graham thought it over. "Hard to say. She's remarkably resilient. Can get adjusted to any situation. That's how she was able to rehabilitate old Vova practically single-handed. The book will help, I hope. I think, as she wrote it, she transferred her love to the man in the book. I guess Vova must have felt that because he resented me and the book terribly." Toni thought there was a slightly complacent ring in the statement. "But never mind that. It's you I want to know about."

"Well," said Toni, flashing him a sudden elfin grin, "go ahead, draw me out."

In the midst of this pleasant occupation, Toni's attention was drawn by a blob of violent color that somehow struck an answering chord in her memory. She looked closer at the wearer of the gown.

"By George," said Graham, also looking, "if it isn't old Kate. We'd better pay our respects."

Kate Whitehead it was, wrapped in incongruous folds of airy tulle. Her face was yellow and her eyes were sunken in their dark sockets. A diamond choker blazed at her throat. By a certain glazed intensity of her stare, Toni realized that she was drunk. But the bony hand that held a glass of Scotch didn't waver.

Her escort, on the other hand, had gone apart like blotting paper. Even his usually well-kept beard had gone straggly and looked like a hunk of false hair carelessly applied to his fat face.

"Hello, m'boy," said Kate Whitehead. "Y'know de Speranski." The latter tried to bow gallantly and his chin bumped the table. "The son of a bitch is drunk. Who's that little piece of fluff you've got with you?"

Graham introduced Toni.

"Oh yes," said Mrs. Whitehead with unexpected cordiality. "The little girl who never smiles. Let me warn you about Graham, my girl. He's tricky. Better leave him to cold calculating gals like Natalia Izlomina."

"Good old Kate," said Graham.

She waved both hands. "All right, all right. Siddown, won't you? I want to talk."

"We can't stay long," said Graham sitting down.

Kate prattled on. "Oh God, I feel so damned low. I've never felt that way before, not even when George broke his neck. I suppose you think I'm crazy to feel that way about an ill-tempered little bastard like Vova?"

"Not at all," said Toni politely.

"Well, I like them bad-tempered. Everybody hated him but me. You did too, you swill-soaked old fool." She prodded de Speranski with a sharp elbow. "Don't you think I know that you've been celebrating all this time? What did he have on you, anyhow? Have you been embezzling?"

De Speranski came to his feet as if jerked out of his drunkenness.

"*Chère madame*, how can you—it's not—I—"

He struggled madly and then sank back into his former state.

Mrs. Whitehead gave him a look of disconcerting shrewdness. "I must remember to check up...Going already, children?"

"Yes," said Graham. "What about you?"

"In a while. One more drink and I'll be equal to mopping up this revolting mess. Run along, my dears. To bed, to bed."

"Poor old de Speranski," said Graham, "she'll check up on him all right. She remembers things, drunk or not." They walked the few blocks to Toni's house in comfortable, companionable silence, Graham's hand warm and hard on hers. The house, a cozy brownstone, had the usual stairway in front. Toni mounted the first step and that brought her face on a level with Graham's.

"Good night," she said. "It was nice."

"May I kiss you?" said Graham, abruptly. Toni nodded. Graham took off his glasses, with a diffident smile. His kiss was far from diffident, however. It was demanding and expert, and Toni, returning it with an enthusiasm that surprised her, sighed and relaxed under his possessive lips.

After a while she pressed her hands across his chest and freed herself. She ran up the stairs and turned to look at him. He was still standing where she left him. His upturned face showed uncertainty and delight, like that of a man who stumbles unawares into a strange and enchanted land.

"I'll call you tomorrow," he said. "Good night, Toni, darling."

And he walked off along the moon-dappled street.

CHAPTER ELEVEN

THE NEXT DAY Izlomin was formally returned to his wife, a mere earthly shell in the actual sense of the word, since most of his internal organs were kept by the Medical Examiner's office. The undertakers immediately got to work on him preparatory to depositing him in a little Russian chapel on 125th Street, where he would lie in state. The funeral would take place on Saturday and everybody expected it to be a very impressive spectacle.

So Toni gathered at the Daillart School of Ballet, where she took occasional dancing classes and where most members of the American Ballet Drama came to practice when they were neither rehearsing nor performing. Janet Banks, a willowy blonde whose one grievance was that her mother wouldn't let her change her name to Bankova, wondered if they would let him wear a ballet costume. Lilon Caritas scoffed at this idea. Of course Vova would wear a dress suit, like all respectable corpses. "Wouldn't he look silly lying in the coffin in a *Spectre de la Rose* costume?"

The heartless titter this provoked subsided as Tamara came in. She sat down next to Toni and began to change into her practice clothes. She said nothing, her sleek head bowed as she concentrated on the task of getting the ribbons of her ballet shoes tied. But when she raised her head Toni saw that she was crying, huge sparkling spherical tears that looked like glycerin.

"Oh Toni, what shall I do? They've arrested Mike."

"Oh dear," Toni thought. She mutely offered a handkerchief.

"They took him away this morning. Now they'll third-degree him until he confesses. And you know how stubborn Mike is. He'll just let them b-beat him…"

"There, there," said Toni. "It's not that bad. Does Torrent look like a man who'd beat anybody to get a false confession?"

Tamara nodded dispiritedly. "With rubber hose."

"Well, he isn't. I know him very well and Mike does too, and he's just as unhappy about Mike being mixed up in this as we are."

Tamara blew her nose and looked anything but convinced.

Love can sure be hell, Toni thought sympathetically, following her into the studio. At least, she added, her thoughts veering to last night, it can be a damned nuisance—for example, when you suddenly find yourself irresistibly attracted to someone who you're perfectly sure is no good for you, charm and pleasing personality notwithstanding. She wondered drearily why she was so sure that there was no future in Mr. Graham. Unfortunately she had a knack for seeing these things very clearly. She had met his type too often not to recognize it—charmers rather than lovers, takers rather than givers, men intense in their pleasures and light in their emotions, men whom you can intrigue and captivate but never attach. It was going to be one of those lamentable relationships which, promising nothing but grief, still has the effect of making all other associations seem shallow and incomplete.

Last night seemed unreal even in spite of the camellias, two scarlet blossoms coolly perfect on their glossy green leaves, that had come this morning. They heralded a phone call from their sender. Toni's heart swooped shamefully at the sound of his voice and to make up for that she virtuously refused to be taken out either for lunch or dinner. She did weaken enough to promise to call him later if there was, as he plaintively put it, "some way of fitting him into the scheme of things." That made her bleakly aware that her unavailability had the traditional effect of making him more eager. She could see herself never relaxing in the constant game of I run and you chase. The prospect seemed grim.

And Eric? Well, she could either stall him along for the remainder of his leave or tell him immediately why, for the time being, she couldn't even think of marrying him. Not too pleasant either way. She hadn't decided which she would do when he called her to tell her that he had run into the parents of a buddy of his who had been in his company before being sent overseas and would have to spend the day with them. He would try to get away for dinner but Toni was not to count on it. Toni cravenly welcomed the respite.

"So thoughtful, Toni," said M. Daillart, materializing at her side. He was a small compact man in his forties, wearing tightish trousers of Spanish cut and blue sneakers. His long iron-gray hair bounced on his head when he walked. "You look as if you had lost your best friend."

"I probably will," said Toni gloomily. Daillart didn't hear her.

"You are watching the next class? It will probably be execrable. They have their minds on other things, no? *Quelle catastrophe, hein?*" He pronounced these words with a singularly cheerful air. "And yet de Speranski hopes to revive *Phoebus* at the end of the season. Only yesterday he told me he wants me to teach the variation to Vassine. 'When all this blows over,' he says. I say to him, 'Things like that don't blow over so easily, my friend.' *Eh bien, messieurs, dames. . .*" Daillart pattered briskly into the studio to take his stand near the piano.

Toni lingered to watch the class. It was a large one—only Mike was missing among the male dancers. Slava was there, kerchief buccaneer-like on his red curls. She enjoyed watching even stock exercises at the bar: the precise flutter of the beats, the gracious arabesques, the sudden upward spring to the toe for the attitudes, with the whole class suddenly transformed into a group of poised Mercuries.

She suddenly felt herself being stared at and traced the stare back to the intense black eyes of Tamara's mamma. Toni gave her a smile and Mme. Ribina leaned forward and hissed, "I want to speak with you a minute, yes, please?"

Before Toni had a chance to answer she had slipped out of the hall. She made off along the corridor, dropping a ballet shoe as she went, and Toni picked up the scuffed pink thing as she followed her into the empty dressing room.

"Thank you," said Tamara's mamma, showing her white teeth. "I am so worried, I keep dropping things all the time." She held the shoe, slapping it against the palm of her other hand. "This is the matter I want to talk to you. My Tamara, she is just a child, she doesn't understand. She has been keeping things from the police. It's very bad, no?"

"Well," said Toni cautiously, "it's a good idea to let the police have all the facts."

"That's what I say. Now the cops think Tamara was the last to see Izlomin. That's no good, if it's murder. She shouldn't have ever had nothing to do with him. A married man, a crazy lunatic besides. Well, he's dead now, God rest his soul. It doesn't matter that he was a no-good loafer. But my Tamara—she didn't talk to him, like she told that policeman. I mean when he went upstairs and got himself killed. He wasn't alone. He was with Mike Gorin. They were talking together on the steps."

"Do you happen to know what about?"

"She wouldn't tell me. She made me swear not to tell the police. So I think I'll tell you. You're friendly with that policeman with the mustache, you tell him, no?" She tossed her head with a sort of guilty defiance.

"Tamara will be mad with me. But it is very bad for a ballerina to be mixed up in murder."

"Mamma!"

Mme. Ribina flinched and spun to face her daughter, who was standing in the doorway, her face blazing with fear and accusation.

"You told. After you promised."

Her mother wisely said nothing. She merely picked up the ballet shoes that she had dropped again and scuttled outside. Tamara made as if to follow her and then changed her mind and turned back to Toni.

"I knew what she was up to the minute I saw both of you leaving the room. Well, are you going to tell? You aren't, are you, Toni? You couldn't. Why, it's like spying on your friends."

"Whoa," said Toni mildly. "Hold your horses. I didn't ask your mother, you know. She came and told me herself. Besides, it was nothing new. If you think you've kept your dark secret about Mike from the police, you're wrong. They've guessed about—"

"They have!" Tamara sank down on the bench among stockings and girdles and began to weep.

Toni sat down next to her. "You better tell me all about it and we'll decide what to do."

In her demoralized state, Tamara told all. Yes, it was Mike whom she had seen talking to Izlomin. Their conversation was low-voiced and earnest and she heard nothing of it until Izlomin started to go away.

"And then—" Tamara clapped her hands to her face. Her voice came muffledly through the spasmodically interlaced fingers. "And then Mike threatened him."

"Threatened him? How?"

"He said, 'God help you if you're still in the building in ten minutes.'" Tamara flung her hands away from her face. "And then they find him dead. Murdered! And it's all my fault. I drove Mike crazy. I made him believe I cared for Vova and that wasn't so. I only care for Mike—it was just to show him—and now—and now…"

"Wait a minute," said Toni. "Let's finish this before we go all tragic. Then what happened? Both of them went up?"

"Both of …? No, of course not. Vova went on upstairs and Mike went back to his room."

Toni stared at her. "Mike went back to his room? You're sure?

"Of course I'm sure."

"Oh, for heavens' sake," said Toni in exasperation. There must have been a note of relief in her voice as well because Tamara eyed her with sudden hope. "You little fool. This story that you've been keeping to yourself is the best kind of alibi for Mike."

"Alibi?"

"Don't you see? Until now they didn't believe that he went back to his room after talking to Izlomin. Slava said so, too, but on account of your idiotic behavior Torrent thinks that Mike was with Izlomin and that Slava was merely covering up for him."

"But—but," Tamara stammered, dissolving in tearful and abashed radiance, "it seemed so—At first I didn't think anything of it. Mike always says things like that and anyhow Vova had killed himself supposedly, so why bring it up? And then, when it turned out to be murder and the police questioned us all over again and Mike wouldn't talk, why I got scared. Toni, will it really help Mike if I tell them?"

"It'll certainly put him in a better position than he is in now."

"But Toni," Tamara looked at her imploringly. Her long eyelashes were stuck in points like a tearful baby's. "I don't have to tell them about Mike threatening Vova, do I?" Her round chin hardened. "Because I won't. And if you do, I'll say you're lying."

"It's your business," Toni told her. "It's always best to tell all. Mike probably has his reasons for saying what he did, reasons that had nothing to do with Izlomin's murder, but as long as he keeps them to himself, they're going to obscure the case and keep the police from catching the murderer. You want them to get whoever killed Vova, don't you?"

"Not particularly," said Tamara, with commendable frankness. "All I want is to get Mike out of trouble. I never did like Vova, really. And look at all the trouble he's caused Mike and me. So you can't blame me, can you, for the way I'm feeling?"

Toni shook her head speechlessly. The mental processes of the ballet dancers always got her down. Their logic, like their leaps, seemed to defy all laws of nature.

As they were leaving the dressing room, Toni heard excited voices in the reception foyer, among which she recognized Bill Stone's amused tenor.

"Sure you can tell who's who," he was saying. "I can tell this is Lilon because of her bad fourth position. And this is Marina, nobody else holds her hand like that."

Somebody else contributed gleefully. "These must be Maurice's feet—the largest in the company."

"And that must be André because he told me he was behind Marina and she tried to trip him up. And here's Tamara. I can tell her round little bottom anywhere."

"Fancy meeting you here," said Toni, who, as a matter of fact, had made a date to meet him here. "I was sure I'd have to come down and make those enlargements myself." She had the keys to Bill's photographic studio, which she used very often, as the boys in the *Globe* darkroom were prone to be a little snooty about "amateurs" working with them. "What's the meaning of all those highly personal remarks?"

Bill grinned at her, his pale blue eyes alight with mirth. He was perched on the edge of the table with the dancers, who had been let out for a brief intermission, milling about him and squealing excitedly as they tried to get a glimpse of the enlargements he had made for Torrent.

"I'm trying to sell them a group picture. I ought to make money on it, too, because everybody's in it."

There was a general hoot of derision. "Yes, but you can't tell who is who!"

"I told you I can," said Bill still grinning. "For example, I know that this must be Elena. I can tell by the shape of the toe slipper and the edge of the tape peeking out." Only Bill could get away with this allusion to Perlova's bunions without making her mad.

Toni looked over his shoulder and understood the joke. Everybody was in this picture, all right, but heavily shrouded. It was the group picture of the "mists."

"Imagine," said Bill, "I can't sell it to the silly kids because they can't see their faces. Faces aren't everything."

The boys and girls crowded around him jostling and rumpling him affectionately. Bill was very popular with the ballet dancers. He made all the girls look glamorous and all the boys manly.

"Bill, darling, I must have this one, I look so wonderful in it."

"I'll have to show this to M. Daillart. He's always after me because I don't turn out enough."

"Tamara will want this." The girl who spoke held up a picture of a radiant Izlomin stretching a beckoning hand to the dusky maiden. Tamara showed no eagerness to take it.

At this point the pianist played a summoning arpeggio and M. Daillart himself appeared and shooed his pupils inside like so many chicks.

Toni helped Bill to get the pictures together and they went through the tedious business of "dating" the enlargements as per Torrent's suggestion.

Later that afternoon, Torrent paid a visit to the "Damon and Pythias of the Ballet" as de Speranski had described them. They lived in a tiny bijou of an apartment on upper Madison Avenue. Damon, in the person of Geoffrey Ffoulkes, opened the door. Torrent identified himself and got a very strong feeling that for some unknown reason his visit was unwelcome just at that moment. Ffoulkes made British-sounding noises of co-operation, however, and ushered Torrent into a charming room with moss-green walls and white moldings. A fire was burning briskly in a small fireplace, its flames leaping in the polished surface of the silver teapot standing on a low table. Two boys, one dark-haired and one copper-pated, and a charming russet spaniel scrambled to their feet to stare at the visitor.

Ffoulkes said, "We've been having a spot of tea. Care to join us? Or something stronger, perhaps? No? Well, what can we do for you, sir?" He fitted a pipe into his strong teeth and his smile flashed at Torrent, around the pipe as it were.

Torrent made the routine explanation. He was wondering why Slava should look so terrified at the sight of him. He glanced curiously at the other young man, who was older than Slava and much younger than Ffoulkes, and who wore a midnight blue turtleneck sweater and a gold bracelet on his wrist. So that was the mysterious Vassine. He didn't look too comfortable, either. The only member of the company who was at his ease was the spaniel, who looked at Torrent trustingly, his russet scrap of a tail thudding on the floor.

Ffoulkes, nothing loath, obliged with the account of his activities at the Civic Opera, affirming de Speranski's story about their negotiations. Here Torrent created a digression by wanting to know about how the rift between the management and the dancer arose in the first place. "Mr. Vassine might tell me that."

Ffoulkes began, "It was all most unfortunate . . ."

Torrent silenced Damon with an upraised palm and a motion of his square chin toward Pythias. "Since it's really his story, don't you know? Well, Mr. Vassine?"

Pythias stammered and blushed. "Well, they'd promised. I mean after all the Gypsy had always been my role and Jeff had even designed a beautiful costume for me, hadn't you, Jeff? And I'd danced with a bad ankle before. You just put on a rubber sock, and if it gets dislocated, you reset it backstage, isn't that so, Jeff?"

The story came out finally between stammers and appeals for verification to Jeff. It seemed that Vassine and Izlomin had both wanted to dance the same part, and for once Vassine got it. During the dress rehearsal he went through a variation with Izlomin, a mimic fight, in the course of which the latter was supposed to pick him up, hold him poised overhead and throw him down. This was a step in which a maliciously minded partner could do a lot of damage. Izlomin did just that.

"He deliberately broke his ankle," Slava burst out. "I was there and I saw it. The dirty swine."

"So after that you resigned."

"We went to Mrs. Whitehead with the story," said Ffoulkes. Torrent let him talk this time, figuring it would be faster this way. "But Vova had gotten there before us. The contract was—ah—abrogated by mutual consent."

Torrent nodded. "Very understandable, too," he said sympathetically. "All the more surprising under the circumstances that you should have written this card." He produced the card Toni had found in the basket of anemones. "Why d'you write this?" he asked casually.

Vassine brushed back a strand of black hair from his broad white forehead. His eyes reached for Ffoulkes. "Well, it seemed—I mean—"

Ffoulkes came to the rescue. "We thought it was a good idea, since we were thinking of coming back to the American Ballet Drama. Sportsmanship, don't you know."

"Almost too sportsmanlike," said Torrent dryly. "One might call it appeasement."

Two red spots appeared on Ffoulkes' thin cheekbones. "Not of Vova, I assure you. The gesture was for the benefit of Mrs. Whitehead."

"I see. How come you decided to come back? I understand Mr. Vassine was contemplating an appearance in a musical comedy. Would he have gotten more or less than he was getting in his former position?"

"More." Ffoulkes volunteered this information negligently. A slight superior smile touched his thin lips. "But there were other things to consider. Admittedly the musical comedy pays much more than pure ballet. But it's a ballerina's market. There is always a danger of a male dancer being reduced to the role of a mere adagio partner. André is a great dancer in his own right. I would have hated to see him reduced to a sort of dancing prop, no matter how much that paid. In ballet there is much more scope for a male dancer. Besides, some of my friends in show business have assured me that this show isn't going to last long. And with de Speranski offering better terms, it looked like a good time to get off our high horses, as it were."

Yes, and to eat humble pie and expose themselves again to Izlomin's tantrums, Torrent added silently. Not that it wasn't a plausible story. Only Vassine's disjointed story had laid bare a store of resentment that somehow didn't go with his mentor's story of sweetness and light. This Ffoulkes was a smooth article.

"Incidentally," Torrent said, taking out the inevitable notes and handing one to Vassine and one to Ffoulkes, "can you gentlemen tell me anything about these?"

He watched the two faces, bent over the threatening messages to a man they both hated, and was rewarded by a reaction from Ffoulkes—a swift cool glance in Slava's direction. Slava, who seemed to be remarkably sensitive about these notes, caught it too.

"I didn't. I tell you I didn't write those goddamn notes."

"Shut up, Slava," said Ffoulkes pleasantly. "Don't be a bloody fool. Nobody's saying you did." He looked straight at Torrent and his lean jaws creased sardonically. "To forestall your question, I didn't write this childish stuff. I don't know who did."

"What about you?" Torrent turned to Vassine who was looking at them in a puzzled way.

Vassine's answer was long in coming. But then he was a slow lad altogether. "No. No, I don't know."

Torrent came back to Ffoulkes' night at the Opera. The latter mentioned his visit to Mike and Slava's dressing room and return to watch Izlomin dance in *Phoebus*. Torrent asked whether anything struck him as odd about his behavior.

Ffoulkes considered. "N-no-o. He was rather distrait, now that you mention it. Brushed by me and never saw me. Probably just as well. That chap had no inhibitions about making a scene."

"You'd known him before you met him in New York?"

"Yes, a long time ago. In Paris and during his London season. Not too well. I was pretty obscure at the time." Mr. Ffoulkes spoke with the casual self-deprecation of one who has emerged from that obscurity. He went on with his story. After having seen Izlomin dance and having paid his respects to de Speranski, he had left the Opera just as the ovations started, stopping only to chat with the doorman.

Torrent, who had already checked with the doorman on that point, nodded and asked Vassine how he had spent his evening. Both Vassine and Ffoulkes seemed surprised at the question. The former explained, however, that he had spent the evening at home, waiting for Jeff to "come home and tell him about everything," and that later they both went to the Russian Rendezvous, where they learned about Izlomin's death.

These particulars learned, Torrent left the room with the moss-green walls. He was conscious of a faint sense of frustration, not that he had any reason to expect anything from the two friends, who were so far shaping up as innocent if not disinterested bystanders. But like the veteran prospector he was, he couldn't help feeling that there was gold in them thar hills if one dug deeply enough, and if one knew just what one was digging for!

CHAPTER TWELVE

FOR THE TENTH TIME Toni found herself nervously fingering the camellias that blazed like twin scarlet accent marks at the throat of her subdued gray dress. It had been too late to take them off when Eric had unexpectedly arrived at Torrent's office where she had taken the enlargements and a tearful and jittery Tamara. He had been released for dinner by his friend's family after having solemnly sworn that he would come back to spend the evening with them. He didn't seem, however, to give more than passing attention to the camellias or to be put out by Torrent's joining them for dinner, even though it meant a delay in the resumption of last night's discussion.

Even with Torrent there Toni felt unhappy and ill at ease, a fact which she strove to hide by chattering determinedly about the crasser aspects of ballet.

"People tend to think of ballet dancers as glamorous little butterflies who live on air as well as tread on it. The sad fact is that, like everybody else, they have to eat."

"I can subscribe to that," said Eric. "That little Marina packed away a mean steak." Toni lifted an inquiring eyebrow and Eric tried hard to look guilty. "Why dissemble? I did take that fragile little ballerina to lunch yesterday when I came to the Opera and found you gone for your interview with Izlomin's widow. Point is, I can join you in assuring Captain Torrent that ballet dancers do eat."

"Moreover," said Toni, "they eat fifty-two weeks a year. Their season covers something like twenty-one performance weeks and fifteen rehearsal weeks, according to the basic union contract. A dancer gets a minimum of forty-five dollars a performance week. This amounts to an average earning of twenty-five a week, out of which they pay for their practice shoes, stage jewelry, ballet lessons, union dues, hotels and taxes. Many of them increase their earnings by modeling in their spare time. But take somebody like Tamara, who looks heavenly on the stage but hasn't the emaciated figure necessary for modeling. She's just out of luck. So here you have boys and girls working like mad, undergoing constant and rigorous training for years, and for what? So they look glamorous to the audience for the munificent sum of twenty-five dollars a week. All that while the managers and directors like de Speranski clean up."

"That isn't true of the stars, is it?"

"No, they make more. But even Izlomin didn't get as much as you'd expect, much less than an actor of his stature would get."

Torrent agreed. "I've been checking up on his estate, and everything considered, the widow doesn't get, much."

"They expected to make a lot of money this summer in Hollywood. Vova was negotiating to appear in some picture as himself. I got that from Anatole Chujoy, the editor of *Dance News,* who usually has his facts straight. Incidentally, he was quite surprised that Vassine is coming back to the American Ballet Drama. According to him, it was all settled about the musical comedy. The contract was to be signed on Thursday (that's yesterday) and Ffoulkes had told him that he was delighted. The show was going to be a great success and André was going to make some money for a change. And then bingo—everything changed."

"After Izlomin died," said Eric thoughtfully.

"Very interesting," said Torrent. "I'll have to check up about the Hollywood plans." He smiled a little, remembering the fury in Izlomina's eyes when he told her that her husband had been murdered. His impression at the time must have been right. She had been mourning a financial as well as personal loss.

Toni was asking, "What about Tamara's little contribution? Does it help Mike?"

Torrent smiled sourly. He had had a long and tedious session with Mike and finally had to let him go simply because there was no good reason for holding him. "I'll have to get hold of him again and ask him politely why the hell he lied and said he left Izlomin in his room, when he actually walked him to the stairs. The fact that she saw him go back to his room helps. Samarkand saw Mike at ten-ten, when *Printemps* was over, and told him to get ready to take Izlomin's place. It's just possible, of course, that he could have slipped out after that to settle Izlomin's hash and that young Mladov is still covering up for him."

"Or what's more likely," said Toni, "they're both being very mysterious about something that has no connection with the murder. Ballet dancers are like that."

"Mike's not the only one who gives us trouble. We've got a whole bunch of people to check up on, everybody whose activities from ten to ten-twenty weren't vouched for by a lot of other people. Now this lets out all the girls on the third and fourth floor dressing rooms and all the boys on the other side of the house."

"The entire corps de ballet, in short. What about the principals?"

"Well, there are the four people who were looking for Izlomin—de Speranski, the Whitehead woman, Izlomin's wife and Samarkand."

"Don't they alibi each other?"

"No. They had separated during their wanderings. Nobody can swear to anybody else's movements at any given time. I am not putting the finger on any one of those people. I'm just pointing out that they could have done it, don't you know."

"Even the wife?"

"Well, we can say that she had equal opportunity with the rest. Motive? We don't know of any, I admit. Now the others. We've mentioned Mike and Slava Mladov who were in their dressing room, or so they say. Tamara Ribina was in her dressing room, alone. Elena Perlova, in her dressing room, alone. They had shut the bathroom door between their rooms so they can't really vouch for each other."

"Come, come," said Eric. "Isn't it a bit farfetched? A woman can strangle a man while he's unconscious. But hauling him up and hanging him—well!"

"I don't know. Ballet dancers are unbelievably strong. Did you ever feel their muscles?" Toni fixed Eric with an accusing eye. "Knowing you, I am sure you did."

Eric inclined his head modestly. "I defer to your superior knowledge of your sex and acknowledge that every woman is a potential strangler."

"On the other hand, I can't see Tamara risking soiling her beautiful white tutu. Now if she had her practice clothes on..." Toni's gravity broke down under their concerted speculative gaze and she laughed. "I'm sorry, but the idea of Tamara...That's the lot, isn't it? Of suspects, I mean."

"I've just thought of another one," said Eric unexpectedly. "What about the guy who was hanging around with la Whitehead? That big blond Willkie effect with horn-rimmed glasses?" Toni choked on her food and Eric broke off to pound her back. He resumed, "He was around at the same time as the Whitehead woman. And he didn't even join in the search, just sat around and nobody paid much attention to him. Couldn't he have sneaked up and...?"

"As far as the opportunity goes, he had it, I suppose," said Torrent. He didn't look as surprised by the inclusion of this new actor as he might have been. "He kept out of the way of the stagehands so that they can't swear that he remained where he was all the time. But—the motive?"

"I can provide one," said Eric with simple pride. Toni looked at him and longed to break a plate over his head. "I got it out of Marina. The poor innocent child didn't even know that I was pumping her. I told you, Toni, that there was a lot to be gotten out of..."

"The motive?" Torrent prompted gently.

"Oh, that he's in love with Izlomin's widow, of course." He attacked his dessert with gusto.

The moon was a huge movie moon and Toni admired it like a movie heroine, from a penthouse terrace where she had wandered while Charles was mixing cocktails. They had spent a pleasant evening together before coming here to pick up the galley proofs of *Lazarus Arise,* an evening spoiled for Toni only by the thought of Eric, who had dutifully gone back to regale his friend's family with more stories about his friend.

Nothing had marred Charles' evident enjoyment of it, not that he was the type to let any emotional commitments bother him, even if there were any in his life. He had chatted about himself happily and unrestrainedly. His life was an open book and he hoped that Toni wouldn't put it down unread. He had been married three times, divorced twice, with the third one coming up. He liked horses, sailboats, French cuisine, Viennese psycho-analysis, Picasso, Piero della Francesca, Bach, South American music, Dickens, Boccaccio, incunabula, Vermont in winter, Connecticut in the fall, silk shantung dressing gowns, Veuve Clicquot champagne, Napoleon brandy, burlesque and boogie woogie. He preferred Rodzinski to Stokowski, Zero Mostel to Jimmy Savo, the *Herald Tribune* to the *Times*, and Willkie to Roosevelt. He was fairly catholic in his taste for women. Toni wondered whether all his women were provided with this complete personality sketch at the outset. She felt tempted to ask him about his sleeping habits, a feature that a certain columnist always mentions in his thumbnail sketches of movie stars, but suspected that this was a subject that was bound to come up of its own accord anyhow.

"What are you thinking about?" said Charles.. He came through the door balancing two amber drinks. "But you won't tell me. You're one of those enigmatic reserved women who keep themselves to themselves."

Toni said that she was merely admiring the moon and relieved him of one drink.

"Funny," said Charles, "the minute I saw you I knew you were for me. Just like a spark. That's a wonderful feeling, that moment of awareness when you catch on fire. You can't equal it no matter what heights of ecstasy you scale later. You liked me too, immediately, didn't you, baby? I can always tell." His arm lay lightly, possessively on her shoulder. She almost resented the quick easy way in which he walked in and took possession. His smile was teasing. "I shall particularly insist that Natalia find a good home for Vova's marmoset. After all, it brought us together."

Toni laughed. "What lovely sentiments, Mr. Graham. You aren't wearing your glasses, I notice."

"Vanity of vanities! When I begin leaving off my glasses they know it in the office as a sure sign that I'm falling in love. But I'm still not sure if I want to give you those galleys of Natalia's book. Supposing you find a boner at this late stage. You've got that sort of an eye. The book is at the binder's now, you know."

"But you promised. Please don't change your mind," Toni protested. She had come up to Charles' apartment not to see his etchings but to get the galleys of the book, which should give her a lot of invaluable information. So she kept telling herself.

"Let me have them right now," she pleaded. "Please, Charles? Before you really change your mind?"

"All right," said Charles, amused. "What a little pragmatist you are. Come on in. You can prowl in the secret drawers while I make another drink."

Toni drew the serpentine sheets out of the drawer of an exquisite waxed birch desk and waved them at Charles. "Is this it?"

"Yes. There are some manila envelopes in the left-hand drawer. Now put it away and forget about it and come here. I want to ply you with drinks and make love to you. Do you want me to?"

Yes, God help me, Toni thought, coming to him.

"No," she was saying a little later. "No, please, Charles, no." She pushed at his broad shoulders to free herself, but her body clung to him like melted wax.

"Why not? You want to, don't you? Darling…"

Toni said, "Yes, I want to. But please let me go." She couldn't recognize her own voice, so unlike her it sounded, weak and breathless and sort of ingenue. "I'm not being coy, really, I'm not. It's just—well, it's messy to get into one thing without settling another. It'd make me feel horrid. Please, Charles."

"The lieutenant, eh? All right," said Charles. He kissed her gently and let her go. "As you will. I'm really a very tame wolf. Sorry I lost control. But to coin a phrase, you do something to me."

"All things considered," said Toni, still in her new voice, "you'd better take me home."

Riding back in a taxi, Toni regarded his debonair profile with something like resentment. He was so sunnily pleased with what for him promised to be another pleasant love affair, of which he intended to savor every moment, while she—well, it was disheartening, to say the least, to start a love affair prepared from the outset to write it off to experience.

A pleasant experience, she admitted, as he kissed her good-bye. Then his smile glazed a little and he said incongruously, "Oh dear."

Toni followed his dismayed gaze and found Eric seated goblinlike on the stoop, watching them with bright interest.

"Look here," said Charles helplessly. "I'm sorry."

"Not at all," said Eric politely and pattered down the stairs. "I mean, it wasn't as if you were forcing unwelcome attentions on the lady. From where I was sitting I could see all signs of enthusiastic cooperation. So I don't have to punch you in the eye. On the other hand," he added thoughtfully, "perhaps I needn't be so technical."

At this point Toni recovered her wits and said good night to Charles in a firm tone of voice. Charles immediately and tactfully retired to the taxi, not without a casual, "See you tomorrow."

"A fine thing," said Eric after the taxi rolled away. "I come back to visit you with a halo around my head after a virtuously spent evening, and this is what I find. I didn't even know you knew the guy. Why, we were discussing him with Torrent and you never…For heavens' sake! Toni, you took my remarks seriously and started an investigation along your own lines, didn't you? Mata Hari stuff, eh?"

Toni steeled herself to the inevitable. "No, it isn't that at all. I'm afraid it's got to be catalogued as One of Those Things. Caps all the way."

Eric stared at her incomprehendingly. Suddenly his face whitened and Toni wished miserably for a crack she could crawl into.

"You can't mean…What's going on? Toni, this is crazy."

"I know it," said Toni forlornly. "But I can't help it." She added inadequately, "I'm sorry to spoil your leave for you. I—I guess we'd better forget what we were talking about last night."

"I guess we better had," said Eric. He drew himself erect, as if bracing himself against the hurt. "Well, he's a glamorous guy. He ought to give you a good time."

"No," said Toni and sat down on the steps, suddenly weary. "I won't have a good time. He's not at all the sort of man I like. He's superficial and cold and frivolous. I'll have one hell of a bad time. It'll be worse than *East Lynne.*"

Eric hesitated, looking down at her. Then he sat down too.

He said gruffly, "Suppose you tell me all about it. What the hell, I've always wanted to know how it felt to be civilized about those things."

The dark blue sky had grown much lighter when Toni finally stumbled into her apartment. Her throat felt scratchy with unshed tears. She didn't know how to cry, a most unfeminine lack in her makeup. She had certainly wanted to. She and Eric had talked on the stoop. They had gone around the block several times and had finally wound up in Stewart's, where they gulped down cups of coffee. All this got them nowhere. Eric kept on saying that it was like measles and the best thing to do was disregard it. Toni claimed that measles or no, she couldn't disregard it.

At one point Eric wanted to know whether Graham's intentions were honorable. Toni said, "Good heavens, no." Upon which Eric turned two shades greener and in a strangled voice asked Toni to do him one favor in view of their long and pleasant association—wait until he got out of town before she went to bed with the guy. He added bitterly that she wouldn't have long to wait. He'd been asked to visit some friends in the country and there was certainly nothing to keep him in New York.

That was the low point. Nothing remained to be said, and Eric took Toni scrupulously to her door in an awful silence.

There was a note left under the door. It said peevishly, "Your cats are making the damnedest racket. How about a little consideration for your neighbors?"

Tom Jones greeted her smugly, his whiskers drooping in a dissipated manner. Toni drove him and his dark paramour into the kitchen, closed the door and stuffed up the cracks with a blanket to deaden the sounds of any further bacchanals. It soon became clear to her, however, that she would never be able to go to sleep and she got out the galleys of *Lazarus Arise*. From the kitchen there came a smothered banshee-like yeowl. She read on. At least, she thought grimly, Tom Jones' love life was running an uncomplicated course.

CHAPTER THIRTEEN

IZLOMIN'S FUNERAL took place on Saturday at noon, as scheduled.

It was a grand and glorious performance, with flowers, tears, swoons and all the appurtenances of a really successful funeral, not to mention the impressive trappings of the Greek Orthodox ritual. Several priests in shining brocade robes and high miters over their bearded faces officiated. The members of the Don Cossack choir supplemented the regular choir, and their voices rose from the loft in piercingly sweet harmonies that seemed to waft the little church heavenward in a cloud of blue incense.

Izlomin reposed before the altar in floral splendor. His coffin was covered by a blanket of white orchids sent by Mrs. Whitehead, and wreaths of white roses were piled high around him, their scent mixing with the heavier odor of incense and melting tapers.

Toni, standing in the back of the church, felt a headache tapping at her temples. The chief priest's treacly bass reverberated in her head. It was a strange feeling to be here, after having read the book, almost as if it were all a part of the same experience. She had devoured most of the book during the night, falling asleep on galley sixty after the sun had already begun to pour its first oblique rays into her bedroom. And now—how strange to think that the motionless doll lying among the flowers was the same Izlomin who had led a turbulent and artificial life, glittered in many ballets and had silly things written about him by professional esthetes. One of them had written madly, "The tenderness, the emotion, the instinct in Izlomin's buttocks transcends that expressed by another actor's whole physiognomy." Even some of the people present at the funeral had been mentioned in the book: Perlova, about whose affair with her husband Natalia had oh so delicately hinted; de Speranski; Samarkand, then a dancer in Izlomin's company; even Ffoulkes, a rising young designer attracted by ballet.

This party at least was well attended, she thought. She saw Slava in a cluster of sobbing ballet dancers who had obviously been overcome by the solemnity of the occasion. Tamara and Mike were also there.

Then the service was over and they all followed the black-garbed widow to the coffin. Some people were bending down to kiss the dead dancer's crossed hands. Toni omitted this venerable Russian custom, contenting herself with a brief look. Izlomin looked young and defenseless, his face smoothed out and a faint smile frozen on the rouged lips. It reminded Toni of a phrase in Natalia's book that had stuck in her mind in spite, or perhaps because, of the fact that it had been deleted. She had written of Izlomin just before he danced *Phoebus,* "His face was curiously smoothed out and seemed younger by years. The defenseless youth of it stabbed at my heart."

This brought to mind another deletion: an incident that had taken place a few days before that same performance. Izlomin was talking about his costume and spoke about a "wig of hyacinthine curls." His tongue got twisted around the word and he couldn't get it out. De Speranski, who was present, had laughed and Izlomin had flown into a dreadful rage and practically chased him out. Toni could see why this particular episode would be deleted for purely political reasons. But the other one? She suspected that it must have sounded like a self-betrayal to the reserved Natalia. It had such a passionate, self-revealing sound, as if it had been torn out of her.

As she was making her way out of the church in a crush of people, her arm was grasped and she turned to look into Charles Graham's blue eyes.

"Hello there. I've been keeping my eye on you. What a show!" Toni agreed.

"Natalia wanted it simple but Kate said let Vova have the kind of funeral he would have liked and charge the expenses to her. You look tired. What happened after I left you?" His eyes crinkled. "I have a feeling I should have stayed to look after my interests. You haven't done anything rash like promising never to see me again, have you?"

"No," said Toni. She didn't think it was necessary to tell him that she had merely promised to forbear sleeping with him until Eric was out of town.

"How about having dinner with me tonight, then? I'm seeing Jay Wallace of *Look-See.* He wants to use the pictures you took on Wednesday night. Right up his alley, he says. And it'll be good publicity for the book. Join us for cocktails, will you? And bring the pictures?"

Toni said she would. "About the pictures, though. Most of the really good ones were taken by Bill Stone, the photographer I work with. I'll bring them as well."

"Another rival? No? Good. Bring them along. I love that weary transparent look you have. Any chance of meeting me sooner?"

"I'm afraid not. I've got to go to a rehearsal. They're training Vassine for one of Izlomin's roles and my paper seems to think that rates a story. I'm beginning to get a bellyful of ballet dancers, dead or alive."

"Too bad. At Twenty-One, then, at six for cocktails. I've got to join Kate now. I'll be seeing you later."

Toni decided that she had collected enough local color to cram down her editor's throat and hailed a taxi. As it was pulling away she saw Mike Gorin striding away from the church and called out to him.

Mike climbed in with alacrity. "Thanks," he said, with a wan grin. "I think you've just helped me to shake off a tail that my good friend Andy Torrent had set on me. You're riding with a dangerous suspect, did you know that?"

"I know it," said Toni and erased the grin entirely off his face by recounting to him her conversation with Tamara.

"She didn't tell me she heard that," said Mike. "Jesus!" His eyes narrowed. "Are you going to tell this to Andy Torrent?"

Toni disregarded his question. "What are you up to, Mike? Why all the secrecy? What did you talk to Izlomin about?"

Mike merely shook his head wearily. "Anything else you'd like to know?"

"Yes, there is. Why did you want to get Izlomin out of the building?"

"Why did…" Mike looked at her and swallowed. "Where'd you get that idea?"

"From what Tamara told me, naturally. She thought you were threatening him. That's not how it sounds to me. It sounds as if both of you were anxious for him to get out safely, and somebody else must have gotten him while he was trying."

Mike's wide shoulders drooped. "At least you don't think I did it." It was a statement, not a question, but even at that it held little enthusiasm. "What are you going to do, go to Torrent with it?"

That was the second time he had asked this and this time Toni answered him. "Yes, I think I will. You'll probably think it's ratty of me but it's best this way. If you killed Izlomin I don't particularly want to protect you."

"You don't think he deserved it, the rat?"

"No, not even if he neglected the beats on his *cabrioles* and faked his *fouettés*," said Toni firmly and was rewarded by a feeble smile from Mike. "The most he deserved was a good beating. Moreover, I know you didn't. You're either being noble or just cowardly. Torrent has got to know all these things or else how is he going to break the case? Tell you what," said Toni in a cooperative frame of mind, "I'll give you a chance to tell him yourself. This is Saturday. You spin your yarn before Monday—or I will."

Mike thanked her ironically and Toni said he was quite welcome. But her heart misgave her as she looked at his brooding face. "Mike, you didn't kill Vova, did you? That's what I'm banking on, you know."

The look he bent on her was as enigmatic as his naturally open Irish countenance would permit. "I don't know," said Mike. "I might have."

The taxi stopped for a red light and he got out before Toni had time to recover.

Toni didn't know what time it was when she got to the Opera but she had a feeling that it was fairly late. She couldn't have made it before, though. For one thing she wasn't going to let Tom Jones starve, just when he probably needed all his *élan vitale.* Then she wasted much of her time trying to get Bill Stone on the phone. Naturally he was nowhere to be found. She had tried his home, his studio, the concern for which he did part-time work. At the latter place they had wanted to know, wistfully, whether she had seen Mr. Stone lately and when he intended bringing in the prints that had been due two days ago.

She telephoned a threadbare hoofer by the incredible name of Zwieback who was Bill's bosom pal of the moment. Mr. Zwieback didn't know Bill's whereabouts, but hoped that when Toni located him she would tell him that he, Mr. Zwieback, had found a wonderful partner and needed some professional pictures for the agent. Toni promised to give Bill the glad news. Those were the assignments on which Mr. Stone never failed. The ones he treated cavalierly were those involving thousand-dollar ads with expensive models and minks.

Toni thought of running down to the studio but decided that she had no time. Anyhow, only Bill could ever find anything there.

She lingered even after she had put on her new soot-black frock romantically highlighted with black sequins. She realized after a while that it was a call from Eric that she was waiting for. Somehow she hadn't expected him to cut himself off so completely. She looked in the mirror and sighed. The dress fitted her almost shamelessly. She had fallen in love with it and bought it in anticipation of Eric's leave and here she was wearing it for another man. She stripped it off and put on another dress, a red and black affair that was more devil-may-care than romantic. Then she put her pictures, the ones she had taken herself, into her capacious suitcase of a pocketbook and ran.

When she alighted from her taxi at the stage entrance, she saw some of the corps de ballet leaving, carrying the tiny suitcases in which every dancer always keeps her practice clothes. The rehearsal wasn't over, though.

"Samarkand is rehearsing *Roi des Chats* and he didn't need us," said Lilon Caritas, a tiny brunette with a face like a rosy kitten. "Wasn't it a lovely funeral? I cried and cried."

Janet Banks said that so did she and the two girls lingered on the stairs talking about the funeral. Toni had a feeling that they were stalling for a reason. Finally Lilon said with one of her excited giggles, "Do you think we ought to tell her?"

Janet Banks replied reasonably, "No, but since you've said that much you might as well."

Toni lifted an eyebrow and waited for revelations.

"We think you ought to know," said Lilon, "Marina called up your lieutenant just before the rehearsal. He told her where he was staying when he took her out for lunch yesterday. Lunch was all right because he missed you and it just worked out that way. But it's not nice to call up somebody else's soldier."

Toni said inadequately, "That's quite all right."

The two moralists exchanged significant looks and Janet Banks said, "You might as well know all. He dated her up for dinner and for after the show. She's borrowing my silver fox, because hers is being repaired. I hate to lend it to her but I have to, because she lent me her evening wrap last week."

Toni said, "Thanks for telling me." She added, feeling that something more was expected, "Er—men are dogs, aren't they?"

They were nodding solemnly as she left them.

The doorman stopped her as she was about to pass him with a cordial nod. "Wait a minute, Miss. Where are you going? Do you have a pass?"

Toni gazed at him with some surprise.

"Why, Patrick," she said, "you know me."

Patrick went on frowning like a bloodhound. "That's neither here nor there. You ain't a member of the company, are you?" He went on darkly. "It's not for nothing I've had cops down my throat for days on end about who goes in and who goes out here. I don't let anybody in I shouldn't. And from now on, nobody goes in without they has a pass, or Mr. Samarkand or Mr. de Speranski is here to say okay. Nobody!"

Toni wondered what Torrent was trying to get out of Patrick. She bent her energies on cajoling him with the result that Patrick sent one of the stagehands to ask permission of Mr. de Speranski, if he could locate him, or Mr. Samarkand in the rehearsal hall on the fifth floor. Toni had about given up all hope of getting in when another member of the corps de ballet came down bringing Samarkand's message to the effect that it was all right to let Toni in.

Once in the building, Toni didn't bother to wait for the slow-moving elevator but hoofed it down the hall and up the stairs like all the members of corps de ballet who had their dressing rooms on the third and fourth floors and who probably kept their figures by never waiting for the elevator. As she sped upstairs, she remembered going up the same way with Torrent when they were looking for Izlomin, and shivered a little.

The stairs were bare and badly lighted. She was on the women's side of the house and most of the girls had gone home while the others were

across the way in the rehearsal hall. The voices of the stagehands perco-
lated through as from another world.

She thought of Skeets, who was apparently going to leave without
saying good-bye to her. She was glad that at least his last evening would
be made pleasant by Marina, who was, as she knew from many reports,
just the thing for a soldier on the loose. She looked for the slightest trace
of jealousy in her reaction as a sick person looks for the symptoms of
normality, because if she were jealous of Eric, why then maybe the infatu-
ation with Charles was not as total as it seemed. But the very thought of
him gave her a funny shivering sensation and she desisted.

Toni had come to the fourth floor landing, which led to the first fly
gallery. On an impulse she walked through the open door and stepping
over the coiled ropes peered over the rail. They were hanging some flats
on a batten. There was a terse command, a humming sound and the batten began rising, dragging the flats and flies along.

It was at that moment that Toni had a feeling of danger, as palpably as
if someone had breathed down her neck. Her knees stiffened with the
realization of the height and her hands tightened on the rail. She listened
tensely. There was nothing, really. Just that strange, almost visceral consciousness of somebody close and silent.

Moments crawled by and Toni said to herself, "This is getting silly."
But it required a wrenching effort for her to relinquish her hold on the rails
and turn around. There was nothing. Or was there a flitting shadow disap-
pearing just beyond the bright rectangle of the door, a hardly audible shuffle
of soft shoes?

"Probably not," said Toni aloud. "Come, come, Miss Ney. Nerves
yet?"

Her heart fluttered uneasily as she moved toward the landing. And
then she saw it—the silhouette of a man lounging against the doorway,
dark against the gray shadows that filled the fly gallery. Toni stared at it
with fear-dazzled eyes. "Hello," she managed to whisper brightly. She
repeated it louder in a voice that she hoped would be heard below. "Hello
there," she caroled with false gaiety. "I know you. You're the Phantom of
the Opera."

Her voice broke off and one of her rare blushes began creeping up
her neck, as her eyes, becoming accustomed to the dimness, recognized
the still, menacing figure. It was a coat on a hanger, probably belonging to
one of the stagehands, hung up on a nail near the door.

Toni slunk away sheepishly. She still had to go up one flight to reach the second fly gallery, the one outside of which Izlomin was found, then she would cross by the back gallery to the other side, where the rehearsal rooms were.

The second fly gallery was even darker than the first and a remnant of her original uneasiness kept her away from the rail, hugging the wall. She turned into the back gallery. Today it looked more like a passage than a balcony. A flat had been brought down just within the rails. It extended almost the length of the gallery, isolating it from the rest of the theater, like a wall. Another flat hung along the wall. In the middle of the passage thus formed there stood a table with an array of paint cans on it. The two flats were being painted. Toni could distinguish the rococo contours of some fabulous palace sketched in on their gray surfaces.

She hesitated. She could hear the piano being pounded across the way and the faint thud of dancing feet. But the sense of danger was strong upon her again and she had to summon the memory of her humiliation downstairs before moving on.

And then it happened. There was a movement behind her, a swift shuffle and somebody administered a neat scientific rap on the back of her head.

"Hey, Clancy, she's coming to. Are you all right, lady?"

Toni said, "I don't know," and struggled to her elbow. She found herself leaning picturesquely against an overalled knee.

"Take it easy," one of the stagehands advised. "The first thing you got to do when you're hurt is lay flat on your back until the doctor comes."

"Don't be silly," said Toni. "I've got a date. What time is it, anyhow? Ouch!" Her hand went to the back of her head. The men exchanged tolerant glances.

"Ain't it just like a woman? No, Miss, you better wait until the police come."

"The police?" Toni's eyes widened. "You called the police? Did you think I was dead or something?"

"Well, you looked pretty bad when Clancy found you. You was under a heap of canvas there with just your foot sticking out, or Clancy wouldn't of seen you."

Clancy said, "So I says to meself—geeze, another corpse. But you kinda moved and groaned, so we figured you'll live. The reason we called the police is they're handier. There's somebody from the homicide squad talking to the guy with the beard downstairs. Say, who slugged you, anyhow?"

Toni would have very much liked to know that herself. She told as much to Captain Torrent, with considerable emphasis. Because by the time he arrived, his ruddy face full of concern, she discovered that her pocketbook had disappeared.

Torrent got her down to Perlova's room and tenderly deposited her on the couch, whence he refused to let her move until a doctor looked at her head and had pronounced that it was "a lovely bop on the conk" but nothing dangerous.

By that time it was after seven and the best she could do about her appointment was to ask Torrent to call up Twenty-One and tell Charles that she couldn't make it. With that off her mind, she relaxed on Perlova's couch, dabbed eau de cologne on her aching temples and answered Torrent's questions.

"I haven't the slightest idea who it was," she told Torrent. "Somebody in ballet shoes or in stocking feet. Not toe shoes, they've got box toes and they tap. And I don't know exactly what time it was—somewhere around five or maybe five-thirty. The rehearsal was still going on, because I heard the piano."

"We'll check on that as soon as your friends come back for the performance, which ought to be soon."

"It is pretty late, isn't it?" said Toni. She grinned ruefully. "Well, I came for the rehearsal but I seemed to have stayed for the performance, haven't I? Why are you looking at me like that, Captain Torrent? Did I say something?"

Torrent was indeed looking at her with a peculiar expression.

"It just occurred to me," he said, "that I ought to put you on a salary."

"Why, did anything drastic happen?"

"Well," said Torrent, "we've finally identified that print on the threatening note to Izlomin. It's Vassine's."

"Well, I'll be damned. Then he wrote it after all?"

"No, the handwriting isn't his. He just handled it."

Toni wrestled with this for a moment and gave it up. "Did you ask him about it?"

"No, I'm collecting other information first."

"Like—?"

"Well, for one thing, I want to speak to the doctor who attended Vassine's mother when she was ill." He grinned at the bafflement on Toni's face. "Didn't you tell me she died of cancer?"

"So I did, but I don't understand... You're on to something, that much is clear to me."

"At least I have a notion. There were a few things bothering me. Like the doorman's testimony and the fact that I didn't see how it was possible with so many people around. You have just taken care of the first one for me." Toni put her hand to her forehead in a distracted way and Torrent broke off contritely. "I shouldn't worry you with these things. I'm going to send you home. What you need is some sleep."

"Sleep," Toni echoed longingly. "Yes, I could do with a little sojourn in Murphy's arms, as Eric says."

Her mention of his name might have been a charm. A wild-eyed Lieutenant Skeets materialized at the doorway, made a beeline for Toni and fell on his knees before the couch. There was a faint alcoholic aura about him but certainly none of the exhilaration that goes with it.

"Toni," said Eric in a panic, "you're all right, aren't you? I was downstairs" (presumably bringing Marina back after supper, Toni thought) "and I heard somebody say that you..."

Toni said, wincing as he shook her in his eagerness, "I'm all right now. Somebody bopped me on the head and took away my pocketbook. But apparently I'll live. I've got a wonderful goose egg, though."

Eric touched it. "Not bad. And that's all the damage?" He smiled palely. "I spend a whole day getting tanked up and you scare me out of it. And all for nothing."

"Well, my head is bursting open at the seams, if that'll make you feel any better." She absentmindedly tweaked the strand of hair that had fallen onto his distracted brow. Eric winced as if the little tug hurt him and rose to his feet.

"Come on," he said coldly. "I'll take you home. You look like a turnip ghost. You can tell me all about it when we get to your place. Stop lolling on that chaise longue—who do you think you are, Madame Recamier?"

Thus urged, Toni tottered out of Perlova's room, solicitously supported by him and Torrent and creating a sensation among the members of the company whom they encountered on the way.

"I'll send a man to keep watch on you just in case," said Torrent, putting them into a taxi. "Take care of yourself, Toni. You'll be all right. You're tough."

"I don't know why everybody thinks I'm tough," Toni complained as the taxi drove away, "I feel as if I've been softened up plenty."

"Any idea who softened you up?"

Toni shook her head and distinctly heard her brains rattling.

"No. I wish they'd left me my pocketbook. The nicest pocketbook I've ever had, damn them. I could put everything into it."

"You probably did too. What was in it?"

Toni told him, as she had already told Torrent, and Eric whistled.

"I will refrain from conventional remarks about all the junk women carry. Those photographs sound promising."

"Torrent said he'll look through the enlargements Bill made up for him and see if there's something. Offhand I can't think of anything important in them and nobody knew about my having them along."

"There's always a chance that you know something that somebody is afraid of and that this was an attempt to silence you and the purse was taken to distract attention."

Toni suddenly had an unpleasant and disconcerting idea. Mike! He certainly didn't want her to pass her information on to Torrent. "But that's impossible," she said horrified. Eric pounced on it.

"Then you do know something! What is it?"

Reluctantly she told him. Eric stared at her, "And you've kept quiet about it! Toni, you idiot. You ought to know better. You should have told Torrent about it tonight!"

Toni was about to say that she had better things to do tonight but thought better of it. By that time they had reached the house and Eric was handing her out as carefully as if she had been a crateful of Venetian glass.

The phone was ringing in her apartment and Toni realized that she couldn't get in. She listened to its persistent ringing while Eric ran down to get the key from the landlady. There's nothing quite as frustrating as not being able to get at a telephone, particularly if you have an idea who is calling. By Eric's nasty little smile she surmised that he had an idea too.

The phone had stopped ringing and her headache had grown·unbearable by the time they got inside. Eric made her bed for her and chastely went to feed the cats while she got into it. It was a heavenly sensation to relax.

The cats came in, their whiskers dripping with milk, and leaped up on her bed to stare at her. Apparently they had entered a less orgiastic phase of their love affair. Tom Jones marched up the bed to rub his nose against her shoulder and after getting his ears scratched went back to the foot of the bed where he and Cleo kneaded the blanket in unison with their front paws as if performing a piano duet and purred loudly.

Eric drifted in and out of the room, plopping cold compresses on her fevered brow. He was munching an apple and the sound mixed pleasantly with the cats' purring. A tiny stream of water trickled toward her ear from the compress, and moments passed peacefully.

The telephone rang. Eric grabbed it, forestalling Toni's frantic attempt. "Hello? Oh, we got home all right and Toni's gone to bed. Captain Torrent," he told Toni in an aside. "Yes, I'll tell her. Incidentally, Captain Torrent, you say you've talked to Mike. Did he have anything to tell you? No? Well, then…"

"Don't, Eric," Toni besought him. Eric gave her a cold look and went on with the story she had told him. Then he hung up and turned to Toni, who was watching him inimically from her bed of pain.

"There, it's done and it's not even on your conscience because I was the one who done it. Torrent tells me that he's talked to people about your little misadventure with very little luck. Apparently he who hits from behind and runs away is the hardest kind to catch and will presumably come back to hit another day. Now why don't you go to sleep? We'll have a hard day tomorrow. Torrent wants you to come to the Opera at one. Says he has an experiment in mind he wants to try out."

"We? I thought you were going away," said Toni. She added sleepily but in an injured way, "without even saying good-bye."

"You fixed that, pal. I'd have a fine time away from New York worrying about whether you were still alive. I only hope Torrent clears this up before I have to leave. As long as you're safe—and what you do with your personal life is no concern of mine."

Toni closed her eyes. She thought it must be sheer physical weakness and fatigue that was making her feel much better at the idea of Skeets sticking around. She burrowed deeper into the pillow. The little yellow pill the doctor had given her was beginning to work.

Eric stayed around for a while, munching his apple in a subdued way. Then he tiptoed out of the room, taking the telephone with him. Since it had a long wire he was able to make himself comfortable on the couch and still keep it within a grabbing distance. He also took the precaution of locating the bell box and stuffing a pillow around it. Presently the phone rang feebly, and Eric answered it, with an apprehensive eye on Toni's bedroom.

"Hello. Yes, this is Toni Ney's apartment. Well, no, I'm afraid you can't talk to her just now. She's gone to bed. That's right, gone to bed." He listened patiently. "Well, why shouldn't she go to bed if she wants to? This is a free country. All right, let's put it this way. She's not feeling well. No, I'm not the doctor." His voice took on a smug expression. "Just an old friend. Good-bye. Oh, wait a minute. Do you want to give me your name so I can tell her when she wakes up?"

There was a minute explosion in the telephone. Eric hung up the receiver and smiled angelically at the ceiling.

CHAPTER FOURTEEN

IT WAS A PLEASANT SUNDAY MORNING but Captain Torrent foresaw no rest. He was mentally girding his loins for a very tough day. He had a fine collection of suspects to crack. Asking them questions hadn't been much good. He had a hunch that telling them would produce much better results and today was the first time he could actually back up his questions with certain ideas and facts. What Eric had told him yesterday about Mike was important. It was another fact to bolster up the incredible conclusion at which he had arrived. Of course, as he had told Toni, there still was that matter of too many people being around. Nevertheless, it was the only thing that made sense and he was going to play it that way.

He rather suspected that Toni with her uncannily sharp eye would be of great help to him. Then he thought of someone else and immediately picked up the phone to call her.

Natalia Izlomina agreed readily. "I was coming to the rehearsal anyhow, Captain Torrent. The only thing..." There was a doubtful little pause. "Will—will the police be present? A lot of them?"

"Mrs. Izlomin," said Torrent bluntly, "what's on your mind?" Natalia said, "Well, I was coming to the rehearsal for a purpose. One of the company has been acting a little strangely. He—this person—I have a feeling as if he wants to tell me something and then he changes his mind at the last moment or there are people around. I thought if I gave him an opportunity…"

"Who is it?"

"It's little Slava Mladov. I think—I am sure he knows something."

Lady, you and me both, Torrent thought. Aloud he said, "If he does come through with anything, will you pass it on to us immediately, Mrs. Izlomin? Even if it's told you in strictest confidence…"

"How can anything about Vova's murder be told to me in confidence?" There was a steely clang in her soft voice. "Don't worry, Captain. I'll tell you everything that Slava tells me—if he does."

She would, at that, Torrent thought, as he hung up. There was no sentimental nonsense about this woman.

Toni listened to Graham's tale of intrigue and perfidy with tightening lips and narrowed eyes. Then suddenly the funny side of it struck her and she began to laugh.

"I didn't feel like laughing, I assure you," said Graham ruefully. "I was furious and jealous and concerned. All in all, your friend gave me a pretty bad half an hour until I heard from Kate Whitehead about what happened to you."

"And right away you felt much better," said Toni dryly. An absurd exhilaration welled up in her. She might, she reflected, have reason to be grateful to Eric after all.

Graham remonstrated feebly and gave up. "Yes, I admit it, I did. Horrible but true. I'd rather have you beaten to a pulp than untrue to me."

"I don't believe I know you well enough to be untrue to you," Toni remarked. She batted her long eyelashes at him and he precipitately moved to the couch where she sat.

"But you will, I hope, ultimately. Darling, don't keep me dangling too long, will you?"

Toni lay passively in his embrace. Only her lips responded to his. Never before had she experienced that sense of complete, helpless abandonment, and it scared her. Some remaining instinct made her keep intact the habitual impassive mask and forced the lips that threatened to grow too tremulously tender into a cool gay smile. There was a puzzled expression in Graham's eyes, as if he too found that her kisses and her smile didn't quite jibe. "Cold little brute," he said softly, and returned to the former.

"No," Toni thought, "you're the cold one, my lad. That's why you feel so safe." She flinched as his hand touched the back of her head.

"By George," said Graham, abandoning her lips and passing his finger gently over the sore spot, "is that from yesterday? Darling, you must have been slugged really hard. Who do you suppose...?"

"I don't know," said Toni. She freed herself from his embrace and walked over to a mirror. An unfamiliar face looked back at her—green eyes soft and dreamy, cheeks flushed, lipstick showing signs of being tampered with. She began to repair the damage. "Somebody who thinks I Know Too Much."

The doorbell rang just as she finished putting on a new mouth. The visitor turned out to be Lieutenant Skeets, natty and bright in his uniform.

"Come on in," said Toni, adding *sotto voce*, "louse."

Eric motioned a guileless, "Who, me?" with his expressive eyebrows. His quick gray eyes lighted on Graham, who was rising from the couch and somewhat ostentatiously tucking away his handkerchief that sported unmistakable traces of lipstick. "Men," Toni thought, shocked, "can be just as catty as women." Eric allowed himself to be introduced anew to Charles, whose hand he shook warmly and whom he called "sir," in a fulsomely respectful tone that seemed to add centuries to the decade between them.

"I've come to take you to the Opera, Toni, if you feel well enough to go. How's the bump?" Eric felt of it and shook his head in deprecation. "Nowhere near the glorious thing it was last night ."

"I was about to tell Toni," said Graham, "that it might be better for her to keep out of this business altogether. Somebody seems to resent her interest."

"That's what I keep telling her too," said Eric. "Don't go poking around where you aren't wanted. But she never listens to me. I'm glad you share my opinion, sir. Perhaps she'll listen to an older man."

They were still talking about her in the third person when she went to her room to tie a veil ribbonwise around her hair and fluff out the bow. That was Toni's only concession to the unnecessary institution of hats. When she came back, she found that Eric was in the kitchen talking to Tom Jones, while Charles was fingering the galleys she had left lying on the table.

"Darling," he said to Toni, frowning a little, "I seem to have made a mistake. Miss Brown will cut my throat for this. I've given you the galleys with author's corrections and they belong in a file. I'll have a duplicate set sent to you." Toni helped him to collect them.

"Ready?" said Eric coming in from the kitchen. "Justice must not be made to wait."

As she went down, squired by Graham and Skeets, she reflected glumly upon her lack of femininity. She was embarrassed and annoyed by a situation in which any other woman would probably glory. She compared her two swains. Eric, slim and mercurial; Charles, big, almost burly, almost hulking, yet with his own brand of elegance. He was sure enough of himself not to be ruffled by Eric's impertinence, although Toni thought she caught something wistful in his swift glance at the latter's uniform. He even liked the younger man and it was obvious that by being bright and young and maliciously witty Eric had added to Toni's desirability.

It would have been nice if Eric's barbs had found their mark, if she could suddenly say to herself, "What am I doing with this middle-aged wolf?" But they didn't work. When Charles said good-bye, smiling his special, intimate and, alas, only too facile smile at her, she felt her heart turning completely over and knew that she was in for a long siege of measles.

In the meanwhile Torrent had come to the Opera a little ahead of time and gone straight to de Speranski's office. He found the door to the inner sanctum closed, and from behind it issued sounds of a battle royal.

Mrs. Whitehead's language, he thought with impersonal admiration, denoted a good agricultural background and a complete lack of inhibitions. After a while he began to distinguish a central theme. "Thief," she boomed with colorful qualifications, "vulture, robber."

Torrent heard a small shocked gasp behind him and saw Natalia Izlomina, all in black, like a well-dressed shadow. She acknowledged his greeting and glanced nervously in the direction of the ruckus. In spite of her embarrassment Torrent fancied he saw an expression of satisfaction flash across her face. "I think I'd better go," she said, "Mrs. Whitehead is so…"

The door flew open and Kate Whitehead strode out. She was dressed in her riding clothes and carried a crop with a heavy silver handle. Torrent wondered whether she had used it on de Speranski. The latter looked as if he had been through a mill that had ground exceeding fine and wasn't too slow either. He made a few failing steps toward his irate patroness, joined his hands together with a slapping sound and brought them close to his chest.

"*Ma chère madame*," he said, and sobbed heavily, "*Notre bienfaitrice*—I can explain."

"Like hell you can," said Mrs. Whitehead briskly, "I know you, you fat sniveling thief. You'd wriggle your way out of anything, give you a chance. But not this one, no, sir."

De Speranski emitted another fat heavy sob and muttered something about restitution.

"You're damn tootin'," said his nemesis with a snort. Her crop swished ominously. "Through the nose. Christ, man, stop sniveling at me in front of people. Have you no sense of decency?" Her small angry eyes fell on Torrent and Natalia. She strode toward them, answering Natalia's uneasy greeting with a curt nod and addressed Torrent vindictively.

"I can't see that you've done much so far. I expected you to report to me on your progress."

"Did you?" said Torrent mildly. She turned on him almost happily. It was as if she was pleased to vent her anger at somebody who would stand up under it instead of dissolving into sluglike abasement.

"Yes, goddamn it, I did. Don't give yourself airs, Torrent. You're no goddamn commissioner, you're a plain copper and your business is to apprehend the criminals."

"It's a hard proposition, Mrs. Whitehead. Most people are reluctant to tell all they know, even those who seem to be most interested in getting the case solved. As a matter of fact, I was going to pay a little call on you in that connection."

He smiled a little as her truculent gaze wavered.

"It appears," said Mrs. Whitehead, in a sort of dying-away salvo, "that I am surrounded by incompetents and thieves."

"I take it," said Torrent, "that I belong in the former category."

Kate Whitehead went back to the blubbering impresario with renewed gusto. "Our fat friend here has been swindling most of the dancers he had imported from abroad, trading on their faulty knowledge of the language and on their being too timid to demand their rights."

Torrent asked eagerly, "Izlomin, too?"

"Oh yes, Vova too. When he first came." A few words explained the situation. When Mrs. Whitehead had acquired the ownership of the ballet she had "bought" all the dancers hitherto under contract to de Speranski.

The latter, however, had managed to keep secret agreements with some of the dancers in which he figured as their agent. Under that arrangement he was able to collect fees from them which he, as director of the American Ballet Drama Company, deducted from their salaries, since he cashed their checks for them anyhow.

Telling this, Mrs. Whitehead's fury boiled again. She whirled on Natalia. "You must have known about it. Vova was a babe in the woods but you knew what was what. What were you doing, splitting the commission?"

Natalia Izlomina met the other woman's furious gaze squarely. There was a small spark of contempt in her hazel eyes.

"If Vova were alive, he would be the first to assure you that in my own very humble way I took as good care of my husband as even you may have wished me to."

She emphasized the words "my husband" delicately but unmistakably. Kate Whitehead flushed a dull red.

"I shall go to the rehearsal room now," Natalia said to Torrent.

"Very good," said Torrent. "I wonder if you'd be kind enough to show Mahoney the way there." He took her to the door, turning his back on the pulsing tension in the room, and beckoned to his burly aide. "This lady will take you to the rehearsal room. Here's a slip of paper with the names of the people I want to see after they're through rehearsing. May I use this office, Mr. de Speranski?"

The crushed impresario made a gesture which seemed to say, "Go ahead, trample on me. What can I do?"

"Thanks. When you are through there, Mahoney, come down and stand guard in the corridor. I've got Williams at the door leading from the orchestra. Don't leave your post under any circumstances, understand? I don't want any of the people I mentioned getting out without seeing me."

"Okay, chief. Lead the way, lady."

In the room, Mrs. Whitehead was smoking a cigarette in quick resentful puffs, like a volcano about to explode. She gave Torrent a tight mirthless grin. "Did you see how that little bitch fluttered her widow's weeds at me? All the same, she didn't answer the question. Or were you so bowled over by her airs that you missed that? God, how I hate those soft, goody-goody women."

"Still waters run deep," de Speranski contributed unhappily. "A Russian proverb…"

"Shut up," said Mrs. Whitehead ungratefully. She shook her crop at him. "I'm not through with you."

"I hope you aren't through with me," said Torrent. "I'd like to ask you a question or two."

"Later," said Mrs. Whitehead shortly and walked out. Torrent sighed. That probably meant that he would have to track her down to her house.

De Speranski, on whom the departure of his "benefactress" had an immediately reviving effect, fell into his chair and extracted a fat dark bottle from the bottom drawer. He poured the brandy into a small glass and from the glass into his mouth so fast that the liquid seemed to bounce. Tears came to his eyes, this time expressive not of self-pity but of pleasure.

"American women," he said didactically, "think dzat to be business-like dzey must be hard as nails. But it really means nothing."

"What do you mean, nothing?" asked Torrent, interested by this fast recovery.

"But of course. It is dzis way, Captain Torrent." He emptied another glass. Torrent noticed that his beard was beginning to settle into its former suave lines. "I am a merchant of beauty. All dzis assemblage of grace and charm and purest art—who brings it to dze American public? I do. Yet I do not own it. Because of persecutions and because at heart I am not a businessman but an artist, a lover of beauty. Therefore I must make ar-rangements. In Europe it is an accepted thing for a—middleman, shall I say—like myself, to receive a little commission. Dzey understand dzere. And Mrs. Whitehead will understand too. What happened just now was *du theatre*. American women like Kate—she must dominate. Make her feel dzat you are dze worm and she dze heel," said de Speranski with deadly seriousness "and she will be happy. Kate makes much noise, but you doubtless know dze old English proverb, 'a dog dzat barks is not as dangerous as one dzat goes about his business quietly.' "

"You're probably right," said Torrent. "But I am interested in the—commission, as you call it, that you got from Izlomin."

"Something we agreed on while Vova was in Lisbon. You see, Cap-tain, without me, Izlomin would have been nothing. I brought him here. I took him into dze Ballet Drama."

"I see. And to use a crass American term, you've been getting your cut from him ever since?"

De Speranski protested. No, only at first. Later he, de Speranski, felt that Vova's obligations to him were repaid and dropped the "commission" of his own will.

"That, I suppose," said Torrent, "was when Izlomin began to get very chummy with Mrs. Whitehead and you thought you'd better go easy. And he capitalized on the situation, didn't he? Not quite the brand of dancer you're used to, eh?"

De Speranski's face got very ugly indeed. He suddenly expressed his feelings about dear departed Vova and Torrent blinked, mildly surprised to hear such crude Anglo-Saxon sentiments issuing out of such a cultured beard.

"I see I'm right," said Torrent. "It must have been unsettling to see him on such good terms with Mrs. Whitehead, with her crude American ideas of doing business." He moved his face closer to de Speranski's, from which the bacchic ruddiness was flowing fast, and added, "You must have been very much relieved when he was murdered, Mr. de Speranski."

At that moment the telephone rang. De Speranski grabbed it as a drowning man grabs a lifeline. As he listened, his face began to regain its color and become suffused with righteous indignation. "Tell her," he said shortly, "I come."

He turned a harassed look on Torrent. "She is in dze box office," he said. "Dzose American she-millioners. Intolerable! She may own dze ballet but a man's box office is his castle."

He stalked out, a portly Coriolanus bludgeoned by the world's injustice. "Wait," said Torrent. "I'll go with you. I want to see Mrs. Whitehead."

In the corridor they ran into the returning Mahoney, who had something to report. "The Mladov kid had something to say to Mrs. Izlomin. He kinda wavered close to her after they started dancing and said something and she kinda nodded."

"All right," said Torrent. "Stay here and don't let anybody leave. I'll be back in a while."

Patrick delayed Toni and Eric so that they missed Torrent. He complained about the undue lot of attention that had been paid him by the police.

"So he says to me, 'Is it usual for Mr. Ffoulkes to talk to you for such a long time?' So I says, 'Why not? Some people are naturally polite,' I says, 'not like other people.' Then he wants to know how did I know that it was right after *Phoebus* and I tells him they was still calling Izlomin out for curtain calls. Then he says I couldn't be sure, could I, with me deef ear, and I explains to him patient-like that that's what Mr. Ffoulkes told me, just as he come out. 'Well,' he'd said, 'Patrick old boy, they're still calling for him.' And then that copper starts asking me about whom I let in for the rehearsal that same day!"

Toni was very thoughtful as they entered de Speranski's office, to which Mahoney had directed them. Nobody was there and Toni sat down in his chair and began to poke at a bulky parcel lying on the table.

Eric teased her, "Are you trying to find out what's in Torrent's mind by sitting in his place?"

"I'm beginning to get a glimmer," said Toni. "Talking of glimmering..." she stared at a rent in the package through which something sparkled and shone. The next moment her hands tore frantically at the brown paper, shredding it in her eagerness to get at the sparkling thing it contained.

"Toni," said Eric horrified, "what in the world...?"

Toni wasn't listening to him. Her face had gone white and her eyes blazed green with excitement. She snatched up a piece of paper in the package and read the words on it aloud.

"The costume in which Izlomin was found."

"What about it?" asked Eric, looking uncomprehendingly at the *Phoebus* costume, its golden sequins glittering madly in the lamp light.

"That's just it!" Toni cried. "The costume in which Izlomin was found. But that isn't the costume in which he danced." She shook him as if to shake the bewilderment off his face. "Don't you understand, Eric? When I saw Izlomin coming down to dance in *Phoebus,* he wasn't wearing this costume."

CHAPTER FIFTEEN

ERIC OPENED HIS MOUTH to say, "But that's impossible," but changed his mind, impressed by the blazing conviction on Toni's face.

"But what was he wearing then?"

"Another costume with sequins—almost exactly the same, except for the sequins."

"Then how come you're so sure?"

"My sequins," said Toni. "I have the same kind on a dress of mine. I told you about it, remember? They're twice as large as the ordinary kind and twice as shiny. You can only get them at one place. Remember, I said that time that he was not as dazzling as he should have been? I meant the sequins. I thought he hadn't gotten the costume he wanted in time and was wearing the spare one with the old sequins."

"But could you tell on the stage?"

"I think so. He would have blazed like a torch. But anyhow I saw him close to. And I particularly noticed that he was wearing the old sequins."

"Why didn't you tell Torrent?"

Toni made an impatient movement. "How should I know? I didn't see him when he was dead. Other people identified him. I didn't look at the costume until now. When I saw Natalia that time, she was going down to telephone the costumer because Izlomin was hitting the ceiling. His costume hadn't arrived. So I naturally took it for granted that it never did arrive. And I didn't know different until now. And now…" She stared at it, her lower lip caught in her teeth.

"And now?"

"Now I know what Torrent is suspecting. And this—this ought to prove it to the hilt! What was it Torrent said yesterday? He could see the solution but there were too many people around. He didn't see how it could have been carried off. Very well, we'll show him."

She picked up the package, grabbed Eric's hand and flew out of the room and down the hall to the stairs, pausing only to tell Mahoney, "We're going to be on the second floor in one of the dressing rooms. Tell Captain Torrent to come up there the minute he comes back. It's very important."

"Phew," said Eric, setting his cap straight. "I feel as if I've been snatched by a witch on Halloween. What now?"

"You'll see," Toni promised him, making for Izlomin's dressing room. The light she snapped on showed it to be exactly as it had been before the police sealed it. The seal was off now, but some feeling of superstitious unease had kept it from being used. Toni looked at the dressing table and made a small sound expressive of satisfaction. Then she turned to Eric.

"Take your clothes off," she said.

Eric's jaw fell. "Darling, isn't this a little sudden?"

"This is no time to fool around," said Toni sternly. She unwrapped the parcel and threw the costume at him, sequined tunic, gold-colored tights and all. "Put this on and then I'll explain to you."

Captain Torrent finally came back from a stormy interview with Mrs. Whitehead, whom he found browbeating the ticket agent about the number of tickets he was leaving for de Speranski's personal friends. The reason for her keeping back her second visit to Izlomin's dressing room was unexpectedly feminine. She simply had hated to give the impression of pestering Vova, who didn't want to see her.

He heard Toni's message from his lieutenant with some astonishment and immediately went up to the second floor, repeating to Mahoney his instructions about sticking in the corridor.

"Hello there," said Torrent and rapped on the closed door.

Toni's voice replied, "You, Captain Torrent? Just two more minutes."

"What are you up to?"

"You'll see."

Toni looked at her handiwork carefully. Her eyes narrowed in an effort to remember. Then she drew a careful outline and a red curly cynical mouth sprang into sudden relief.

"There!" said Toni.

She opened the door. "You can come in now."

"Well, I'll be damned," said Torrent, staring at the figure that rose to meet him out of Izlomin's chair. It was the dead dancer come back to life and ready to dance *Phoebus*. The arrogant golden mask with the slanted eyes, the curly mouth, the eyes slanting wickedly between the bulging brow and the prominent cheekbones—they were all there.

"Isn't it strange," said the apparition in Eric's voice, "how women are always trying to make you over?" It came out in the middle of the room, glittering, and attempted to execute an *entrechat*, failing miserably.

"That's what was bothering you, wasn't it?" Toni asked, wiping the gold greasepaint off her hands. "You figured there must have been a substitution because Izlomin was acting too strangely to be true, but you didn't see how anybody could get away with it in front of so many people. Well, there you are. He looks good enough to deceive you right now. Imagine how it would be on the stage, or for that matter backstage in the shadows."

"Amazing," said Torrent, peering closely. "I mean the structural similarity."

"Well, Izlomin had a sort of face that was easy to model on somebody else's. All those distinctive features, like his cheekbones and forehead, and then the fact that everything was covered over by golden greasepaint that shone so that you missed the differences."

"That profile…"

"Putty. Miracles can be worked with putty. Not on everybody, of course. You can't make a small nose out of a large one. But Eric has a small nose that swoops like a ski slide so I could build a bigger straight one by filling in the gap from the bridge to the tip of the nose."

"Tampering with God's handiwork," Eric put in virtuously.

"Then you just draw in the mouth and so on. I had to work fast so you can see the seams. But there was plenty of time last Wednesday. The choreography helped, too. Izlomin never came near the others. And then the glitter—"

"That's right," said Torrent. "Probably the true Izlomin was gotten out of the way before the ballet started and his costume was used. And then they had to get the costume back on him again…"

"No," said Toni quickly. "The substitute didn't take off Izlomin's costume. He wore the other one—the spare one."

Torrent shook his head in his turn. "Couldn't have. The spare costume is still at the tailor's. We checked on that. The tailor's boy arrived at the last minute with this," he indicated the tunic Eric was wearing, "and took the spare one back with him, to fix it the same way."

"Then there must have been a third costume, because this one wasn't worn," said Toni. She went again through the story of the bigger and better sequins and an expression of deep satisfaction settled on Torrent's face.

"That clinches it," he said.

"It does tell you very plainly who the substitute must have been," said Eric. "Somebody about the size of Izlomin, with the sort of face on which Izlomin's face could be built."

"And who was a good enough dancer to duplicate Izlomin's style and even to improve on it," said Toni.

"Somebody whom Mike was willing to protect."

"And who had another friend, pretty good at making costumes."

"Somebody possibly whose doctor had prescribed morphine scopolamine pills for his dying mother in order to make her last days bearable." Torrent smiled wearily. "Yes, I got that bit today. And you gave me a clue yesterday about how he got in, by saying that you came for the rehearsal and stayed for the performance. You see, I was going to play the few facts I had for all they were worth and I thought that making the substitute put on the costume would unnerve him to the point of breaking down and maybe make other people remember. Izlomin's wife had felt that there had been something odd about that *Phoebus*—and so did you, Toni. But this bit about the costume just clinches it. Now I can go ahead without any histrionics."

"The only thing is I can't see him doing it all alone," said Toni thoughtfully.

"I didn't say he did," Torrent answered. He smiled at their puzzled faces. "I'll go down now. Join me downstairs after Eric is himself again, will you?"

The screams came when he was halfway down the staircase—prolonged, agonized screams, that cut like a knife through the Sunday stillness of the Opera House. Torrent could never remember afterwards how he made the rest of the stairs. For aught he knew, he may have slid down the banisters. Mahoney was no longer on guard in the corridor. The door to the stage was still swinging a little from—presumably—his exit. Torrent made for the stage, where the screaming was still going on.

It was dark there and Torrent could just make out Mahoney's solid figure frozen in a stunned attitude. A little way from him stood Natalia Izlomina, her hands clasped to her white face. Both of them were looking up into the flies.

Torrent looked that way, too. The flats that hung from the grid like a gigantic Monday wash were being queerly agitated by something that made a tearing, crashing sound as it hurtled through them. Head thrown back, Torrent's eyes searched the swinging ropes, the swaying flats and the flying shadows, and saw that something black was falling toward them, halting momentarily as it caught on a rope or crashed through a flat. It seemed an eternity, while the muscles in his throat ached and Natalia's screams battered at his ears, until the last obstruction had been cleared and the black thing landed on a packing case with sudden and horrible finality. Now it was a smashed puppet, its carrotty head hanging from the edge of the packing case.

Natalia screamed again and hurled herself at Mahoney, hiding her face in his shoulder.

"He fell," said Mahoney, hoarsely and unnecessarily. "From the back gallery, I think."

Torrent heard the door slamming behind him as he began to walk toward the body, and the agitated voices of Eric and Toni were asking what had happened. Their queries came to a gasping stop as they saw, and then Eric asked, "Who is it?"

At the sound of his voice Natalia lifted her face from Mahoney's shoulder to see who had spoken. For a moment her eyes rested on his glittering figure uncomprehendingly. Then they dilated with renewed horror. She opened her mouth and a sort of paralyzed hiss issued from it.

"No," said Toni, quickly, "it's not—it's only Eric."

Her explanation fell on deaf ears. Natalia had fainted dead away. Her body slid through Mahoney's clumsy hands and dropped to the floor, as limp and lifeless as the smashed body of Slava Mladov at the other end of the stage.

Mahoney told Torrent, "I was in the corridor, like you said, and she comes around. She goes to your office and doesn't find you there so she comes back and wants to know where you are. I tells her I don't know. Then she tells me she's supposed to meet somebody on the stage and it's important for somebody official to listen to their conversation. Could I maybe sneak in after a while and do that? I tell her no, on account of you want me outside. She kinda oh dears for a while and then goes in herself. About five minutes goes by and then she starts screaming. I rush in and...Jesus!" The ordinarily stolid Mahoney mopped at a damp forehead. "I can tell you, chief, it was strictly no good."

"All right, don't go and faint on me," said Torrent unkindly. "See how Toni's doing with Mrs. Izlomin. I'll come up to take a look at her in a moment."

Mahoney limped away on his errand. To add to his discomfiture he had stumbled over a long piece of rope lying in an unseasonable place at the back of the stage and had sprained his ankle. Altogether he was pretty unhappy about the whole thing.

This was half an hour after the accident—if accident it was—had occurred. The Medical Examiner, the fingerprint men and the police photographers had arrived and men were swarming up in the grid and on the fly galleries trying to reconstruct the path of Slava's falling body among the flats.

All the people who were in the building during the rehearsal were detained. The dressing rooms hummed with excitement and hysteria and the hardier members of the company were kept busy with cold water and smelling salts.

Lieutenant Skeets had contributed considerably to the excitement by trying to get upstairs in Izlomin's costume. First he bumped into Mrs. Whitehead, who took one look at him, let out a whoop and fainted into de Speranski's arms. Then he found himself a center of screaming girls still in their practice clothes. Considerably unnerved, he beat a retreat to the stage and ventured out only upon being provided with Torrent's coat and scarf to hide his embarrassing incandescence. He was now hard at work in Izlomin's dressing room removing all traces of his temporary reincarnation.

Natalia Izlomina sat upon the couch of the same dressing room in which Toni had nursed her own injuries the day before and took a thirsty sip from the glass of water Toni offered her. Toni, who had been with her ever since she had been brought to the dressing room, thought she had recovered very quickly. There had been a wild stare upon recovering consciousness, a few wild words and then a set blank face and a desperate effort to keep calm. Occasionally a spasmodic shiver would shake her whole body. But the story that came out between her chattering teeth as she faced Torrent was coherent enough.

Up in the rehearsal hall, she had sensed very strongly that Slava wanted to speak to her. She gave him an opportunity to do so and he begged her to meet him before he saw Torrent. She had wanted him to tell her right then and there what was troubling him, but he had refused. He finally asked her to meet him on the stage, "where nobody would see them."

"Was it your impression that he was afraid?" Torrent asked.

"Yes. Afraid of many things. Of you and other people. And even of me. He kept saying that I'd hate him when I found out but he must tell me himself. And at the same time he wanted me to go away so that nobody would suspect what he was telling me."

Then Samarkand had called on him for his *pas de deux* with Perlova and Natalia had thought it might be a good idea to look in on the other rehearsal room where Vassine was going through his paces. After staying there a little while, she went down to speak to Torrent before going to the stage to wait for Slava.

She had waited for several minutes. And then—then there was a noise up in the flies. Torrent pounced on that.

"What kind of noise?"

"I don't know. I can't remember. All I know is that suddenly I was looking up, straining my eyes and my ears. I couldn't see much because of all the flats hanging there, but there was a movement of some sort somewhere around the back of the second fly gallery. And then something was coming down, crashing through the scenery." She clamped her teeth down on a fit of shivering.

"Just another question and I'm through," said Torrent. "Did you hear the boy make any sound as he fell?"

"Yes," said Natalia in a whisper. "Once he screamed, I think. I was screaming so hard myself that I couldn't…"

"All right," said Torrent. "That'll be all."

"Wait," said Natalia, leaning forward. "She told me somebody pretended to be Vova. They must have killed him before he let them do that. Who was it?"

"Madam," said Torrent. "I think I can safely assure you that by tonight we will be able to tell you who was responsible for your husband's death."

Izlomin's wife sighed and leaned back, tension flowing out of her body. "You will tell me as soon as you know?" And at Torrent's nod, she slowly closed her eyes.

Torrent eyed with cold dislike the agitated faces that lined the anteroom to de Speranski's office. He was very much annoyed because the result of his questioning was, as he had inwardly predicted, exactly nil. What had made it particularly futile was the fact that two rehearsal rooms were being used at the same time since the company had to rehearse new ballets and at the same time other people had to be trained to take the places of Izlomin and Barezian, claimed, respectively, by the grave and the army. As a result, people were constantly shuffling between the two rooms and there was no pinning them down at any special time.

Nor had the principals in Izlomin's murder anything to contribute by way of information about Slava's death. Vassine and Ffoulkes had gone out in the corridor for a breather. Since they had been together all the time they provided mutual alibis, but under the circumstances Torrent was skeptical about the value of their testimony. Mike had gone down to his dressing room to fetch a new pair of ballet shoes. Torrent had fastened on that because if he had crossed the back fly gallery he might have seen something. But Mike explained that he was no longer using his former dressing room, having moved to the other side of the house with the rest of the men, so that he had no occasion to cross the back gallery but just went straight down. Nobody had kept track of Slava's movements. He had just faded out unobtrusively after having finished his *pas de deux* with Perlova.

And so on down the line. Nothing to answer the questions that were bothering Torrent, one of the most annoying being what Slava Mladov was doing on the second fly gallery when Natalia Izlomina was vainly waiting for him to keep his appointment with her on the stage.

Torrent got up abruptly. The roomful of faces, blank or apprehensive, followed his movements like a lot of sunflowers attending the progress of the sun. But two of them, no, three, returned his look steadily. They knew what was coming.

"Class dismissed," said Torrent brutally. He was tired and there was a hard day's work still ahead of him. "All of you can go, except Mike Gorin, André Vassine and Geoffrey Ffoulkes. The three of you will come with me for further questioning."

CHAPTER SIXTEEN

TONI SAT on the pony-skin-upholstered couch in Charles' apartment and sipped delicately at an amber and potent drink. She had not really wanted to see Graham. What she had wanted was to go home and relax, which was impossible in his presence with her every nerve, every blood vessel aware of him. But apparently she could no more resist seeing him than a child can resist a sweetmeat, even before dinner when it knows it shouldn't.

Charles' eyes glowed with solicitude as he plied her with drinks and asked her questions. Toni could have done very nicely without the latter. On the other hand she was afraid that, with a reasonable amount of drinks and persuasion in Charles' best manner, she could be induced to forget her promise to Eric. So it was lucky, she supposed, that Charles wanted to know exactly what had happened and how Natalia was.

"She was only one of the casualties," Toni told him. "I'll never forget the sight of your friend Mrs. Whitehead keeling over into de Speranski's arms."

But it had been a windfall for de Speranski, who faced Torrent with a dramatic statement that Mrs. Whitehead had been with him every minute, was completely ignorant of the whole affair and should immediately be sent home. Thus he made a spirited bid for his patroness' good graces and at the same time gave them both an alibi.

"That old battle-ax," said Charles unfeelingly. "But how awful for Natalia." He got up leaving his drink unfinished. "I'd better find out how she is. Can't have my favorite lady authoress going on the blink."

He went to his room to telephone and Toni prowled restlessly through the room, looking at the books that lined the walls. There was a sizable section on psychology, she noticed, and remembered with faint amusement Charles telling her about how he had himself psychoanalyzed when his third marriage started going bad. Mr. Graham apparently went to be psychoanalyzed the way other men go to Turkish baths. "My best friends are psychiatrists," he had said with a twinkle, "and I practically consider myself one. You must tell me your dreams sometime."

Charles came back reassured. "She's resting easily," he said and grinned as Toni replaced a book. "Poking among the complexes, eh? I didn't know you were interested."

"Oh, I've read my Henderson and Gillespie. I can tell a hawk from a handsaw and dementia praecox from paranoia," said Toni airily. She gave him a sidelong glance. He looked worried, she thought. Still about Natalia? She remembered unhappily what Eric had said. Charles stood near her, his arm around her shoulders, and his kiss brushed her temple, gentle and somehow distrait.

"That girl has had a lot of trouble," he said. "The shock of losing one's husband in such a ghastly way…"

"Not to mention the still greater shock of thinking him come back from the grave to haunt one," Toni chimed in and was instantly ashamed of herself. She was being nasty about another woman! What could be ailing her?

Charles went on gravely. "You've read the book. You know what sort of life she's led. It's kind of important that nothing more happens to her."

Well, what else can? Toni thought. She said, "Important? To you?"

Charles' eyes seemed to acquire a sort of impenetrable blue glaze. "Yes, I suppose so."

"Are you in love with her?" Toni asked suddenly. Her voice sounded only mildly interested but there was panic in her. I shouldn't have asked. It must be because I'm tired.

"I don't know," said Charles, watching Toni. "Perhaps."

Toni ruffled through the pages of another book. Her lips felt dry. She said idly, "Well, then, why not go ahead and woo and win her? Isn't that the phrase? Without dissipating your energies on the sidelines."

Charles laughed suddenly. "It's all very simple to you, isn't it, darling? It's more complicated than that. The only thing I know is that for some reason it's vitally important for me that she doesn't get hurt. I can't explain why. It ties up with some vague childhood memories or something. She looks like a governess I was in love with at the age of six, a soft-spoken, smooth-haired girl, very much like Natalia. It's all very tenuous really. Nothing like the rather primitive emotion I have for you."

"Oh, you have," said Toni feebly.

"Didn't you know?" said Charles and grinned. "I'm crazy about you. I'm in love with you. So you needn't worry."

The word "love" came so easily to his lips and Toni wondered how much it meant. Yet she felt oddly comforted, even about her shadowy rival. Perhaps he wasn't so cold after all, if he was troubled with those uncertain emotions, mysterious even to himself. Perhaps...

She said lightly, "I'm not worried, darling. I'm starved."

"Darling," said Charles, "how human of you."

Geoffrey Ffoulkes gave Torrent a cold look for look. He said, "You have no actual proof."

"We can show," said Torrent, "that the man who was dancing *Phoebus* was not Izlomin. And we can show that Vassine was in the building that day. Meanwhile all this stalling is giving me other ideas. About Mladov's death. He was ready to spill the works, wasn't he, when he so providentially died?"

Vassine's face puckered up and tears ran down his beardless cheeks. He looked like a miserable little boy.

"Oh God," said Mike and looked away. Torrent regarded the weeping dancer and stroked his chin. He spoke to the two detectives who were leaning against the door. "I'll talk to him alone. Take the others out."

"Jeff!" said Vassine in accents of utter terror. "I can't, Jeff. Don't let them."

But it was Mike who spoke up. "All right, Torrent, we'll talk. The fellows here will correct me if I go off base." He gave a weary grin. "It'll be a relief to get this thing off my chest."

And indeed as he talked, the air of furtive depression that he had worn ever since Izlomin's death lifted. He might have been reporting for a committee in his capacity as shop chairman.

So sure was Toni that Torrent would call her that she insisted on Graham's taking her home early. When he did call, however, he provokingly refused to tell Toni what she wanted to know. He had instead a request to make of her. It seemed that her pocketbook had been found and would she come down as early as possible tomorrow morning and check on its contents.

"I had been wondering what Slava Mladov was looking for on the fly gallery before meeting Mrs. Izlomin downstairs. I told them to turn the place upside down and that's what they found. Incidentally, he was the one who slugged you, all right. The pocketbook was full of his prints."

So Slava had been the threatening presence she had sensed behind her. It made sense, Toni decided. He had been helpfully forewarned of her coming by the message sent to the rehearsal hall by the conscientious Patrick, and he had sneaked out and lain in wait for her. But why?

Toni helpfully offered to come over and look at the pocketbook. "Tomorrow morning will do," Torrent told her. "I still have a little work to do on our friends."

"Then they did…"

"They certainly did," said Torrent grimly. "A very busy little bunch they've been, too." He refused to talk beyond that and presently hung up.

Not long afterward another call came through, this time a long distance call from the wilds of New Jersey. Toni was wondering who it could be—she didn't know anybody in those parts—when a familiar diffident voice greeted her.

"Bill Stone," Toni cried, sitting up straight. "For heavens' sake. Where have you been? Where are you?"

Bill wasn't quite sure. "Must be quite a distance from New York because I had to pay forty cents to get you."

"You're in New Jersey," Toni informed him. "The operator said so. Do you know that I've been trying to get hold of you? Your employers are going mad. You're supposed to hand in some pictures of a mink coat or some such thing…Are you there, Bill?"

The meek and silent presence on the other end of the wire gave an apologetic little cough.

"As a matter of fact," it said mildly, "I was in New York on Saturday evening. But I left almost immediately. I was a little blue, on account of the fire, you know, and I thought different surroundings might give me a lift. It did too. Cows are wonderful animals. So soothing. And photogenic, too, though you'd never think so. Thought I'd let you know where I am in case you want me."

"Wait a minute," said Toni, "what fire?"

Bill explained. He had spent most of Saturday somewhere in Coney Island. He mentioned a girl he'd met who could twist herself into pretzels but was really a good scout and deserved the breaks. He came back to New York at about seven and arrived at his studio just in time to see the tail end of a fire that had inexplicably broken out in his studio. Luckily none of the equipment was damaged. But all the negatives had gone up in smoke.

"Prettiest sight I ever saw—green and red and yellow, like witch fire," said Bill, dismissing in his characteristic way a catastrophe that would have made any other photographer howl like a coyote. Bill did admit to having felt a wee bit discouraged. So he hopped a milk truck run by a guy he knew and was now chasing the blues away by photographing cows on a milk farm. Here the operator demanded more money, and Bill, apparently unable to oblige, hung up with a cheery good-bye.

Toni sat quite still, thinking. Finally she picked up the telephone and called Eric at his hotel. She was beginning to get certain ideas which she wanted to share with him. But she was told that Lieutenant Skeets had checked out during the day, without leaving any address.

"A practical joke gone wrong! My God," said Torrent disgustedly.

He was rereading for the fourth time the transcript of the statement made chiefly by Mike Gorin, but with contributions by André Vassine and Geoffrey Ffoulkes and signed by all three of them. The statement began with Mike's frank admission that he had always thought that Izlomin was a stinker who had taken advantage of his position to lord it over his fellow workers, to hog all the roles and keep artists who were his equals or even betters from getting a chance.

"We always thought it would be a very fine thing if someone could hog his favorite role the way he was always hogging others'. Particularly *Phoebus,* because he really looked forward to dancing that. At first we (Mike was referring to himself, to Vassine and Slava Mladov) just talked about it, then we took to learning his steps—just for fun. Then Vassine had to leave the company and we got to considering getting back at Vova really seriously. Slava even talked about maybe pulling the same trick on him as he had pulled on André. And that's when we thought of getting him out of the way for a little while and substituting someone else for him. It would have been a great blow to his prestige because he was being publicized as unique. And one day Slava came in all excited because he'd been able to spy on Izlomin's private lesson with Daillart and learn the steps of the variation."

Vassine had interrupted here to say scornfully that the vaunted variation wasn't too hard. "It looks good to make God knows how many *entrechats* when you're jumping down from a high place but it's much harder to do a real *entrechat huit*." He added smugly. "Or an *entrechat dix*."

This made their scheme a little more real. Vassine still had in his possession the morphine scopolamine pills the doctor had prescribed for his mother, and they thought of using that for a Mickey Finn. The indefatigable Slava had even gone to the length of getting a new key for the bathroom door connecting their two dressing rooms.

All this was merely in the realm of daydreams as long as Izlomin was attended by his personal dresser. But by this time the game had taken hold of their imaginations and it was fun to figure out every possible facet of the thing. Ffoulkes, who also hated Izlomin, joined in the game and even duplicated Izlomin's *Phoebus* costume for Vassine. But the most they could count on was a little private performance by Vassine, to which most of the company would be invited, to demonstrate that Vassine was much better than Izlomin in the role the latter had created for himself. That was their idea of a *premier danseur*'s revenge.

And then fate played into their hands. Izlomin's valet got ptomaine poisoning and would be unable to attend his master on the opening night. It was a matter of common knowledge that Izlomin never let anybody else touch him. Now they could play their joke on their enemy.

"Jeff was wonderful," Vassine had said naively. "We couldn't have done it without him. He got the costume all fixed up that night and he practiced making me up until I looked just like Vova. And he rehearsed us until we all knew exactly what to do."

The next day, Vassine had visited the Opera House during rehearsal and had stayed in the building until the performance without being noticed. Slava and Mike had come to the Opera House early and smuggled him into their room, hiding him in the closet behind a lot of costumes. The fact that Izlomin followed a very strict routine had made things easy for them. While Izlomin was taking his shower, Slava had sneaked into his room and dissolved the pills in his glass of orange juice.

Presently Ffoulkes had come up from de Speranski's office—a meeting he had arranged in order to have an excuse to be present on the scene—and stayed long enough to make Vassine up. Mike, Slava and Vassine had entered Izlomin's room (using the key Slava had previously procured) to find that the drug had worked. Izlomin was sprawled at his dressing table, out like a light. They lifted him out of the chair and laid him on top of all the costumes in the trunk, where they knew he would remain unconscious for the next hour or so.

Vassine had interposed at this point. "That's when I must have left that fingerprint on Vova's notes." He explained further, exploding a small bombshell as he did. After they had lifted Vova from the dressing table, Vassine, who had slipped into his place, found that Vova had been writing a note which he hadn't finished, probably being overcome by the drug in the midst of writing it. His uncapped fountain pen was lying near by where it had dropped out of his hand. A tidy soul, Vassine had put the note into a drawer where he saw several other similar notes. He didn't read them at the time but later when Torrent had showed one of them to him, he had recognized it. "But I kept quiet, didn't I, Jeff?"

Torrent reread that part and shook his head at himself. This was something he had overlooked—the possibility that Izlomin had written the notes himself. It was perfectly logical, however. Izlomin had good reason to wish not to appear a victim of a persecution mania. He had hit upon the device of writing threatening notes to himself in disguised handwriting. But what could be the danger he had felt? Could he have somehow got wind of his colleagues' crackbrained scheme? Torrent made a note to compare the disguised script with Izlomin's actual handwriting, and returned to the transcript.

Izlomin had been safely stowed away in the trunk and Mike and Slava had gone down to dance in *Aurora's Wedding* when Kate Whitehead knocked on the door. Vassine had been prepared for such an eventuality and acted on his instructions. He was not disturbed after that and just sat around waiting, alone with the unconscious Izlomin who was peacefully sleeping in the trunk. The conspirators had deemed it wise to close the trunk, but they had taken the precaution of wadding the black velvet cape into a ball and stuffing it under the lid to prevent it from closing. Izlomin was lying on top of the costumes that had been piled into the trunk, his face very close to the sizable crack, so that they anticipated no trouble about his getting enough air to breathe.

The ballet went off beautifully. Izlomin's habits and general ill nature had been so well established that nobody spoke to or otherwise bothered the impostor, who was able to make his way to the ramp unmolested. After that all he had to do was dance like an angel, an easy and relaxing task after what he'd been through. And then suddenly the idiotic school-boy prank had backfired and became a tragedy.

Torrent again savored the tension behind the neatly typed pages of the transcript. "I'd just gotten through with my solo when Slava came up to me. The kid was green. He said, 'Something is wrong with Vova. I feel it. Go up and see.' He could say nothing more because he had to go on. I looked for Jeff but he'd already gone up. When I came up, he was just opening the trunk. It had got closed somehow and the lock had snapped to. We looked in the trunk and there he was, stone dead, in the same position we'd left him in. The way it looked he must have moved and pulled at the wad of thick velvet we'd stuck in. It'd worked its way inside and was over his face, with his hand tangled in it. The lid had closed over the single lap of the mantle and the lock had clicked to shutting off all air.

"We just looked at him. Then Jeff looked him over and listened to his heart and took a mirror and pressed it against his lips and there was no breath on the mirror. Then he said, 'We'd better get him out of here.' I guess he sort of took charge. I was so stunned I couldn't think of any-thing. I just did what he told me to do. He went around getting all the fingerprints off all the places he could think of and he washed that glass out. Then we picked Vova up and carried him upstairs. We knew nobody would see us, because everybody was downstairs dancing. We sweated plenty when we passed the first fly gallery but old Gus there was too busy with the lights to notice us. I didn't know then what Jeff had in mind, but when we got to the second fly gallery and dumped Vova there, he sort of listened and said, 'They're finishing below. You've got to go down in time to take your curtain call and warn André. Tell him to go to his room and talk to no one.' So I left him there and went down."

Here Ffoulkes' cool crisp voice had cut in. "You see, we hadn't planned our getaway because we hadn't expected this particular development. André wouldn't have cared if anybody did recognize him while he was taking his curtain calls. But this changed matters."

Torrent had wanted to know why Ffoulkes had stayed behind and Ffoulkes had explained urbanely that he intended to string the body up and fake suicide by hanging. "That seemed like the only solution. Unfortunately I found that I couldn't do it without help. So I had to go down."

Mike, in the meanwhile, had arrived backstage too late to take his bows with the rest of the company. Vassine was on the stage alone, getting his ovation, and he just stood and watched him, ready to get hold of him as soon as he was through. After a while Jeff joined him and explained his idea. The immediate problem for the latter was to create an alibi for himself. This he tried to do by ostentatiously saying good-bye to de Speranski and leaving the stage and, presumably, the building. What he did, of course, was to go to the second fly gallery where he had stored the corpse and wait for reinforcements.

Mike followed his instructions implicitly. He had grabbed the smiling and triumphant Vassine right after the last curtain call and carried him off to the dressing room before anybody could get close enough to him to recognize him. Slava had lost his nerve completely and couldn't be induced to go up and help Ffoulkes. So Mike left him with Vassine and had gone upstairs and...

"Well," Mike had said, twisting his broad shoulder in a queer little gesture of revulsion, "Jeff and I—we hung the body."

Vassine, too, had followed instructions faithfully. He had had to wait in the dressing room with Slava until *Printemps* had started, since that cleared the floor and made it safe for him to venture out. There had been nothing for him to do. He couldn't even change into his own clothes, since he couldn't be seen in his own person. So he was still wearing his Phoebus costume and his makeup when he made his way up to the deserted dressing room on the fifth floor where Ffoulkes was waiting for him.

Torrent read this with glum appreciation. It had been a bold stroke and it had succeeded. As Izlomin, the boy had been safe. Tamara's brief glimpse of him as he was talking to Mike, who had just come down after doing his hangman's stint, had only served to mislead the police. Once upstairs he had removed his makeup and put on his street clothes over his tight-fitting costume, so that no betraying glitter showed. It was a matter of a few minutes for him to get dressed. Then the two of them had stolen downstairs.

"That was the really ticklish part of the business." The statement—or rather the understatement—was Ffoulkes'. "But luckily everybody was getting dressed for the surrealist ballet, which is quite a job. We got downstairs without any mishaps and nobody was hanging around the corridors. André hared it into the little cubicle near the stage entrance where Patrick keeps his togs, and I engaged Patrick in a conversation. For one thing, I persuaded him that this was right after the performance of *Phoebus*—he's rather out of things way out there and is deaf besides. I thought I'd have to pull a stunt like getting faint and sending Patrick for water so's to get the coast clear. But that proved unnecessary. A boy came up bringing flowers, for Perlova, I think, just as I was getting ready to stagger about a bit. Patrick had to take them inside and André popped off and was outside in a second. I followed him immediately."

It was most inconsiderate, Torrent thought, of Slava to kill himself or to get himself killed just at this time. He particularly wanted to know what had made the boy so sure that something was wrong upstairs. The others had ascribed it to intuition and didn't question it. Perhaps, Torrent thought, they had reasons of their own for not pressing the point. Slava may have remembered something, some carelessness that had spelled death for the drugged man in the costume-crammed trunk.

And then there was the matter of Slava's attack on Toni. Why? Because of the information she was going to pass on to Torrent? There were other questions—too many—they buzzed in his brain like so many gnats. He tossed the typewritten pages on the table and yawned. Tomorrow he would deal with them. Tonight he wondered whether the three prisoners were getting any sleep. He doubted it.

But he was wrong. Mike was sleeping the heavy sleep of exhaustion for the first time in five days. André Vassine slept too, as children sleep, leaving the worries to the grown-ups. Only Geoffrey Ffoulkes lay awake, his face gaunt and stony, his eyes straining against the darkness.

CHAPTER SEVENTEEN

WHEN TONI SHOWED up at Torrent's office the next morning, Torrent, clean-shaven and grim, showed no signs of fatigue after his grueling

Sunday. He gave Toni an approving look because she had come early and let her look at the statement. Toni raced through it and turned a troubled face to Torrent. "Pretty bad, isn't it?"

Torrent agreed. "Manslaughter in the second, probably."

"I feel sick about Mike. Just because they wanted to take a crack at Izlomin, who was a louse… After all, it was just an accident, wasn't it? Or do you have your doubts about that, too?"

"We shall see," said Torrent evasively. "Nothing is the way it looks in this screwy case."

"Not even Slava's death? Have you come to any conclusion about that?"

Torrent shrugged his shoulders. "Hard to say. He died of a broken neck sustained as a result of his fall. He was alive when he struck the stage. There are contusions, of course, and it's difficult to say whether he got them as he was falling down or before that. This is one type of death that is impossible to determine. You can't tell whether a guy fell down because he wanted to, because he got dizzy or because he was pushed, unless there are witnesses."

"Then you think…?"

"Either he killed himself because he didn't want to face the music or he was killed because he wanted to spill things. While he didn't strike me as a type that would commit suicide, there's no doubt that he was scared out of his wits." Torrent tossed Toni's pocketbook to her. "I want you to look it over and see if anything is missing."

Presently the top of his desk was littered with articles from Toni's "suitcase." Among them were three lipsticks, a pair of nylon stockings just back from a repair shop, a small bottle of yeast tablets for Tom Jones, five thick copy pencils which Toni adored and stole shamelessly by the dozens from her office and a pamphlet luridly entitled "Repent and ye shall be saved."

Toni wrinkled her nose at it. "Could Slava have put that in? I can't quite see him as a boy evangelist…Oh, I remember now. Columbus Circle. Everything seems to be here," she checked for torn lining, "except—except my keys."

Torrent came over to investigate. "No keys?"

"Nope. I might have lost them myself, of course. I do all the time." She enumerated them—a key to her apartment, to a locker in the Daillart School, to Bill's studio, to her safe deposit box where she kept her War

Bonds, and some trunk keys—and listened to Torrent issue instructions for a search in Slava's rooms.

"The photographs are all here," said Toni, thumbing through them rapidly, "so I guess he wasn't after them." She took a deep breath. "Incidentally, Captain Torrent, do you suppose I could have those enlargements back if you're through with them? I've got to show them to a magazine editor and Bill is away on one of his jaunts and now I can't get into his studio."

She held her breath for the fraction of a second it took Torrent to make up his mind in the affirmative. He didn't seem to get the connection that to her guilty mind seemed to loom as obvious as a mountain.

But then of course she hadn't mentioned the fire in Bill's studio.

"I've got to find out for myself first," said Toni to herself defensively as she left Torrent's office with the enlargements tucked under her arm.

The business of the reconstruction of the crime (after a confession is obtained) is a routine and humdrum one, with everybody very polite and the culprits preternaturally obliging and cooperative. This one was no different. The squad of plainclothes men, with its forlorn nucleus of prisoners, got to work as soon as Torrent came in with the District Attorney. He had stopped for a minute in de Speranski's office to pick up the two Izlomin pictures with their inscriptions for comparison with the threatening notes. As they ranged up and down stairs and corridors retracing the moves made by the prisoners last Wednesday, they might have been a bunch of interior decorators or plumbers or anything else except what they were. And when Mike and one of the detectives (representing Slava Mladov, deceased) put another detective (impersonating Vova Izlomin, also deceased) into a trunk, Mike seemed an unconcerned spectator, lending a hand in good fellowship.

"At this point," said the District Attorney, "you, Vassine, were left alone with the corpse—I mean with the unconscious man." Vassine, perched gracefully on the chair in front of the dressing table, nodded affirmatively. "Now you can't actually swear that Izlomin was not a corpse when you left the room."

"Yes, I can," said Vassine unexpectedly. "Slava had told me to check up and see if he was all right before I went down." He sounded naively righteous about it, like a little boy whose mother had told him to be sure and see that the window was closed before he went out to play and he did.

"Let's see what you did," said Torrent. The boy blinked at him. "Do just what you did that night."

"Oh…" Vassine rose from his chair and went to the door, moving as gracefully as a young panther. Then he veered back. "I'd almost forgotten," he explained smilingly. He approached the trunk, lifted the lid, peered inside, mimed a little gesture of approval. "I saw he was all right," said Vassine, "so I just went on."

He turned away from the trunk looking at Torrent for approval. The latter's face went stony as he saw what was going to happen. The boy's thigh had brushed against the thick wad of velvet that was hanging over the edge of the trunk and pushed it inside, so that the lid slid over the single lap of cloth, closing the trunk. A muffled cry of protest came from inside the trunk, and Vassine spun around.

"Don't move," said Torrent, his voice steely. He went down on his knees to look. The rough fabric had produced enough friction so that a tiny crack still remained. He stared at it, not sure whether it was large enough to let Vassine out of the bad situation he had created for himself.

"He just did it now by accident," said Mike. "It doesn't mean he did it that night."

"I believe I told you," said Ffoulkes, "that the lock of the trunk had snapped to. That isn't the case now, is it? Even though André did let the lid slip—and I am sure he hadn't that night."

Torrent shifted his eyes from Ffoulkes' pale face. "Hadn't you, my boy?" he asked Vassine. "Then perhaps you had better show us what you did do."

Vassine stared at him dumbly, the full significance of what he had done gradually percolating into his somewhat slow-moving brain. You could almost tell to the second when it finally did, as the blood receded from his cheeks and a white line appeared under his enormously dilated pupils, like a scared colt's.

"André," Geoffrey Ffoulkes' voice was gentle, "show them what you did that night. Show them how careful you were." He added softly, "Take it easy, old boy. You're all right."

Vassine let out his breath with a hiss. Silently he went through the same routine. His movements had lost their easy grace. He moved now like a wooden automaton. There was something pathetically unconvincing about the careful way in which he eased the lid down over the wad of black velvet.

Finally he straightened up, seeking and not finding reassurance in the too-bright smile Ffoulkes had pinned on his concerned face. He said in a loud, uncertain voice. "That's how everything was when I left."

"All right, son," said Torrent quietly. "Let's get on." The little procession moved out of the room and the man who had been taking the place of Izlomin popped out of the trunk like a jack-in-the-box, complaining, "Geeze, I don't wanna do that again. I got claustrophobia."

But as it turned out, he did have to do it again. After the reenactment was completed and the prisoners sent back, Torrent returned to the dressing room with the D.A. The victim of claustrophobia unwillingly climbed back into what he mutteringly called a living grave and Torrent and the D.A. practiced slamming the lid on him.

"You see," said Torrent after a few attempts, "as long as any of that velvet is on the edge of the trunk, a tiny crack remains. You'd have to assume that he'd deliberately slammed it down with all his might."

The D.A. shook his head. He was a slight wiry man, who prided himself on being able to make up his mind like that! "But that crack is so tiny," he said. "Would such a small supply of air keep a man alive?"

"You must remember that Izlomin was unconscious and the amount of breathing he did was minimal. There are cases of people buried alive, during the London blitz, and dug up alive, simply because they'd been knocked out and not doing much breathing. I'll get the M.E.'s opinion on that. And then, of course, they claim that Izlomin's hand was clutched in the mantle, indicating that he'd pulled it in."

"Naturally they'd claim that."

"We might as well check on that too. McCloskey!" said Torrent replacing the wadded cape, "I want you to clutch at this stuff and pull it in."

They watched the thick folds move and the wad disappear. The lid came down with a little bump. Torrent bent over it and shook his head. "Same result," he said. "You can't close it completely that way. The only way you can do that is like this." He gave the lid a sharp rap. There was a dull click and the lock snapped to. The man inside the trunk gave a muffled shout and began hammering to be let out.

"Give the gentleman air," said Torrent with a grin, as he accompanied the D.A. out of the room.

The latter said peevishly. "I don't know exactly what you're driving at. As far as I can see, you've given me a good case as it stands. This Vassine could easily have slammed the lid down hard enough without meaning to. He doesn't seem to be too bright. Or," he added thoughtfully, "maybe you're right. Maybe he did slam it down, meaning to."

"That isn't exactly what I—" Torrent began. The D.A. wasn't listening.

"Let's go over the file again. I want to see how it works out from this angle."

"Smoke?" inquired Torrent. He emptied the ashtray into the wastepaper basket before moving it near Ffoulkes. It had been heaped high with cigarette stubs, for Torrent had spent an hour in chain-smoking, ceiling-gazing solitude before he finally had Ffoulkes brought in.

"I wanted to talk the situation over with you before formally charging you," said Torrent, picking his words carefully. "You're the oldest of the three and you would probably understand what is involved better than either of your friends."

Ffoulkes inclined his head in courteous acknowledgment. Torrent went on to explain the possibilities. One was manslaughter in the second for all three of them. But there was another. The D.A. thought he could prove that Vassine was the one directly responsible for Izlomin's death.

"You could be held as accessories, but the D.A. is thinking of concentrating his guns on Vassine."

"What does that mean?" said Ffoulkes. For the first time he looked really terrified.

"Probably murder in the second," said Torrent shortly. Ffoulkes leaped to his feet, his thin hands leaning on Torrent's desk.

"They can't do that. It was an accident. They can't charge the boy with deliberate murder!"

"The D.A. thinks he can play it that way. He even thinks he might be able to get the first degree, but I don't believe so. You see, Vassine's performance earlier today made things look pretty bad. And then there is plenty of evidence that Vassine hated Izlomin's guts. The D.A. is pretty sure he can convince the jury that he closed that trunk deliberately. It might turn out to be a good thing for you and Mike. You see, two parties cannot be tried for the same cause unless acting in concert, and it was Vassine alone who closed the trunk, causing Izlomin's death from suffocation. The two of you might get away with just assault and battery."

"The hell with that," said Ffoulkes savagely. He seemed nowise consoled by the prospect. "André charged with murder! Oh God." He sank into his chair as if his knees had given way. "It's monstrous—monstrous! I never dreamed…"

"One doesn't, does one? But there are always complications." Torrent's voice was odd and Ffoulkes lifted his head out of his interlaced fingers and looked at him.

"You don't believe it's right, do you? To punish André as if he had deliberately…"

"No, I don't. But then, unlike the District Attorney, I don't believe Vassine did this. The trouble is that I can't prove anything. The murderer is damn clever, don't you see."

Ffoulkes threw him a look of wild incredulity.

"But you can't just sit there and let André…Just because you're too incompetent to get the evidence you need! By God, this is fantastic!"

"I'd like to tell you my theory," said Torrent, "since you're concerned by your friend's situation and since, the way things are working out, you mightn't be affected." Ffoulkes' thin face was suddenly convulsed and he gave a short bitter laugh. "You see, I can't quite see Vassine actually closing that trunk. The click it makes is pretty loud and would have turned him back, unless he did have lethal intentions, which also seems unlikely in view of his rather gentle character. The murder was done by a much smarter man, one who could plan quickly and ruthlessly." Torrent lit a cigarette. "I'll tell you what I think, Mr. Ffoulkes. I believe that when you reached the trunk, it wasn't locked."

"Wasn't locked," said Ffoulkes dazedly.

"That's right. And what's more, Izlomin wasn't dead, only in a deep coma induced by the drug and the lack of air."

"But he was dead, I tell you. There was no life in him. And the trunk was locked. Ask Mike, he saw it."

"I'm not talking about what Mike saw. You got there before Mike did, didn't you, Mr. Ffoulkes?" Torrent held up his hand smiling. "Let me rave a little longer. Merely speculating, as it were. You said he was dead, but you were mistaken, and Mike was too upset to check up. You got Izlomin to the second fly gallery without rousing him from his stupor but my profound conviction is that he was still alive then."

"But you yourself said that he was already dead when we hung him. The doctor's report…"

"Right. He was dead all right when you hung him. But there was plenty of time to take care of that. You're about to ask who. Well, you had the opportunity yourself. You sent Mike down ahead of you, didn't you?"

Ffoulkes stared at him for a long while. "You're mad," he said finally. "What motive have I for doing something so incredibly stupid?"

Torrent took a deep draw on his cigarette. "More speculation. You had another friend of whom you were very fond, as fond as you are of young Vassine, and Izlomin was responsible for his death."

"So you know that," said Ffoulkes softly and his gray eyes filmed over with a shadow.

Torrent went on. "As I told you, Mr. Ffoulkes, this is merely a lot of theorizing on my part. Right now you're in no danger. But I do hold it my duty to tell you that I'll try my damnedest to get enough evidence on you in time to save your friend from a life sentence or worse. That'll be all." He tilted his chair to an upright position and stubbed out his cigarette. The interview was over.

Ffoulkes didn't move from his chair. He seemed to be in the grip of a rending struggle. Finally he drew a deep breath and smiled at Torrent.

"You win," he said. "How could I suspect that you would be so clever?"

"That's right," said Torrent with a certain degree of complacency. "I didn't have a thing on him. But he'd maneuvered himself into a spot where he could remain safe only at the expense of Vassine, and he didn't want to do that."

The time was late in the afternoon and the listeners were Toni and Eric, somewhat reserved as to each other and, conversely, warm and admiring toward Torrent, who was wolfing down a belated meal in their company.

"From the very beginning I had that sense of expert stage management. It was Ffoulkes who supplied the props and made up the star and coached the other actors. He even prompted them when things went wrong. It made me wonder…"

"Then you think," Eric said, "that he had worked it all out beforehand?"

"No, not exactly. He played around with the idea, the way all of them played around with the idea of impersonation. And when he went up to check on Slava's hunch, the temptation to put it into operation was irresistible. He hated Izlomin so thoroughly, don't you know. I think Mike intercepted him just as he closed the trunk and then he sold Mike the idea of Izlomin being suffocated by accident. Mike believed everything he told him. He had a great respect for his friend Jeff."

"But to take such a chance..." said Toni.

"Well, he figured that having involved his friends in a murder for which all of them considered themselves responsible, they'd keep quiet about the prank. That way Vassine was safe because there was no way of tying him up with the mishap. And with Izlomin's background, there was a good chance of the suicide theory being adopted."

"What made you pick on him?"

"Elimination. The closing of the lock made it look deliberate. It had to be done by someone who knew that Izlomin was in the trunk. It was out of character for Vassine to do it, the D.A. notwithstanding. Slava never got upstairs. He tried to but was held back by de Speranski. Mike got to the dressing room after Ffoulkes had been there some time. That left Ffoulkes. And there was only one way for him to do it."

"Couldn't somebody else have slammed the trunk accidentally?"

"Two reasons against it. Nobody admitted to even being near it, I mean at the time when the sinister role it played was unknown. And then, during the time *Phoebus* was being danced, everybody was busy every minute, either on stage or getting ready to go on. Their absence would have been noticed, as Mike's was."

Eric thought it over. "Still, I keep thinking that you've got a very flimsy case. If Ffoulkes had chosen to keep quiet—"

"But he didn't, you know, said Torrent. "He confessed."

"To save poor dopey André Vassine. It makes me feel sick, somehow." Toni sighed. "I had my own candidate all picked out..."

"Who?"

"Slava Mladov. He knew that something was wrong because he was the one who made it so. And he killed himself because he couldn't stand the gaff."

Torrent smiled at her indulgently. "You're just saying that because you don't like to see the living suffer, isn't that it?"

Eric snorted and remarked acidly that he personally had never noticed in Toni any disinclination to see the living suffer.

The dinner over, the three participants scattered in all directions. Torrent went back to his office to tie up loose ends, and Toni to the Opera House to see a rehearsal. As for Lieutenant Skeets, he didn't say where he was going and Toni didn't ask him. When beautiful friendships start to disintegrate, they go fast.

The American Ballet Drama Company was suffering from a bad case of jitters. At first finding itself with all its *premiers danseurs* in *durance vile*, it had to fall back on predominantly feminine ballets like *Giselle* and *Les Sylphides*. De Speranski, sounding like the coach of a flu-ridden football team, sweated over a new lineup (Shishkin for Vassine, Damian for Mladov, Gray for Gorin). Then Vassine and Mike were released, not without an ominous hint from the D.A. that they might be pulled in again if they proved uncooperative about testifying against Ffoulkes, and the company switched back to its original program and was now frantically rehearsing *Coppelia*.

The piano tinkled bravely in one of the Opera House's rehearsal halls and Vassine went through a dispirited *pas de deux*, with Perlova as Swanilda. He moved woodenly, like an unskillfully manipulated puppet, his arms stiff and his eyes vacant.

"André," said Samarkand wearily, "this is supposed to have life, romance. The last two bars, please." He pranced spiritedly through the steps with Perlova drifting into his arms like a silk scarf coming to rest. "See?"

Vassine shied at being addressed and burst into nervous tears.

"Oh God," said Mike. "Again." He turned to Toni with a ghastly little grin. "He's been crying all the time, poor little bastard."

"Poor André," said Tamara softly. She sounded dutifully sympathetic but somehow she couldn't force her pretty face into the proper lineaments of woe. Her lips curved upwards irresistibly and she kept nestling close to Mike, nuzzling her dark smooth head against his shoulder. In her dark practice clothes she resembled nothing so much as a black kitten that had got her saucer of cream and didn't care about anything else. Mike was back, unscathed. All was well.

The dancers crowded around Vassine, cooing concernedly. "Leave him alone, Paul," said Perlova to the *regisseur*. "He'll be all right tonight."

Samarkand's eyes crossed wildly as if begging each other for sympathy. "Very well. The *czardas*, please. Gorin, Ribina."

Tamara and Mike had just taken their places at the head of the corps de ballet when the door was flung open and Mrs. Whitehead strode in, a pale and distracted de Speranski at her heels.

She stopped in the middle of the room and included the entire company in a single basiliscan glare. Her voice rang out harshly in the scared silence.

"There's no room for goddamn murderers in this company. Not for that Irish hoodlum over there and not for that sniveling little fool, who belongs in jail with his murdering friend." She strode over to the shrinking Vassine and shook him by the shoulder. "So your boyfriend wanted to build you up and couldn't do it any other way except by getting rid of Vova. Well, by God, after I'm through with you, you won't dance anywhere."

"Leave him alone, said Mike, his broad chest rising and falling. "It's dirty business to kick a man after he's down."

Vassine got up and shuffled toward the door. There he turned and spoke, haltingly but with dignity. "Jeff never did it. If he had I'd have known. I'm not very bright but I'd have known. He just said he did because of me and now there's nothing I can do." His liquid black eyes were bright with pain. "As for dancing I don't ever want to dance again—never again if Jeff…" He walked out blindly and Mike whirled on Mrs. Whitehead.

"I'll get out, but I want you to get this straight first. I'm not sorry about doing what we did, though I certainly didn't want it to turn out this way. Vova had it coming to him. He was a stinker and a bully and it would have taught him a lesson. It's all your fault anyhow," Mike roared, warming up. "If you hadn't fallen for him and hadn't pampered him like an old fool, this would never have happened!"

"Gorin!" De Speranski screamed in a voice as shrill as a whistle with sheer horror. Mike ignored him. Later he might recall this moment with dismay but right now it had all the plunging ecstasy of a toboggan ride down an alp.

"He's been playing you for a sucker, only you didn't have the sense to see it. Dear Vova," Mike mimicked savagely. He shook a finger in Mrs. Whitehead's astonished face. "And don't you be smearing me or André by calling us murderers. We'd be in jail if we were. We're no more responsible than a guy that knocked another guy cold and then somebody else came along and cut this other guy's throat. As for dancing for you—you can tear up my contract and be damned to you. I'd be better off in the army than dancing my legs off for a fliggertigibbet old fool like yourself."

Slam! Another exit. Toni wanted badly to applaud.

"Mike! Oh Mike," Tamara screamed and burst into tears. A sympathetic groan rose around her and Samarkand inquired with a ghastly smile, "Well, what are we going to dance tonight? Do we change back again?"

"Change back again!" Perlova screamed. "Changes, changes, changes, every hour, changes. I can't stand it. No, no, no!" She threw her arms around the weeping Tamara and had hysterics.

It might have been a signal. The company, which had been rehearsing steadily since morning and had been shuttled from one ballet to another, suddenly cracked and dissolved in tears and laments.

Kate Whitehead had been staring at the door which Mike had slammed, with a peculiar expression on her hatchet face. She now started and said helplessly, "Oh for God's sake," and hastened to leave on the crest of mounting hysteria.

"Dzere's an old Russian proverb, by King Solomon," said de Speranski, " 'everything passes.' One must remember dzat at moments like dzis!" He tugged at his beard with such violence that a hunk of it came out, and followed Mrs. Whitehead, still clutching it in his palsied hand.

Late that evening, Captain Andrew Torrent, still in his office, began to run into complications. There was, for example, the report that had been forwarded to his office from one of the precincts. It dealt with the matter of a fire in the photographic studio rented by William Stone. One of the tenants on the same floor had seen a slender red-haired youth going into the studio only a little while before the fire broke out. Later the same man came across the pictures of Slava Mladov in the Monday papers, and was much struck by the resemblance to the visitor, eventually giving a positive identification.

Torrent's sandy brows drew together as he studied this piece of intelligence. The prowler had used a key, he noticed, and remembered Toni's lost keys. He called up Bill Stone and to his mild surprise found him home, just back from a milk farm, as he blithely explained.

A few minutes later he hung up with a definite impression that something peculiar was going on and that it had something to do with pictures. He gathered in his mind all the facts about pictures.

Toni had wanted Bill's photographs on Saturday and couldn't get them. She was slugged that same Saturday, but the pictures she did have with her were not taken out of her pocketbook, so that obviously they hadn't been what Slava wanted. Now Bill hadn't been so lucky. His photographs and negatives had gone up in smoke. It looked as though Slava had attacked Toni, abstracted the keys and used them to get into Bill's studio and burn all the negatives. He wasn't interested in the photographs Toni had with her. He must have been interested in those she didn't have with her. It stood to reason that he must have wanted a picture taken by Bill Stone on Wednesday night. And wanted it badly.

Torrent wondered whether Toni had gone through the same train of thought before she had asked him so ingenuously to return the enlargements. He rather suspected she had. A telephone call failed to reach her and he decided that it could wait until tomorrow. He was just putting on his coat when his telephone rang again.

"Mr. Harris wants to speak to you." Torrent sighed and settled down to a long talk. The handwriting expert was a long-winded conversationalist. Moreover, Torrent expected nothing new from him. But this time something he said arrested him.

"When you speak of forgery," said Torrent, correcting what he thought to be a slip of the tongue, "you mean 'disguised handwriting.' And you are referring to the threatening letter that Izlomin wrote to himself, the one beginning '*Prenez garde…*'"

The telephone croaked an emphatic negative. It went on to amplify and Torrent sat up bolt upright as if a current of electricity had been shot through the receiver into his unsuspecting ear. There was a look of wild incredulity on his face.

"Oh, *mon Dieu*," said Perlova peevishly. Her face shone with cold cream and an impatient foot in an old toe shoe tapped on the floor. She hated to be seen in undress but Torrent had been firm though polite. "All this fuss about—I don't even know what to call it."

"Isn't it true," Torrent persisted, "that Izlomin, far from trying to have an affair with you, as you had stated, avoided you and even tried to ease you out of the company?"

Perlova slammed the jar of cold cream down and glared. "I can tell you that better men than Vova have tried to make love to me. Besides, he knew that it was no use. I was too much interested in my Kotik. My poor Kotik. Where is he now? Where have they taken him? War is a cruel thing, Captain Torrent." Her large blue eyes filled with tears. "If not for war, he would be here to protect me from such insinuations, that I am not good enough for a *salaud* like Izlomin, God rest his soul."

"Madam," said Torrent in desperation, "please believe that I have no desire to inflict any humiliation on you. As a matter of fact, I can't imagine any man in his right mind not wanting to have an affair with you and I can assure you that there must have been a very discreditable reason for Izlomin's—er—abstinence. But I do have to check on it. You and Izlomin were—well—intimate in Paris, and Izlomin didn't even try here?"

Perlova gave him a long and thoughtful look. "That is true," she said, evidently satisfied as to his attitude, "what you have said. I have tried to be nice to Vova when he first came, just to make him feel at home, but it is true, he was quite stand off. Very different from Paris, I assure you. I have some letters that were very…I'll show them to you. Anyhow, here he was very careful to act as if there had never been nothing. Perhaps he was afraid to hurt his chances with Mrs. Whitehead." She flashed a smile of feline malice. "He wasn't so careful about people who didn't know him half as well. He let de Speranski go around saying that he had been a very close friend and adviser."

"And that wasn't true?"

"But no, not at all. You remember that picture de Speranski keeps in his office?" Torrent nodded grimly. After what he had been told, he had good reason to remember it. "I happen to know that Vova had meant it for somebody else and not de Speranski. De Speranski had got hold of it and claimed it meant him. And Vova let him, because he needed de Speranski here in America. In Paris, de Speranski was glad when he could get within ten feet of Vova."

Torrent thanked her fervently. To his great surprise he found himself kissing the narrow hand that was extended to him, in a true continental manner. But its owner had given him some useful information—and the hand was very pretty.

CHAPTER EIGHTEEN

TONI THREW DOWN the Tuesday morning paper in which she had just read about the latest development in the "Ballet Murder," that is, the fact that Geoffrey Ffoulkes had been brought before a magistrate and charged with murder in the first degree. A tiny voice said deep inside her, "Now it's up to you."

She called Tom Jones, her voice loud and cheerful enough to drown out the other, and engaged in a prolonged romp with him. Cleo, who at first sat apart with an aloof and slightly scornful expression, as if to say, "such childishness," gave up and joined in the fun.

"Why," said Toni, grabbing her after a long chase, "you aren't such a femme fatale after all. You're just a little more than a kitten, aren't you, for all those airs? I'll miss you when I have to give you back. And that'll be pretty soon, because you've taken to biffing Tom Jones again now that you don't need him."

Cleo hung from her hands, limp and boneless, and purred. Toni put her down and Cleo walked to the icebox and stamped an imperious foot. She wanted her vitamin tablets for which she had an unholy passion. Tom Jones, who had to have his yeast tablets either crammed down his throat or craftily smuggled into his system in powdered form in his meat, watched her munching them with incredulous horror.

Toni went back to her breakfast and paper. She turned to the theater section, to the review of last night's ballet.

" 'Mikhail Gorin,' " she read, " 'was in exceptional form all during the arduous program where he had to take the place of André Vassine, who was prevented from dancing by indisposition. His customary virile and sturdy style brought him hearty applause.'

"What the hell goes on?" said Toni, remembering last night. For a moment she wondered crazily whether another impersonation had been pulled on the unsuspecting audience and critics. But her suspicions were dispelled by a breathless telephone call from Tamara.

It seemed that last night Kate Whitehead had caught hold of Mike just as he was shaking the dust of the American Ballet Drama forever from his feet. She had agreed, incredibly, that she had probably been an old fool, and at any rate had spoken hastily, and she asked Mike to forgive and forget and dance.

"I don't believe it," said Toni blankly.

"But it is true!" Tamara giggled. "She did all the talking and that was lucky because by that time Mike had cooled down and was scared. He'd never talked to an older woman like that before. But she didn't mind. She said she liked his spirit. So they shook hands, and Mike danced. And I thought you'd like to know that we're going to get married as soon as Mike gets a marriage license."

"How wonderful," said Toni. "Congratulations and all that. How come you suddenly decided?"

"Well, I thought we'd better. On account of Mrs. Whitehead. Ladies her age get funny ideas, you know," said Tamara sagely. "The way she looked at Mike I thought maybe she thought he'll take Vova's place. This way she'll know from the start that it's no use. Besides, Mike's sure to be called into the army soon, so maybe I'll be a war bride like Perlova."

Toni again said she was delighted and asked about Vassine. Apparently in the first flush of her conversion Mrs. Whitehead was even willing to let him dance. But Vassine had gone completely to pieces. "Like Petrouchka after the Moor kills him and he becomes a rag doll," said Tamara with unexpected insight.

The picture came to haunt Toni with implacable vividness, hovering in front of her breakfast table like a dumb ghost at a banquet.

"There's just one thing I have to do," Toni apologized to it. "I've got to be pretty sure."

At the Forty-second Street Library, the information clerk who passes on the call slips cocked his cultured head and gave Toni a mistrustful look.

"Are you a college student? Because, if so, you can get these books in your college library." Toni replying in the negative, he said dubiously, "Well, this certainly looks like a reading list for a psychology course…"

A couple of hours later Toni, back home again, called Charles Graham at his office. "I'd like to show you Bill's pictures," she said. "Yes, I got them after all. There's one in particular you've got to see…Tonight, then." She felt strangely weary when she hung up, as if she had walked a long way, though actually she had only taken the first and for her the hardest step. She knew that after she had her little talk, something else would be over.

She turned on the radio and an earnest voice out of a soap opera said, "Love isn't everything, Ellen. There are more important things—such as integrity."

"Aarrgh," said Toni and shut it off. She prowled restlessly around the room, Tom Jones and Cleo frisking playfully at her heels.

"You wait," she told Tom Jones balefully, "Tomorrow your little playmate will be gone, then you'll be sorry you've been so unsympathetic. You can console yourself with your integrity then, only you don't even have

much of that. I know who swiped that piece of roast chicken I left on the
table last night."

Tom Jones winked a round amber eye and gnawed at her ankle gently. Toni petted him unhappily. But perhaps I'm all wrong—seeing things
that don't exist. What I read in the library didn't make sense. Perhaps
somebody seeing it from outside will show me how impossible—she shook
her head. No, she knew only too well that she was right. She had gone
over everything time after time, just as she had gone over that picture with
a magnifying glass, and it added up to the same thing.

She went over the whole thing again as she filled the bathtub and
plunked in an extra handful of bubble powder. Toni always took a bath
when she was troubled in spirit. To a psychiatrist it would probably be a
dead giveaway of something discreditable, at best a wish to return to the
womb. "Well, said Toni grimly, climbing into a fragrant and frothy bath,
"that's exactly where I wish I were."

The white bubbles whispered and broke around her in frothy peaks.
Cleo batted at them with a curious black paw. She was sitting on the edge
of the bathtub, her black tail dragging in the water. She didn't share Tom
Jones' wild fear of water, that made his infrequent washings a nightmare
to him and Toni both.

"You silly cat," said Toni. She lay back and felt the tension soaking out
of her.

The first sign she had of anything wrong was the reaction of the two
cats. They had turned their heads simultaneously in the direction of the
door, their ears down. Then both of them streaked out to investigate.

"What in the world—" said Toni and didn't finish. She suddenly felt
cold among all the whispering bubbles.

"Hello there," said Natalia Izlomina, smiling, as she came into the
bathroom. She looked very chic in a beautifully cut black suit, a demure
black Quaker hat with a veil sitting on her smooth brown hair with just a
tiny suggestion of pertness. She wore black pumps and stockings ("Ny-
lons," Toni thought, with an incongruous twinge of envy) and her small
hands, gloved in black suede, were tucked into her muff. There was no
effect of mourning in spite of all this blackness. Perhaps it was the gardenias at her throat and in her muff. Her round face was rosy and her thin
mobile lips were but slightly touched with the palest coral.

"Sweet, isn't it?" said Natalia, catching Toni's glance at the gardenias.
"Charles sent out for them when I came to his office. So nice of him."

So that's it, Toni thought. She was there when I called. She must have listened in somehow, perhaps on an extension wire in the next room, and overheard.

"I got an impression," Natalia went on smoothly, "that we ought to have a talk, so I came up. The door was open, so I walked in."

Like hell you did, Toni said silently. You used the key to my apartment that Slava had stolen out of my pocketbook. And it was more than an impression that you got from eavesdropping on me and Charles. *You knew.*

"Dear me," said Natalia, settling herself primly on the hamper, "what a silent little girl you are. I hope you don't mind my walking in like that. Women with bodies as pretty as yours need not be ashamed to be seen in the nude. Besides, you're very well covered. You mustn't mind me."

"What do you want?" Toni asked. There was a thick lump of terror in her throat and her voice came past it shrilly. It was like the time she swam out too far and suddenly knew that she wouldn't be able to swim back.

Natalia's eyes were hard, like two pebbles. "I want that picture."

"The one," said Toni, "where you aren't."

"How long have you known about it?"

Toni gave a difficult little smile. "I was sure after I found out that Slava had burned the negatives in Bill's studio."

"That's what I thought. That was his idea, you know. I thought the best thing would be not to call attention to it. But when he heard you making the appointment with Charles at the funeral and then you came up to the Opera House and nobody was around—that looked like too good an opportunity. He was a little fool." Natalia's voice was gentle and cold. "But it didn't really matter. You began to suspect when I fainted, I think. I saw you watching me when I came to and I knew that I must have said something stupid."

"It wasn't anything you said," Toni assured her. "It was just the way you acted, like Lady Macbeth."

"I had a shock," said Natalia simply and Toni swallowed a gulp of nervous laughter at the understatement. ("Not to mention the still greater shock of thinking that one's husband had come back from his grave to haunt one…"—when had she said that?) But there was really nothing to laugh at. She had to do something—scream, somehow overwhelm this soft-spoken, dangerous woman.

And then Natalia smiled, a horrible, intimate smile as if she had crept into Toni's brain and could read her thoughts. Her hand stole out of the elegant little muff with the gardenia pinned on it and there was a tiny elegant toy of a revolver in her hand. Toni watched fascinated as she took a towel off the rack and wrapped it around the revolver.

"To deaden the noise, you know," Natalia explained softly, "if I have to shoot. Now, my dear, where do you keep that picture?"

Toni's mind whirred like a stalled machine as she answered mechanically and truthfully. Could it be that Natalia merely wanted to destroy the picture, that she would do away with the proof and let the witness live?

Natalia's next act puzzled her. She moved to the sink and poured some water into a glass with her free hand. Then her hand went into the muff again and took out a little bottle with pills.

"Slava slipped this into my purse when your policeman friend allowed me to go that night Vova died," she said chattily, spilling them into the glass and pounding at them with the handle of Toni's toothbrush to make them melt more quickly. She held the glass to Toni's lips. "Drink this."

Toni shook her head. "No," she managed through stiff lips.

"Drink this," said Natalia quietly. She might have been a nurse coaxing a recalcitrant patient. "It won't kill you. It'll merely put you to sleep for a long time and give me time to make arrangements."

Toni strained away. Her elbow struck the bottle of bubble powder on the edge of the bathtub and it fell in with a small tinkling sound. Both of them started and forgot about it immediately.

"If you won't drink it, I'll shoot you, " said Natalia. "It's more of a chance but I'll take it."

Toni drank it, in the same spirit as a man who walks through a crowded hotel lobby with a gun in his ribs. All this stuff about disarming an opponent with a gun is all very well, she reflected grimly, but not in a soapy slippery bathtub. She tried to swallow as little as possible, letting most of the stuff dribble untidily down her chin. As she sank back her hand found and held the small bottle that had slipped into the tub.

Natalia again seated herself on the hamper. Toni could see her own reflection in the mirrored door—a girl out of a beauty salon ad, in a cluster of white soap bubbles, now going a little flat—a girl with dark hair piled high on a small shapely head, with huge scared eyes in a pale triangle of a face.

That's me, she thought curiously. And in an hour what will I be? For she knew that Natalia's "arrangements" were merely a euphemism. If she'd swallowed enough of the drug, in spite of her precautions, she'd fall asleep and be pulled down and drowned. And if she hadn't swallowed enough, she'd be shot.

Her heart began to beat in heavy thuds that made the water shiver. Talk to her, distract her attention before it's too late.

She said to the patient watcher, "But why did you kill Vova?"

Natalia's smile was ironic. "Haven't you figured that out? I thought you knew everything."

"No, not everything. It has something to do with his madness, hasn't it? It wasn't the brand you claimed—it was something worse?"

Natalia smiled but said nothing. She just sat there, chic and alert, and watched Toni and minutes ticked by.

Eric might have called, Toni thought with an illogical but bitter sense of injury. He'll be sorry…He who never hesitated to call her in the middle of the night and wake her out of a sound sleep…Her mind slid away from the word…Reposing in the arms of Murphy…Can't the telephone ring?

But the diversion she was looking for came from Cleo, who looked at the visitor with a calculating yellow eye and sank her claws into her leg. Natalia winced and her eyes grew angry. She kicked at the cat viciously. Cleo let out a pitiful startled howl as she hurtled out of the bathroom.

"You mean bitch," said Toni through her teeth, and hurled the bubble powder bottle into her face. It was a good accurate throw, but like most dancers Natalia had good fast reflexes. She drew her head back like a snake and the missile merely grazed her face, breaking against the wall. Toni, surging out of the water like Venus from the waves, only faster, slipped and sat down again with a mighty splash.

"Very well," said Natalia. "It didn't work. Be quiet now."

She no longer looked chic. There was a scratch on her face and her black suit was splotched with water. Toni noticed with satisfaction that her nylon stocking had a long run in it. She heard Cleo meowing pitifully outside and shivered with hatred. Tom Jones appeared in the doorway. He hissed and withdrew to a distance where he sat, intoning the deep ululating chant of an angry cat.

Natalia threw a calculating look at Toni and leaned forward to let more hot water run into the bath. A warm bath is more conducive to sleep, Toni guessed. And suddenly she gave in, as if the homely little action had drained the resistance out of her. Natalia must have dosed the drink to capacity. The little she had swallowed was already beginning to work.

She said, in a feeble attempt to fight off lethargy, "You won't get away with this."

Natalia shrugged her shoulders. It was the first Gallic gesture that Toni had seen her use. "They can only hang you once. After one has killed twice—no, three times—one doesn't mind killing again. And without you pointing to me, there is a very good chance that I won't even be suspected."

Twice? Three times? Then she had killed Slava, too. But how? And whom else?

She didn't ask these questions aloud, but after a while Natalia started to speak, as if she sensed that she needn't watch Toni so carefully any longer.

"No," she said reflectively, "the man you knew as my husband was never crazy. That wasn't why I had to kill him."

She went on and on. The voice became a drone that swelled and ebbed in Toni's ears and soon she stopped listening. Her eyelids weighed a hundred pounds each. She tried to keep them open and they dropped, as if hung on defective hinges. Her chin slipped into the water and that woke her up with a faint shock of terror. She dragged her arm across the edge of the bathtub and dropped her head on it. The wet flesh of her arm felt strange to her cheek, something alien, not belonging to her at all. Her body hung in the watery space like a pale weed…

The black figure across the way swelled, enormous, with a big white face and a rapidly moving mouth—then it shrank until it was no bigger than Cleo. Of course—Cleo—silly cat dragging tail in water—might fall in—and—drown—like—Ophelia—with weeds—and—wreaths—and…

CHAPTER NINETEEN

…OF HER BONEs are coral made,
  Those are pearls that were her eyes…
  …suffer a sea change
  Into something rich and strange…
  But I don't want to—air, air…She struggled upward through the sea green water that swirled around her and broke the surface, screaming.

"All right, darling," said a voice she knew. "You're all right. You're not drowning…Eric's here. Eric won't let you drown."

She clung to him, gasping and whimpering. His khaki shirt was so beautifully rough against her cheek and his arms were a tight hurting ring of steel, lifting her safely out of the nightmare.

"Take it easy, baby," said Eric. He added with a faint chuckle, "A Shakespearean scholar yet."

"Oh Eric," said Toni with a shuddering laugh. She was never so glad to see anybody. She rubbed her cheek against his, savoring its warm touch, and kissed him with abandon. She knew she was being hysterical and didn't care. "Oh, Eric, I am alive, aren't I? And not a cold clammy corpse?"

"Don't be silly. Would I be hugging a corpse? What do you think I am—Mad Joanna? Drink that coffee."

Another voice spoke up as she was gulping down the scalding brown liquid. "Hey, Lieut, if she's okay, about that information the chief wanted?"

Toni sat up and looked around. She was on her own bed, decently though not attractively clad in her oldest dressing gown, ordinarily used by Tom Jones for his siestas, and Mahoney was sitting alertly in the chair opposite her with his notebook ready.

He tipped his hat to her formally and said, "Hello, Miss Ney."

Toni said fervently, "How lovely to see you. Are my cats all right? That woman…"

Eric reassured her. He added, "Torrent wants the dope that the Izlomin woman was after. It'll save him time. Something about a picture, isn't it? If you're not up to it, I'll tell them to go to hell."

"I can do it," said Toni briefly. She reached toward her night table and got out the large manila envelope with the pictures. She ruffled among them swiftly and drew out the one she wanted. It was the one with which Bill had amused the kids at Daillart's a few days ago.

"I don't get it," said Eric, frowning at it. "Just a group picture of veiled figures—the mists, aren't they? What's in it anyhow?"

"She *isn't,*" said Toni. "Look, there are all of them in a semicircle— all in the same position, arms outstretched, right feet pointed toward the audience. That's the moment the cymbals crash and they are frozen in that position for a minute before they begin running again. Well, she isn't among them. If Torrent'll check up, he'll see that there is one missing."

Eric scratched his dark pate. "Is that all? How do you know that she's the one?"

"Because of a little piece of sartorial advice I gave her. She had sprained her right ankle and had to wear a bandage. That would have looked bad for her next number, in which she was supposed to prance around as the queen of the Scyths. I suggested that she wear large barbaric bracelets around the bad ankle and she took my advice. Nobody else wore anything like that. As a matter of fact, you can identify all of those people, veiled as they are." She told him of Bill's playful sallies about that. "He was doing pretty well, with everybody entering into the spirit of the thing and helping him. It must have scared Natalia plenty when she heard about it. And it scared her little protégé Slava, who was there at the time, even more. That's why he felt he had to slug me."

"The little woman who wasn't there," said Eric. "Presumably she was up in the dressing room putting the lid on old Izlomin."

"That's right. That part of the ballet was the only time she could slip away. It was a mob scene, sort of, and one of the mob missing wouldn't be noticed, since they all wore those veils and had no special pattern to follow except that Indian snake dance effect. And it was so dark backstage that she could easily slip back again from among the trunks and packing cases that litter the floor, and mingle with the dancers when they were throwing off their shrouds to emerge as Greeks or Ethiops or what have you. I was backstage when some of them came down in those mist costumes and I noticed even then how they sort of melted into shadows. That's all about that picture."

Mahoney took the picture and bore it away reverently, saying as he went, "The chief'll be here to see you this evening."

"You'll have an earful for him," said Eric. Toni nodded, her eyes darkening with the memory.

"It's not only her husband," she said. "Slava, too, though I don't know how."

"Yes, we heard," said Eric. "We were right there, Mahoney and I." He grinned at her amazed face and explained.

He'd been feeling uneasy about her ever since she had been attacked and decided to keep an eye on her. So he had rented the one-room apartment next to hers, in strict secrecy. After Ffoulkes had confessed, he thought his job was over and he was ready to move out. And then this morning Torrent called him and asked him to stick around. He had a shrewd suspicion that Toni was keeping something from him and, outside of being pretty sore, he was worried about her. So Eric hung around, waiting for reinforcements. He heard Toni come back from the library, and an hour later heard the advent of her visitor. The unorthodox method of the latter's entry made him uneasy and he had tried to eavesdrop. Mahoney found him with his ear to the keyhole. First the two of them heard nothing. Then there came a yeowl from Cleo followed by the indignant noises made by Tom Jones. "I knew something was wrong then, because I couldn't hear you soothing your cats' ruffled feelings. I was all for breaking in. But Mahoney thought he'd better use a gadget he had for opening locked doors—very quiet and probably strictly unconstitutional. We came in without being heard. There was just the sound of running water and for a minute I felt extremely silly."

"That was when she was warming my bath in order to relax my nerves. Ugh!"

"You didn't keep up your end of the conversation, but we found your guest a most stimulating talker. Pretty soon she started moving about in the bathroom and we walked in to find her grabbing you by the ankles preparatory to dunking you. When she saw us, she dropped you and took a potshot at us—doubtless irritated at our intrusion into a strictly feminine *tête-à-tête*. She missed and we disarmed her and I fished you out." Eric sighed. "You looked awful pretty—all slim and white and drowsy. A sleeping mermaid. But you scared me into fits and I gibbered and squeaked like a Roman ghost on the ides of March until the doctor came and said to let you sleep it off. Then Torrent dropped in with some friends to take a look at you and take your girlfriend away."

"I hope everybody had a good time."

Eric grinned. "Oh, Mahoney had you bundled up by then. Said to tell you he's a family man and you shouldn't mind because he's got a daughter your age who's even skinnier than you. Then we waited for you to wake up. I stayed around because I had an idea you'd be scared when you came to."

Two small tears suddenly crawled down Toni's cheek.

"Don't," said Eric. "Gosh, I've never seen you do that before. You must have been in a stew all right."

"It's not that," Toni mumbled. "It's you. You've been so good—watching over me—and saving my life—and everything—and I've spoiled your leave for you."

"Never mind that," said Eric gently. He bent down to kiss her and Toni was conscious of an unexpected thrill of pleasure. Nothing like being saved from a watery grave to make you appreciate a good man's kisses, she reflected.

"Why don't you try to sleep, dear?" he asked.

"Sleep," Toni shuddered. "I'll never sleep again. Unless—well, if you wouldn't mind holding my hand for a while."

She was asleep in five minutes, holding on to Eric's hand.

That was her last glimpse of Eric. When she awoke again, she found that he had folded his tents and silently stolen away, leaving a brief note about being called back to camp and not wishing to disturb her slumbers.

Her love life had certainly gone sour, Toni thought. Eric was gone. And she knew what the sight of her in the witness box helping to convict Natalia would do to Charles. She had no time to brood about it because Torrent had come in and was extracting from her all the information she possessed and answering her questions in return.

"What was her reason for killing Vova? I was too far gone by the time she started talking about it. I'd thought that was something having to do with his being crazy in the wrong way." She went on to explain. "It's something I read in the galleys Charles Graham gave me. She speaks in her book of how a little while before he went insane, he took to looking younger than his age. She even mentioned his 'young smoothed-out face.' That rang a bell. I looked it up and it's a symptom not of schizophrenia, which he is supposed to have had, but of something worse—dementia paralytica or maybe cerebral syphilis. I know this," said Toni modestly, "on account of I looked it up in Henderson and Gillespie this morning at the Forty-second Street Library. There were a few more things like that and they were carefully deleted. Like his not being able to pronounce certain words. I guess Natalia realized at a rather late date what she had let slip. Syphilitic paresis is not quite as romantic as having schizophrenia on account of the woes of the world being too much for you. But then there was a difficulty. Paretics in that advanced stage very seldom recover—and never enough to be the good physical specimen that Izlomin was. So I guess I was wrong about that."

"You're incredible," said Torrent. "As a matter of fact, Izlomin did die a paralytic."

"What's that?"

"Word of honor. The man you knew—the one on whom your pals played that idiotic prank and whom she left to smother in a trunk—that wasn't the real Izlomin."

"Then who was he, for heaven's sake?"

"A distant relative," said Torrent and grinned. "Honestly. It's the damnedest yarn but it's true. The original Izlomin, the great dancer, did become hopelessly insane, a helpless paralytic incapable of performing the simplest motions. Natalia took him out of his sanatorium and looked after him herself. She tried to create a sort of mad prince of ballet myth around him—nothing as sordid as gradual paralysis. The reporters who were occasionally allowed to see him really saw somebody else pinch-hitting for him—a distant cousin of his, also a dancer, though an unknown one, whom Natalia engaged to pose as Izlomin. It was his extraordinary likeness to him that gave her the idea. For four years she worked on him, teaching him all she knew—and she was a good teacher—and pounding into him all the tricks of the Izlomin personality, until at the end the man was actually Izlomin himself. The war gave her the chance she wanted. After the Germans invaded France, she fled from her villa with the man she had trained, leaving the body of the other buried in the little garden."

"She killed him too," Toni breathed, remembering Natalia's precise voice saying, "After one has killed twice, no, three times..."

"You know about their arrival here and the sensation he made. They got away with it. After seven years those of his old friends who were here couldn't remember too well."

"Anyhow," said Toni, remembering the book, "the real Izlomin was sort of an enigma to everybody. Even his affairs were violent but impersonal."

"At any rate it worked. But there wasn't much love lost between the two. Izlomin, I believe, hated sharing his hard-won earnings with Natalia. But there was no way he could ease her out. They had too much on each other.

"I think she hated him mostly because she really did love the real Izlomin. Not when he was a paralytic and a hindrance to her but when he was young. She was sort of hipped on youth anyhow—it comes out in the book."

"She must have been. She had an affair with the Mladov youngster, who was half her age," said Torrent, and Toni remembered Kate Whitehead's nasty cracks about Natalia's motherly affection for young Slava. "Well, that gave Izlomin his chance. He wanted a divorce. He really fell for Tamara, I think, because he told her that Natalia would give him a divorce, which was entirely different from the line he pulled on all the other women, including Whitehead. He was threatening to divorce her using the only grounds that are acceptable in New York because, like the bastard he was, he didn't want to part with any alimony. He might not have got the divorce, but the scandal would have been pretty bad for her, with the book coming out and all. Her stock in trade was being Izlomin's faithful wife who saved him from worse than death and here was the faithful wife being threatened with divorce for adultery. And she herself was so used to this picture of herself that being exposed was something she couldn't face."

Toni demanded, "How did you find out about Vova not being Vova at all?"

"What started me off were the notes Izlomin had written to himself. After I found out about them from Vassine, I sent one of the notes to a handwriting expert together with two samples of Izlomin's handwriting, to wit, the inscriptions on the two photos of him that de Speranski had. One was written in 1935 and one in 1943. I hoped Harris would verify the fact that the handwriting on the note was Izlomin's disguised handwriting. He stumbled on to something much more important. The 1943 inscription was, he claimed, a forgery of the 1935 inscription.

"Well, you see where that left me. Someone was a phony. Harris and I spent a sleepless night checking on all the samples we could lay our hands on. We got from Perlova some letters the real Izlomin had written her and from de Speranski some correspondence with the false one. The results were the same. The Paris Izlomin and the one we knew here were two different men. Nor was it just a difference due to Izlomin's being cured of his madness. Harris rather thought that the threatening note was written in the second man's natural handwriting, though he couldn't swear to that.

"That's when we began to wonder about Izlomin's wife. She would certainly know if her husband was a phony. Obviously she was in on it.

"Checking with de Speranski and Perlova, who knew him in Paris, jibed pretty well. De Speranski had apparently simply made up his connection with Izlomin in Paris and so pseudo-Izlomin had no hesitation about cultivating his friendship. But Perlova knew him in Paris very well indeed and what do we find? He avoids her like the plague and tries to ease her out.

"And then it occurred to me that I'd been working from a false premise all that time. The murderer was somebody who knew about Izlomin being in that trunk, and I had taken it for granted that nobody knew about it outside the four plotters. But that needn't have been the case."

Toni interrupted him impulsively. "That's what made me think of her, too. Slava sort of pointed to her. He was mad about her and it was just possible that he would confide to her about the wonderful joke on Vova. And then his peculiar actions seemed to point that way too. He suddenly knows 'intuitively' that something is wrong with Vova. Why? He must have seen something suspicious. And who would be the only person he would protect, withholding her identity from his friends? Why, Natalia of course, the beloved one! Then he got that premonition awfully early in the ballet—so the cause for it must have occurred even earlier, that means in the very beginning."

Torrent agreed with this. "We figured along those lines, too. Yes, Natalia knew from the beginning what the boys wanted to do. Did you notice how easy it was made for them? She got rid of the valet for the fateful night, by poisoning him. She left the glass of orange juice where Slava could easily drug it. She scrupulously avoided entering the dressing room at the critical time, even though she must have known that the voice that answered her—even though monosyllabically—wasn't Izlomin's. And I suspect she even taught the steps of the variation to Slava, because Daillart swears up and down that it was impossible for anyone to have spied on him and Vova. Yes, she was the one who set the stage, all right—not poor old Ffoulkes."

Torrent chuckled suddenly. "She had one bad moment, though, and you and I were both there to see it. She wanted Izlomin to be found dead in that trunk. She was tickled pink when I went to look for him—the more official the better. And then Izlomin wasn't there—those lunatics had lugged him away! Then, too, it must have made her furious the way they had bungled everything. I told you that she was mad as hell when I told her about his being murdered.

"But even so she was in a pretty good spot. Slava's knowing about her bothered her only a little. She could count on his loyalty to her up to a point, particularly since she had made him believe that she did it all for him. And then he got jittery. He was just a kid, after all, and his knowing about her made him dangerous. So she got rid of him."

"But how?" Toni asked. "You saw Slava fall from above while she was waiting for him below."

"It was pretty ingenious, at that. After openly making an appointment with Slava she decoyed him to the back gallery and slugged him there. Incidentally, her possession of your key shows that she must have seen him after talking to him in the rehearsal hall, because he had no opportunity to give it to her before that. She left him there unconscious, after making certain arrangements. She propped him up on the rail of the back balcony—there was a flat being painted there, remember, that would hide him from view—then she took one of those long ropes that lie in coils there, looped an end of it around his feet and let it hang clear down to the stage floor. Then she went down, pulled that act on Mahoney about wanting him to listen—she had heard me instruct him not to leave the corridor under any circumstances—went on the stage, pulled the rope and began screaming. Both Mladov and the rope came down. Remember Mahoney spraining his ankle on a rope that wasn't supposed to be there?

"The rest you know for yourself."

"Do you mean to say," Toni asked, "that she did it all just because Izlomin was threatening to divorce her? Couldn't she bargain? After all, he wasn't completely secure in his position. I suppose she couldn't fight back much, because after all there was that little matter of a dead husband. Still, it doesn't sound like enough of a motive."

"Nor was it, by itself. Mrs. Whitehead gave us another one. I remembered something she had said the first time I questioned her. She had spoken about a surprise she was preparing for dear Vova. She had located his favorite aunt and smuggled her out of France and was now bringing her to the United States."

"Good lord," said Toni, visualizing the effect of such a surprise on both parties, the aunt as well as the nephew, who was a relative, all right, but not the right one. "No, it wouldn't have done at all."

"Natalia, to whom she had boasted about it, thought so. She saw immediately that she had to get rid either of Vova or the aunt. On consideration she decided on Vova, particularly since the practical joke his rivals were about to play on him gave her such a good opportunity. It might seem at first like killing the goose that laid the golden eggs. But with the divorce business threatening, it looked as if there wouldn't be many more forthcoming. While with Izlomin dead, there would be no exposure and she could go on with her lucrative career as his wonderful, self-sacrificing wife."

"You were certainly able to find out a lot in a few hours."

"Well, we figured out a good deal of it and Natalia told us the rest before she died. I guess she thought we might as well know how clever she'd been."

"Died!"

Torrent looked at Toni's shocked face. "Didn't you know, Toni? Didn't Eric tell you? Natalia Izlomina shot herself when she was caught trying to murder you. She died a few hours later."

"I keep telling myself that it's probably better this way," Toni said wretchedly. Charles had come back with her to her apartment after a dinner during which neither she nor he alluded to the subject. Now it had to be mentioned. "But the fact that it happened here, in my place, makes it lousy. As if I'd actually trapped her." She raised her eyes to Charles' face. "I suppose it makes you hate me."

"Hate you?" Charles was shocked. "You little fool, why should I hate you? How silly. As you say, it's much better this way. No trial, no publicity, nobody involved. I must say she showed sense in doing it that way. But then she did have plenty of sense. Her trouble was insane pride and a completely one-track mind. She had concentrated on building her life on a myth and preserving that myth at any price."

Toni listened to him speaking so coldly and wondered. His blue eyes were unclouded by any shadow. "What a grave face," said Charles, tilting it and kissing it lightly. "Smile, darling. Don't worry about her any more."

"Frankly," said Toni, "It was you I was worried about. You told me…"

Charles got up and walked over to the fireplace. He wore a half guilty, half laughing look. "Yes, I know what I told you. You see, baby, you're so damned sharp. What with your observant eye and your peculiar friendship with that cop, I thought you might get too interested and tumble on to some embarrassing facts."

"You sound," said Toni slowly, "as if you had done that…"

"Well, not exactly. I just had a feeling. I guess I knew Natalia better than anybody else did—you know, that peculiar author/publisher relationship that you read about in magazines. After all, I'd worked on that book with her. Inadvertently she had drawn a pretty clear picture of a very different kind of madness. She was bright enough to take my hints and delete all the betraying passages, but not before they had told their story to a pretty good amateur psychologist like me. Then I could see that she hated Vova and she did love the man in the book. And besides, Kate had told me about the surprise and I couldn't help thinking it was funny that

Vova should die just before his devoted aunt, who knew him so well, arrived on the scene. All those were merely conjectures and none of my business, which was putting out that book, and I did hope I'd get it out before anything broke. A reputable firm like Graham Dobbs can't put out a fraud once it knows about it, but we're not averse to making money on it once it's out in the market. It would have sold like mad, fraud or no."

Toni stared at him. "Then all you said …"

Charles again flashed his charming apologetic grin. "Forgive me, darling? I thought I could get you to lay off for a little while if I sold you a bill of goods, because you were—fond of me. The idea of hunting down a possible rival—I knew you were a young woman of sensibilities."

"I can't say the same of you," Toni commented, still staring at him. "You are a cold brute, aren't you? Colder even than I thought."

"Now I know you're angry with me," said Charles, looking worried.

"Not at all. I'm merely sorry that I have helped to inflict a financial loss on you. I'd thought it was merely an emotional one."

"Ah, but it's both. I've put a lot into that book. When I think of all that brilliant promotion going down the drain…We could use the part dealing with his career until he went mad, but unfortunately most of the book is about how he was rehabilitated by Natalia. However, it's no use thinking about it. I'm going to forget the whole thing and I hope you will too. And," said Charles softly, coming back to her, "I am not cold."

Funny how things change, Toni thought. Like turning a pattern and getting an entirely new one—quick as a flash and quite inalterable once it happened. She waited until Charles finished kissing her and said, "Do you mind if I finish the evening by myself? I'm a little tired and there are things I'd like to think out alone."

Charles gave in after protesting. "But you'll see me tomorrow, won't you?"

"Of course," said Toni and smiled at him sweetly if perfunctorily.

She forgot him the minute the door closed behind him. Her mind was busy framing a telegram to Lieutenant Eric Skeets and she had it all worked out by the time she had reached the phone.

"CURED OF MEASLES AND READY TO MARRY YOU WHENEVER CONVENIENT. I LOVE YOU. LOVE SPELLED L, O, V, E. TONI."

THE END

Toni Ney's first case,
Painted for the Kill, (0-915230-66-6, $14.95)
is also available wherever fine
books are sold.

A catalog of Rue Morgue Press
vintage mysteries is available
by calling
800-699-6214
or writing
The Rue Morgue
P.O. Box 4119
Boulder, CO 80306

About The Rue Morgue Press

The Rue Morgue vintage mystery line is designed to bring back into print those books that were favorites of readers from the 1920s to 1960s. Authors include Joanna Cannan, Joan Coggin, Glyn Carr, Manning Coles, Elizabeth Dean, Norbert Davis, Craig Rice, Clyde B. Clason, Maureen Sarsfield, Juanita Sheridan, James Norman, Torrey Chanslor, Sheila Pim, Charlotte Murray Russell, and Constance & Gwenyth Little. The editors welcome suggests for reprints. To receive our catalog or make suggestions, write The Rue Morgue Press, P.O. Box 4119, Boulder, Colorado (1-800-699-6214).